COMING OF WINTER

BY TOM THREADGILL

COMING OF WINTER BY TOM THREADGILL
Published by Lamplighter Suspense
an imprint of Lighthouse Publishing of the Carolinas
2333 Barton Oaks Dr., Raleigh, NC, 27614

ISBN: 978-1-946016-55-3
Copyright © 2018 by Tom Threadgill
Cover design by Elaina Lee
Interior design by Karthick Srinivasan

Available in print from your local bookstore, online, or from the publisher at:
ShopLPC.com

For more information on this book and the author visit: www.tomthreadgill.com

Brought to you by the creative team at Lighthouse Publishing of the Carolinas:
Eddie Jones, Darla Crass, Brian Cross, Judah Raine, and Stephen Mathisen

Library of Congress Cataloging-in-Publication Data
Threadgill, Tom.
Coming of Winter / Tom Threadgill 1st ed.

Printed in the United States of America

for Janet
the smartest decision I ever made was to let you catch me

ACKNOWLEDGMENTS

Writing is work. I learned that quickly after I tried to pen a novel for my wife on our 30th anniversary. When I proudly showed her the first few pages of that book, the expression on her face told me all I needed to know. When your own wife struggles to find something nice to say about your writing, you know it's time to get serious. Fast-forward several years, many writing conferences, tons of instructional books and gobs of edits, and you have the final product in your hands.

Several people provided invaluable assistance along the way. Thank you to the good folks at Lighthouse Publishing of the Carolinas who held my hand through each step of the publication process.

To my agent, Linda S. Glaz, I hope the headaches have been worth it. You listened to me whine, cry, and pout my way to this point. Your encouragement and commitment got us here. Thanks for keeping the faith!

Finally, thanks to Janet, my wife, who never stopped believing, even after my early efforts. I didn't make our 30th anniversary, but I did beat our 40th. Deadlines are meant to be flexible, right? I love you, babe. Always have. Always will.

Oh, and I should wrap this up by telling you this novel has nothing to do with that first attempt at writing a book. Not even I would give my wife a novel about a serial killer for our 30th anniversary. I'm not that dense. Everybody knows serial killer books are for the 35th anniversary.

CHAPTER ONE

The tub grinder's twenty-four steel hammers each swung more than five hundred times per minute, converting the hay bale—and Catherine Mae Blackston—into cattle feed. Shreds of both spewed onto an already six-foot-high mound of steamy, soggy, and nutritious bovine dinner. Mason Miller used the front loader of his tractor to drop another bale into the rotating contraption. The racket dulled as the hammers bit into the thick mass of organic material, wet from the late January rain common in west Tennessee. At nearly nine feet high, the machine could spit out twenty or thirty tons of mulched product per hour. Overkill for what he needed, but they didn't come much smaller. He waited until the device chewed the hay below the lip of the tub, then hopped out onto the muddy ground.

An oil-spotted canvas duffel bag lay beside the grinder, a freebie from the farm co-op. He dropped to one knee and removed a work glove. The frosty ground soaked his jeans, but he was a farmer. Cold or hot, wet or dry, the work had to get done. He reached inside the bag, being careful not to peek, and let his fingers dance through the contents. After baking so long, most of the bones were on the verge of falling apart. Their collagen gone, the skeletal remains were as brittle as those sand dollars the boys found in Panama City last summer. He grabbed a couple of the bigger bones and held them up for a better look.

A rib and the left femur. Or maybe the right. Much easier to identify them when Catherine was still alive—or at least in one piece. A shame to waste them, but he couldn't exactly toss these to the dogs. Proper disposal might save complications later.

He shook his head and sighed. Stupid. In the beginning, he'd taken what he needed and left the rest of the body where it lay. What was he thinking? Why leave anything for someone to find? This way worked better. It was like the signs in the parks said. Take nothing but photos and leave nothing but footprints. Except of course, he tried not to leave footprints and didn't need any pictures. He kept everything he wanted close by and recycled the rest.

One knee popped as he stood, eliciting a grunt followed by a chuckle. If the joint ever needed replacing, at least he knew where to find another one. He tossed the bones into the grinder and jumped back into his tractor.

A gust of icy wind scattered chaff from the pile and blew a murky cloud toward him. He closed his eyes and leaned out the open door, letting the particles peck his face. The earthy scent of wet hay, mingled with the barest touch of Catherine, enveloped him. He tilted his head back and savored the weightlessness within himself.

He loved it all. Rising early and working the soil, tending the livestock and the crops. It was an honest day's work a man could be proud of.

A peek at his watch told him it was almost noon. No need to quit working. The boys would be here soon enough with lunch, most likely racing to see who would get there first. Ten-year-old Lucas had five years and a foot-and-a-half on his younger brother, but he sometimes let Andy win. And even when he didn't, he made sure to keep it close. Good boys. Both were quick learners too, always willing to help around the farm. He was truly blessed to have such a wonderful family.

He glanced toward the house, hidden a few acres away behind a rise. The boys would be here in a couple of minutes, out of breath and begging to drive the tractor. He'd sit behind them and eat his meal while they took turns steering. Just like his father had done for him.

Nurturing the bond between his family and his land was the best part of being a farmer. Things like teaching the boys to treat their mama and their heritage with respect. Not being afraid to get their hands dirty and work long, hard hours to achieve success. The simple joys of a clean life.

Mason closed his hand around some bones and grinned. Lunchtime. Maybe Paula would send out leftovers from last night's barbecue. He had a sudden hankering for ribs.

CHAPTER TWO

The plastic clock's hollowness bored its tick-tick-tick directly into Jeremy Winter's brain. The Bureau's shrink said he had anger management issues. That his temper could flare without warning. No kidding. With not much to do except listen to the seconds tick by, anyone's blood would start boiling. He chucked a pen at the clock, leaving a tiny blue ink spot and divot on the freshly painted white wall. The writing instrument landed on the carpet next to two other pens and a pad of yellow sticky notes.

Anger management issues. When did everything become an "issue" instead of a problem? Didn't matter anyway, as long as he got clearance to work. "Employee bears watching," the psychiatrist had noted. *Well, watch away.*

Twenty-three years as a Special Agent with the FBI and this is how they reward him. Moved from D.C. to St. Louis, his coworkers and girlfriend Maggie left behind. Reassigned from tracking serial killers to working white-collar crime. Dropped in a sterile office with a new desk, a fake plant, and not enough pens. And no explanations. What the Bureau wants, the Bureau gets.

And they wondered about his anger issues. Forty-seven's too old to try to understand the moronic decisions made by government lifers who'd made a career out of making sure the right form was used at the right time and ... whatever. He sighed and flexed his shoulders to relieve the tension. It didn't make sense.

He'd been fresh off a successful capture on the West Coast. The Boxcar Butcher (as the media named him) rode trains across the country, hopping off whenever he felt like it to rob and kill in remote areas. Lived in the victims' homes until he grew bored, then jumped back on the rails.

He'd murdered a dozen they knew of, and likely more of his victims were waiting to be found.

So sure, why let Jeremy finish his job? Why not ship him halfway across the country and reassign him to a desk? A perfectly logical decision by a bunch of idiotic—

Deep breath.

He took a sip of his lukewarm coffee and slapped the creamy white mug down hard enough to slosh a few drops on the desk and floor. Good. Stain it up. He guzzled the remaining java and dropped the cup into the bottom drawer. No way the cleaning crew was going to wash that thing again. A quick rinse every week or two was all the mug needed. More than that and the ceramic would never get a chance to soak up the flavor.

The phone on his desk beeped, interrupting his thoughts and bringing him back to the present. Phones should ring, not beep. Too early for Maggie's call, and she'd phone on his cell anyway. Doubtless another real estate agent with a "Welcome to St. Louis. Can I show you around?" call. No clue how they'd got his name and number, but if the Bureau had a Realtor's resources, most of their cold cases could be solved overnight. He pressed his lips together and glanced upward before snatching the phone.

"Agent Winter," he said, eschewing the "Special" prefix. Nothing special about sitting behind this desk.

"Hey, G-man. How are ya?"

G-man. No one had called him that since Afghanistan a dozen years ago. The voice sounded familiar, kind of gravelly with a nasal whine. He closed his eyes and kneaded his forehead, trying to recall a name, or at least a face. Nothing came. "I'm good," he said. "I'm sorry. Who am I speaking with?"

A snicker came through the phone. "You don't remember me? I'm hurt."

Jeremy blew a blast of air out his nostrils and squeezed the phone. "Who is this?"

"Okay, okay. This is Randy. Randy Clarke. Been a long time."

Randy Clarke? Why was he calling? They'd never been friends, barely even acquaintances. Two guys in another world. What happened there stays there. Isn't that what the commercial says? Except it *doesn't* stay there. The FBI psychiatrist's report—which Jeremy wasn't supposed to have seen but, hey, that's why it was good to have friends everywhere—

said most of his anger stemmed from his time overseas. Brilliant. And the shrink undoubtedly made ten times what he did. "Yeah, it's been a few years. How are you, Randy?"

The man cleared his throat. "Um, that's why I looked you up. I could use your help."

Jeremy leaned back, closed his eyes, and waited for his heart rate to slow. "What kind of help?"

"The kind that involves the police. I need to find someone."

If he wanted law enforcement included, at least it's legit. Probably. You never knew. "What's going on, Randy?"

"It's my ex-wife. Ex number three to be precise. I can't find her. She hasn't been answering her phone, so I called some of her neighbors and they said they haven't seen her for a while. Her car's gone too."

Jeremy scratched the back of his neck. "That doesn't mean anything. Maybe she went on vacation or something."

"It's been over a month, and the last two alimony checks haven't cleared. Last time I was a couple of days late she called the cops on me. Wanted to send me to jail over eighty-three dollars."

Jeremy dragged the side of his shoe across the battleship-gray carpet. Guess they couldn't find a gloomier color. Likely, a trillion-dollar government study said it would hide stains while improving morale. Wrong and wrong. "That what this is about? Alimony?"

"No, well, kinda. I mean, if she doesn't want the money and isn't gonna call the cops on me, then sure, I'd like to quit making payments. But I'm telling you, something's wrong."

He rubbed his palm across his forehead. "Listen, if you're that concerned, talk to the local police and let them look into it. If there's anything suspicious, I'll do some digging."

"I did talk to them and they told me there was nothing they could do. They checked out her house and said everything looked okay. Talked to a few people at her job too but didn't find out anything. They said that maybe she wanted a change. Maybe she did, but she didn't say anything to me."

"Sure, sure. Did they put her vehicle in the system in case anything turns up?"

"Yeah, but they're not looking. Said if they find her, they'll let me know. In other words, go away. How long do I have to wait before I can stop sending the checks?"

Jeremy rummaged through a drawer to find something to write on. Never any notepads or pens when you needed them. "That's a question for your divorce attorney."

"Yeah, but he charges me if I call him."

I can understand why. "Tell you what. I'll make a phone call and see what I can find out. Honestly, this kind of stuff happens all the time. People decide they want to get away for a while. Maybe start over. You'd be surprised how many folks simply walk away from everything they own for whatever reason."

"Thanks, G-man. I really appreciate it. And you'll let me know what you find out?"

"Sure thing. Give me a day or two. Now, who are we looking for?"

"I suppose you'll want her full name, huh? Everybody calls her Kate, but her given name is Catherine Mae Blackston. Catherine with a *C* and *M-A-E*. She lives in Huntingburg, Indiana. That's little ways from Jasper, if you know where that is." He gave her address and social security number.

Jeremy thumbed through the stack of file folders on his desk. "Got it. Like I said, give me some time. I've got a few other cases going, but I'll make a phone call, maybe even take a drive over myself. Get out of the office for a day."

"Great. Thanks again, man. And listen, seriously, how're you making it? You know, since Afghanistan?"

"Better. It gets better." Most days.

"Yeah. It does." A few seconds of silence. "So, I'll wait to hear from you."

Jeremy nodded. "Yep. I'll be in touch. Hang tight, Randy. Bye."

Hang tight? Do people even say that anymore? Maggie would be calling any second now. She's the language expert. Maybe she'll know.

Her ability to mangle phrases was becoming legendary within the Bureau. Just last week, she'd lectured a room packed with new recruits and told them you can lead a horse to water, but you don't look him in the mouth. Not that most people would call her on it. At least not more than once. He was an exception.

She allowed him to tease her because she believed in "respecting her elders." Uh-huh. Like the not-quite-ten-year age difference was such a big deal. Besides, his love of country music left her plenty of opportunities to retaliate.

The cell phone vibrated, and he glanced at the caller ID. The hairs on his arms stood and he closed his eyes, picturing the woman on the other end of the line. No anger issues here, and nobody could adjust his attitude like she could. He spun his chair and faced away from the clock.

"Hey, Maggie."

CHAPTER THREE

Jeremy parked his government-issued Taurus and stepped out into the early February dullness of southwestern Indiana. The frigid air stung his cheeks and he clapped his hands together while checking out Catherine Mae Blackston's house. No sidewalks or driveway. Parallel ruts in the yard beelined up a gentle slope to the squat one-story home. The houses on either side had large trees screening them, but not Miss Blackston's. No landscaping of any kind. A barren yard surrounded a faded yellow brick house topped with mismatched shingles.

A white Huntingburg police car pulled up behind him and a cop stepped out. Big guy. Six foot two, around two twenty-five, and on the short side of thirty. Stocky build with a round boyish face and short brown hair. The man straightened his dark blue uniform shirt, adjusted his badge a millimeter to the left, and brushed a hand against his service pistol before hustling over to Jeremy.

"Officer Troy Obion," he said as he extended his hand.

"Special Agent Jeremy Winter. Pleasure."

The policeman ran his hand along the hood of the FBI vehicle. "Nice car. Didn't know you guys got the Interceptor version. Last year's model?"

"Yeah. It doesn't have all the upgrades, but it's got enough to do what I need it to." Which lately isn't much. He nodded toward the house. "Does she own the place?"

"Rented. I picked up the key from the landlord so we can go inside. I went in a couple of days ago when we first got the call, but maybe you'll see something I didn't." The policeman shrugged. "She's got a lot of nice stuff in there. Doesn't make sense that she'd up and leave it all, but people do some strange things."

"Yeah, they do. Job security for us, I suppose. Although I could do without most of it."

Officer Obion shuffled his feet and licked his lips. "Yes, sir. I bet you've seen a few pretty intense situations."

Jeremy peered closer at the cop. "How long you been on the force?"

"Going on my third year now."

"Yeah, I've been in a few tough spots. People will surprise you, Officer Obion. Sometimes in a good way. Usually not."

"Yes, sir."

"Her rent paid up?"

"Yeah. She was actually a month ahead. The property owner loves her. Says he's never had any problems. Had to fix her stove a couple of times, but other than that, he never heard a peep. The rent check showed up on time, and the neighbors don't complain."

"She got a job?"

Officer Obion pointed down the street. "You passed it on the way in. A furniture factory. She works, um, worked in one of the assembly rooms. Several friends there, but no one close. No boyfriend as far as we know."

Jeremy nodded, shoved his hands in the pockets of his overcoat, and headed for the front door. "Let's take a look inside."

The two stood on the cracked concrete slab that served as the front porch while the officer dug the key from his jacket. A thick brown doormat with *Home Sweet Home* printed on it welcomed visitors, though from the newish look of the mat, not many guests ever stopped by.

The policeman pointed toward Jeremy's left leg. "I hope you don't mind me asking, but you get injured in the line of duty?"

Good eye for detail. Most people didn't notice the limp. It'd been part of him since Afghanistan. One he'd worked hard to hide. Never failed, though. Every time he thought he'd tamed the angry scar that circled from his inner thigh to outer calf, somebody would show up to tell him otherwise. "The limp? Yeah."

"Man, you guys see a lot of action, don't you? Sometimes I think I should transfer to a bigger city. You know, test myself. See if I've got what it takes." He unlocked the door and pushed it open, motioning for the FBI agent to enter first.

"Test yourself, huh? Tests are easy. You know the information. Have time to study. It's the pop quizzes that'll kill you." Jeremy stepped into the small living room and waited, giving his eyes time to adjust to the dimmer environment.

The cop stood next to him, stamped his feet on a small oval entry rug, and swung the door closed. "So, did you pass or fail? Your pop quiz, I mean."

Good question. "Depends on how you're grading. I'm here, so yeah, I guess I passed. But realistically? Not sure."

Officer Obion raised his eyebrows but kept silent.

Jeremy took another step into the room. "Has anything been disturbed since the last time you were here?"

"Not as far as I can tell. Got some pictures on my cell if you want to take a look, but doesn't seem like anything's out of place."

"No, that's okay. Let's get through the house first."

He held up his phone. "No problem. If you want to see the pictures later, I'll email them over. These things are amazing, you know? The photos are backed up automatically, and I can look at them from any—"

"What about her mail?"

The officer gestured toward the front of the home. "Her mailbox is across the street. The thing was crammed full, and I figured the mailman gave up on trying to get more in there, so I caught him a few streets over. Sure enough, he had a pile of stuff for her. Said he couldn't give it to me, but I talked him into driving back over and filling her mailbox again. He'd stuff the box and I'd empty it. Did it three times before I got it all. Mostly junk and a few bills. I put everything on that coffee table if you want to go through it."

"Later." Jeremy moved into the kitchen. A few pinkish plastic plates rested in the dish rack that sat on the green-speckled white laminate counter. Nothing in the sink. No crumbs. Trashcan nearly empty. "She kept a clean home."

"The house is a little dusty now, but the whole place is like this. Bed's made, bathroom's spotless. Do you think if she was going to up and leave, she'd bother to keep it like this?"

"Possibly," Jeremy said. "Maybe she didn't want the landlord to have to do much before renting it out again. Not burn any bridges, just in case. Could be someone else cleaned up the place, though." He moved to the refrigerator. Nature photos, mostly of trees, lakes, and birds, covered the white appliance. He slipped on a glove and lifted one of the pictures so he could see the back. "Printed at CVS. She probably took these herself.

Recognize any of these locations?"

The officer scanned the photos quickly. "Could be most anywhere around here. If I had to guess though, I'd say she took them over in the park. Lots of folks in these parts like to spend time there."

"The park?"

"Yeah. Hoosier National Forest. Couple of hundred thousand acres spread across the state. It'd take someone better than me to pinpoint the location more than that."

"Probably won't be necessary. Any other photos like these?"

The policeman led him into the bedroom and pointed over the dresser. "She had this one blown up, I guess."

The framed picture was a winter scene with sunlight peeking through bare tree branches covered in ice. Snow covered the ground in a pristine blanket, and a deep-blue sky outlined the trees. In the background, a gray-blue lake spread to the photo's edges.

"Any idea where she took this one?"

"Gotta be over in the park for sure," Officer Obion said. "No other place around here with a lake that big. The picture's not recent, though. No snow that deep for the last couple of years."

"Uh-huh. Is her camera here?"

"I don't remember seeing it but wasn't really looking for one." He reached for a dresser drawer, and Jeremy grabbed his arm.

"I'd prefer we treated this as a crime scene until we know otherwise."

The policeman's face reddened. "Sorry. I've got a pair of gloves in the car. I'll go get them."

"No, that's okay. I'll finish up in here. Look, I know this isn't my jurisdiction, but what are the odds of your department searching Hoosier National Forest for her car? Parking lots, back roads, maintenance sheds, all of it."

The officer's eyes widened, and he ran a hand across the top of his head. "That's two hundred thousand acres. It'll take an awful long time to cover that much ground. There's only two Forest Service officers. A few of the county sheriffs help out when they can, but still ..."

"Understood. But based on what we've seen in here, where do you suppose our best chance of finding her would be? If she's even really missing, that is."

The officer shifted from one foot to the other. "Yeah. I'll talk to Chief

Bowers, but I can tell you what he's going to say. There's no evidence of a crime. If something changes, then we'll take the time to go looking. We're a small department, Agent Winter. Lots of jurisdictions would need to get involved in a search that big. No offense, but this is a local matter anyway. At least as far as we know right now."

Jeremy breathed deeply. "Of course. I don't want to step on any toes here. I told a friend I'd check into it for him, and I did. If you don't mind, I'll finish looking around the house and then be on my way back to Saint Louis."

Officer Obion smiled and nodded. "No problem. I appreciate you understanding."

"We're all on the same team here, right? Plenty of real investigating to do without making work for ourselves. I'm sure Miss Blackston will turn up soon enough."

"It's not that I don't want to do more. I do. It's just that—"

Jeremy placed his hand on the policeman's shoulder. "I understand. Really. Don't worry about it. I'm sure you'll get another chance."

"Another chance?"

"To get involved in something like this. Missing woman. No clue what happened to her." He motioned to the photo on the wall. "Wondering if she's there. Waiting to be found."

They both stared at the picture for a few seconds.

"Eh," Jeremy said. "What am I saying? She's probably living the good life in the Bahamas with a new boyfriend. Let's wrap it up here. I can get back to Missouri in time for dinner."

"I know what you're doing, Agent Winter."

Jeremy arched his brows and cut his eyes toward the officer. "Is it working?"

The policeman smiled. "I'll let you know after I tell the chief we need to search the park."

CHAPTER FOUR

S ix hours later, Jeremy stood on a small rise in Hoosier National Forest. In front of him was Denbo Cemetery, its meandering rows of timeworn gravesites tucked into a corner of the clearing. The trees surrounding the sacred ground stood vigilant in the gusting wind, silent and unmoving. Tombstones, most broken or eroded by age, poked above the frozen earth, reminders of the skeletons sleeping below. Through bare branches, the brown fairway of a golf course was evident, every bit as empty and abandoned as the graveyard.

"That didn't take long," he said. "Her car looks like it's been here for a while. Wonder why no one called it in?"

Officer Obion shrugged. "Who knows? Not a lot of activity in this part of the park, especially this time of year. No reason to come back here. Once we put the word out about the missing vehicle, didn't take any time to find it. Not like it was hidden or anything. Wish we'd looked sooner."

"You followed procedures. Nothing to regret there."

"I don't know. Sometimes it's okay to break regulations, don't you think?"

"I'm probably not the best guy to ask." Wispy vapor clouds punctuated Jeremy's words as his warm breath clashed with the freezing air. "It's beautiful out here."

"Think so? Seems kind of gray and depressing. Could just be the cemetery, though. Me, I prefer autumn. For the colors mainly. But I don't get out this way much. I'm more of a fishing guy."

Jeremy tilted his head back toward the parking lot. "They find anything in Miss Blackston's car?"

"Not yet. No purse or ID, but there is a padded black bag with a big zoom lens in it. The camera's not there, though. Doors were locked. No sign of a struggle. We're going to tow the vehicle in and let the guys from Indy come down and take a look at it."

"Good. This place get many visitors?"

"Not according to the Park Service. It's at the end of the road, so unless you're intentionally coming here, you're not going to find it. Kind of an odd place to take pictures, though. Especially this time of year."

Jeremy turned toward the officer. "Different strokes for different folks, I suppose."

"Excuse me?"

"Oh, sorry. Dating myself again. Just meant that this place might be pretty interesting to some people. Gravesites back to the early 1800s. No other people around to bother you. Seems to me there's a sort of, I don't know, peace? Maybe solitude's a better word. I could see spending some time here."

The policeman raised his eyebrows. "If you say so."

Jeremy leaned his head back and let the sun warm his face. His lips and cheeks burned, chapped by the wind. He sniffled and touched the back of his hand to his septum, shooting pinpricks of pain through his nose to now watery eyes. Have to pick up some Vicks on the way home.

Slamming vehicle doors broke his reverie. Several voices intermingled and blew across the field, giving notice that the search team had arrived.

Jeremy extended his hand. "Thank you for your help. I'm heading back to Saint Louis."

The policeman's forehead creased. "You're not staying while we do the grid search?"

"Nope. I'd only be in the way. You'll let me know if you find anything else?"

Officer Obion scratched his chin and squinted. "You don't think we're going to find her, do you?"

"You might, but I doubt it. If she came here, it was to take photos. Can't think of any other reason to be out here this time of year."

"And?"

"And where's her purse? If she was only going to snap a few photos, why bring her purse? Why not leave it in the car? No one else around. Lock the door and put the keys in your pocket. One less thing to carry. I might be wrong. Wouldn't be the first time. But my guess is she made it back to her vehicle."

"And then?"

Jeremy strode toward his car, slowing to allow the policeman to catch up. "That's what we have to figure out."

"We?"

"You. Your jurisdiction, your case. If I can help in any way, I will."

The policeman pulled his cap lower and hurried toward the search team. "Agent Winter, I'm way ahead of you."

CHAPTER FIVE

Mason Miller zipped up his brown denim jacket and surveyed the farm from his back porch. Just ahead was the vegetable garden, its bare earth coated in frost. A ways behind it, several acres lay fallow, waiting for the corn he'd plant for this year's Halloween maze. And beyond that, four hundred acres of pasture and farmland. Couldn't see them from here, but his small herd of cattle was over the rise on the right, back behind the new maintenance garage. Off to the left a hundred and fifty feet or so, past the gravel driveway and new storm cellar, the old barn stood guard.

On the northern edge of Crockett County, Tennessee, smack dab in the middle between the towns of Friendship and Halls, the land had been in his family for four generations, maybe longer. The official records and unofficial rumors got a little murky much further back than that. No matter. He'd pass the farm on to his boys and they'd do the same.

It used to be that handing down your land was a foregone conclusion in these parts. The family and farm stayed together. Sure, you might lease out your fields for a season or two, but the land always stayed in the family. A fertile heritage and secure future. Plenty of folks had given up. Sold out and moved on. But that wasn't going to happen here. This was their farm. Now and always. Through good times and bad.

Mostly bad. He'd cheaped out on the crop insurance eight years back, and hail had destroyed virtually all of the soy beans he'd planted that year. Some of his equipment had been repo'd, and every year since had been a struggle to catch up. Even the bumper crop of corn two years back had barely managed to meet the farm's financial needs. He'd had plenty of offers to buy the land, but that wasn't going to happen. Not while he lived.

Besides, once you figured out ways to release the stress, you could get past anything. And nothing relieved his tension like taking a day off and going hunting. Stalking his prey until finally pulling the trigger. Deer, rabbit, coon, duck, didn't matter. The killing was what was important, but getting some good eats didn't hurt none either. Almost everything he shot could be fried or cooked up in a stew or ground into meat for burgers.

Almost everything.

He pulled his dingy green ball cap lower, pushed his glasses up on his nose, and trudged through the muddy slop to the old barn, glancing back twice to make sure the boys weren't following.

Thick wood slats, faded to gray and rotted at the ends, covered the building's exterior, standing in stark contrast with the silver metal rooftop. Paula had questioned his decision at first. She said it was pointless to spend good money on a roof to protect a decaying structure, that the weight of the metal would knock the building over. He knew better, and she'd quickly come around to his way of thinking.

They'd been sweethearts since high school and married as soon as they graduated. After a few years in a small apartment, they moved into his family home. Mom had died years earlier, and Dad just kind of faded away after that. He started sleeping later, eating less, and going days without leaving the house. He even stopped whittling. His death came as a blessing to Mason. Watching his father shuffle through life was a painful lesson. The slow downhill slope toward the grave was no way to go.

The farm became their life and they threw everything into it. Paula rarely grumbled, could be a bit stubborn sometimes, but she loved her family more than anything. She'd stood by his side through thick and thin. There'd been a lot of thin.

He reached the old building and paused. His granddad built the barn and its bones were still solid. Sturdy. The wind had no trouble finding its way through the cracks, but that helped keep the dust down. The old equipment needed a place to stay, and it didn't seem right to store the relics in the new barn with its shiny tools and tractors and other gadgets. There was a connection between the old tools and the land and family. A historical link that needed to be maintained and nurtured.

The old barn was his place to relax and unwind in peace, with no thoughts of weather or farm loans or crop prices. This place was off-limits to unwelcome visitors, which pretty much meant everybody. The secrets inside were his to keep.

Mason unlocked the heavy double-door and shoved one side open. The midday sun lit up the interior, spotlighting the wispy dust particles that constantly floated around the structure. Fluorescent lights swayed over the workbenches, but their harshness wasn't what he wanted today. He grabbed a kerosene lantern off the ground, lit the wick, and pulled the door closed, locking it from the inside. Sunlight shot through the walls in a few locations and he inspected each narrow beam, deciding none of the boards warranted replacement yet. He inhaled deeply, savoring the musty smell of dirt and hay. Sometimes other odors crept up from below. Rotting meat with an odd hint of sweetness, heavy enough to coat your nose hairs but not so bad that you turned away. At least not anymore.

He placed the lantern on a workbench and ran his tongue over dry lips. Tradition hung on the walls, reminders of what a good, honest life was meant to be like. It was the same every time he came here. He spent time looking and remembering. He ran his fingers gently over the scythes and chains that had been in the family for years. He fingered the once-smooth handles of the shovels and pitchforks, now splintery with age. He inspected the old oilcans and wrenches and hand drills, made sure the horseshoe still pointed up so the luck didn't run out onto the ground. Pliers and saws and hammers and everything he could ever want were there, all touched by his father, and his father before him. Corn hooks and sickles stacked to one side, hog scrapers and drawknives lined up on the wall, and bull leaders and pulleys piled on the floor. Tools that were made to be used. They had a job to do, and all were still useful if you had an imagination.

He glanced over to a distant corner, too far for the lantern's light to reach. Always the darkest part of the barn. Tarps hung from the rafters, covering the walls and blocking the sun. A plethora of vintage tractor parts sat piled there next to the entrance to the old root cellar. The underground space had also once served as a family refuge against tornadoes but had long ago been replaced by the concrete bunker closer to the house. A haphazard stack of broken pallets, crumbling barrels, and oak logs lay next to a cast-iron stove, its open mouth begging to be fed.

Soon.

He pulled on a pair of stained leather work gloves and grabbed the hog scraper, a small drawknife, and a pulley. The pitchfork and lantern joined the collection, and Mason took another look around the barn. One day, all this would be passed on to his sons. Such good boys. He'd teach them the importance of traditions, just as his dad had taught him.

Heart full and chin high, he hummed as he stepped toward the storm cellar, careful not to trip on the faded orange extension cord snaking along the ground and under the cellar's doors. The pitchfork scraped the floor behind him, leaving four fingernail-like scratches in the dirt.

It was a good day to work.

CHAPTER SIX

A fter finishing his work in the root cellar, Mason trod back to the
house, kicked his boots against the back steps until the biggest
chunks of mud had given in to gravity, then stepped onto the
rubber mat just inside the back door. His glasses fogged, and he let them
slide down his nose before untying his shoes and leaving them. His plans
for Saturday did not include watching Paula mop the kitchen floor.

Oak logs popped in the living room fireplace and shot a faint scent of
smoky autumn through the house. He wandered in and stood with his back
to the fire. His wife sat on the flower-pattern sofa, a book in her hands and
legs tucked under her grandmother's handmade afghan.

"Done for the day?" she asked.

Mason shook his head. "Sounds like those dogs are back. Got the
cattle all stirred up. Best go deal with 'em once and for all."

Paula looked up from her book. "Want me to go with you?"

"Nah. I'll take the boys. About time Andy learned a few things and the
target practice will do them both some good."

"They're still in their room. Playing video games, I imagine. Good
luck getting them off that thing."

Mason kissed the top of her head. "Never met a boy who would rather
shoot a fake gun than a real one. We'll be back soon enough."

She returned to her reading. "Mmm hmm. You boys be careful."

"Always are. Boys! Let's go!"

A mumbled response filtered into the room and Mason sighed. "Okay
then. Guess I'll take care of those stray dogs myself. Just need to GRAB
MY RIFLE."

Muffled thuds were followed by screams of "Wait for us!" and bangs against the walls as the two boys jockeyed to be first.

Mason winked at Paula and headed to the gun safe. "Told you. Boys, get your boots on. It's a little muddy, and we're walking. Don't want to scare off the dogs with the four-wheelers."

"Make them wear their coats," Paula said.

"You heard your mother."

Andy's bottom lip jutted forward. "But Dad, it's not even—"

Mason tilted his head forward, raised his eyebrows, and peered over his glasses at the five-year-old boy. Nothing else was needed.

After a twenty-five-minute walk to the pasture, the three slowed their movement and crept toward the barking. The dogs didn't pose an immediate danger to the cattle, but if the canines got hungry enough, and a few more joined them, they could seriously injure one of the cows. And come spring when the calves were birthed, the dogs would be a real threat. They'd gone feral and at this point were no better than coyotes. Best to deal with them now.

Mason motioned for the boys to stop, and they squatted to get a better view. The cattle wandered about slowly, seeking any grass that had survived the winter. Near them, four dogs, none with collars, yipped and panted. None of them over thirty pounds probably. All of them filthy.

"Okay," he said. "Choose your target."

Lucas, the oldest, spoke first. "The little brown and white one."

Mason nodded and scrubbed a hand across his chest, enjoying the pride swelling within. That would be a tough shot. Small dog. Hyper. Probably got a lot of Jack Russell in it.

Andy pulled his camouflage ball cap lower, the old bright orange *T* sewn on the front now nearly pastel. He squinted and bit his bottom lip. "I'll take that black one."

Bigger dog. Part Labrador and part who-knows. Good choice.

"You sure, boys? Remember, aim steady and true. One shot, no suffering. Aim for the front third of the chest. That'll end it quick."

"Dad," Lucas said, "can I go for a head shot?"

"This isn't a zombie movie, son. You want to aim for small targets like that, shoot cans down by the creek. Hunting's about doing what's right by your prey. End it quick."

"Yes, sir."

Mason brought his rifle up. "They're going to run as soon as they hear a shot. Get ready."

The boys each placed a knee on the ground and leveled their weapons at their chosen dog.

"Got your targets?"

Grunted acknowledgments.

"Good hunting, boys. Here we go. Deep breath. Hold it. Now let it out slow. Three. Two. One. Fire."

Three reports sounded in the span of a half-second. Mason lowered his rifle and watched the fourth dog scamper off over a rise. The cattle moved a few feet away, then resumed their search for food.

"Got him, Dad!" Andy said.

Lucas patted his brother on the back. "Good shot. Let's go see where you hit him."

Mason stood and stretched. "Let me have your rifles. I'll walk over there with you to check it out, but then I'm headed back. You two drag the carcasses to the far edge of the pasture. Leave them there for the coyotes and vultures."

"Why can't we leave them here?" Andy asked.

"Think about it," Mason said. "Do you want to attract coyotes around the cattle? Course not. Drag those dogs out somewhere secluded and everybody's happy."

The young boy brushed his palms along his pants. "Oh. They're kind of yucky, though."

Lucas laughed. "Yucky? Wait until you gut your first deer. Won't seem so yucky then."

"This is the year, right, Dad?"

"Depends on whether you get one, I reckon."

Andy extended his arm and held a pretend rifle. "Pow! One shot and I dropped a thirty-pointer."

Mason laughed and tugged the bill of his son's cap. "We'll see."

As they neared the animals, a low whimper floated toward them. One of the dogs wasn't dead. Small as the Jack Russell was, any shot probably killed it instantly, and Mason knew his own target had seen its last day. Andy's Lab must still be alive.

"Come here, boys. Remember what we talked about? Doing what's right by your prey?"

Both boys nodded.

Mason exhaled loudly and patted Andy's back. "I'm afraid one of the dogs is still alive. It happens. Who knows why a bullet does what it does once it gets inside an animal? But what do we have to do now?"

"Finish it," Andy said. "Put the target out of its misery."

"Yep. Wouldn't be right to leave an animal like this. That's why no matter what you're hunting, if it runs off after you shoot it, you track your prey and finish it. Leaving an animal to suffer is, well, just about one of the worst things you can do."

Lucas bent over until he was eye level with his brother. "It's your dog, Andy. Want me to do it for you?"

"No," Mason said. "No. This is your brother's responsibility. He can handle it. We'll wait here."

The young boy looked unsure. "How close do I need to get to it?"

Mason flipped open the sheath attached to his belt and removed his hunting knife. Four-inch fixed blade with a drop point. Orange handle with leather strap. Good for getting the job done.

He handed the knife to his son. "Take this. You can do it. Keep a tight grip on the handle. The blade's good and sharp. Don't want to cut yourself with it. Just like we practiced, remember?"

Andy took a deep breath, then squeezed his lips together in a look of determination. "I can do it."

The boy marched toward the whimpering animal, slowing his approach as he neared. He stared at the dog for a heartbeat, glanced back, then knelt beside the wounded canine. His shoulders rose and fell in time with his breathing.

Mason shifted his stance. Can't see the boy's face. Fear? Hesitation? Excitement? Lucas's first knife kill had been professional. Unemotional. Matter of fact.

Andy's knife rose and fell, punctuated by a sharp yelp. Then quiet, save for the sound of the cows moving slowly away.

Mason didn't need to see the boy's face. He knew his expression. He'd seen it in his own reflection on many occasions. The joy of a successful hunt. The surge of adrenaline. The raw supremacy that came from taking a life. And the knowledge that nothing, *nothing*, could equal that power.

It'd been that way for Mason. He'd been six years old when his dogs treed a raccoon and he'd shot the varmint down. Even with its left front leg practically gone, the coon was still very much alive. Provoked and irate, the animal was a threat to him and his dogs. If his dad had been with him, he'd have made him shoot it again. Not get too close. Its razor teeth could easily tear into his skin, and this coon was a whopper. Maybe sixteen pounds or more.

Mason had dropped his rifle and unsheathed his knife. He could still remember the pounding in his ears as his heart shoved the adrenaline through his body. The tingling in his fingers. And the desire to finish it.

He'd told himself the animal was suffering. Be merciful. Make it quick. It's the humane thing to do. All true.

But not the real reason.

Andy stood beside the dog and bowed his head. Mason edged closer and placed a hand on his son's shoulder. A tear dripped down the boy's cheek. Might be a couple more years before he understood the power he'd unleashed. "You did right. Nothing to fret about."

"Dad, do animals go to heaven?"

The boy's got his mother's soft heart. "Well, I never gave it much thought, but I suppose they do. Can you imagine a place with no animals? Doesn't sound much like heaven to me."

Andy bent and ran his hand over the Labrador's head. "Do you think he'll be mad at me when he sees me there? For not getting a clean kill?"

"Mad? Of course not. He'll probably run up to you, all wagging his tail and stuff, and lick your face. You did him a favor, son. Sent him on to a better place."

The boy poked out his lips and looked up at his dad. "He'll be happier there?"

"Much happier."

Andy thought for a moment. "So killing's a good thing then."

Now he's getting it. "It can be." He nodded and squeezed his son's shoulder. "It sure as heck can be."

CHAPTER SEVEN

Jeremy moved his mouse in a circle, following the white arrow as it arced around the monitor's wallpaper. It'd taken a buddy in IT to bypass the laptop's restrictions and install the unapproved drawing, but the picture of the tiger was his new favorite. A fluffy orange body accented with thin black stripes. Two long fat legs and two short skinny ones. Thick Groucho Marx whiskers below bright yellow eyes. All adding up to a truly regal beast. Rebecca, Maggie's five-year-old daughter, was getting better with her crayons.

He glanced back at the paperwork in front of him. Another white-collar case. Insurance fraud this time. Staged auto accidents. Serious stuff, to be sure, but not why he joined the Bureau. He drummed his fingers on the arm of the pleather manager's chair. Got to focus. He cleared his throat and stared at the file, forcing himself to ignore the itch at the back of his brain.

Fourteen suspiciously similar vehicle accidents within the past two months. Each in a remote area. No witnesses or ...

Not happening. This case was entry-level stuff, better assigned to rookie agents. He clasped his hands behind his head and leaned back in the chair. Pleather. What is that and why does it smell like plastic rubber?

It's gonna be a long day. He cut his eyes toward the manila folder in the bottom left drawer of the desk. The itch needed to be scratched, but just a quick look.

Catherine Mae Blackston. Two months had passed since they'd located her car, and still nothing. No hits on her credit cards. The camera hadn't shown up at any pawnshops or on eBay or Craigslist. She'd disappeared. Ceased to exist. She could've left voluntarily of course, but Jeremy had doubts. Strong ones. Maybe it was the paranoia of having seen so much of the darkness people were capable of. Present company included.

His cell phone vibrated on the desk, dancing in a semi-circle before he picked it up. A warm wave washed over him when he saw the caller ID. Maggie.

"Good morning, stranger," he said. "I was just sitting here admiring this stunningly beautiful tiger drawing. Rebecca got the whiskers perfect."

Maggie laughed. "Uh-huh. Looks like he's got a mustache. And shouldn't you be working instead of critiquing my daughter's masterpieces?"

"I am working. I've got a couple of interviews scheduled today on this auto insurance scam. Doing a little bit of prep."

"Gonna wrap up the case soon?"

Jeremy leaned back in his chair and stared at the ceiling. "Probably. The gang doesn't seem too professional. One of them will roll on the others soon enough. The dominoes will start to fall."

"Sounds like they've got the house of cards stacked against them."

His heart fluttered. Nobody could mix their words like Maggie. "Oh, they do. I give it two days, maybe three. So, what've they got you working on now?"

"Eh. A possible dirty judge. Some questionable sentences given out to a couple of major drug dealers."

"You sound thrilled."

"No, it's okay. Keeps me close to home."

"Must be nice. I was thinking about maybe arranging a trip to D.C. or something. Fly up and spend a couple of days in the office. Possibly drag it into a long weekend?"

"I've got a better idea. Rebecca's pre-K has spring break coming up in two weeks. How about we come to Saint Louis? They've got a good zoo, right? You know how much she loves animals. And it would do us both good to get away for a while."

Jeremy rubbed his fingertips together. Would she want to stay in his tiny one-bedroom apartment? He could sleep on the couch, and they could have the bedroom. It'd be the first time they'd spent the night in the same place, but did anyone care about that stuff anymore? Did Maggie? He thought he knew her but hadn't considered this situation. What if Rebecca wasn't coming? What would he—

"You got awful quiet all of a sudden," Maggie said. "Is there a problem?"

"What? No. I mean, well, my apartment's kind of small but you—"

Her voice lightened. "I already promised Rebecca a place with an indoor pool. I'll find us a place as close as I can if the dates work for you."

"Oh, sure. There's a few nice places not far from my apartment. I'll take some time off and chauffeur you two around to see the sights. The zoo, Grant's Farm, the Arch, all that stuff."

"Sounds fun, as long as I get control of the radio. None of your twangy country stuff. I have to protect my daughter, you know."

He laughed and propped an elbow on his desk. "Protect her? She needs to be educated. Develop a bit of culture and appreciation for the finer arts."

"Uh-huh. We'll see. Listen, I've got to get to work. I'm *really* looking forward to seeing you. It'll be fun."

His face flushed and he swallowed hard. Love this woman. He glanced at the file, still open on his desk. A small photo of Catherine Mae Blackston was paper-clipped to the corner, smiling at him. "Yeah, Maggie. Can't wait. Maybe I can bounce a few things off you while you're here. Get your thoughts."

"A case you're working?"

"Officially? No."

"Ooh. I'm intrigued. Well, I don't know, Agent Winter. Can you handle a female partner for a few days? Especially one with a young daughter in tow?"

Heat flashed through him again. Easiest question he'd have all week. "Depends on what you mean by 'handling.' You two just get here."

She chuckled. "It's obvious you haven't spent much time with five-year-olds, or you wouldn't be so brave. Gotta run, but watch your email. Oh, and I sent you a care package too. Let me know when you get it. Talk to you soon."

"Hey, before you go ... I saw they posted another opening for an intelligence analyst. You ought to think about it."

After a couple of seconds, she sighed. "Jeremy, we've been through this. I like my job."

"Yeah, I know you do, but think about it. A lot less travel. More time with Rebecca. Those are good things, right?"

"Yep, still good. Just like the last time they had an opening and you brought it up."

"Maggie, I just think—"

"You think it's safer." A twinge of sarcasm and anger crept into her voice. "I get it," she said. "I have a daughter to think about. Only unmarried, childless women should be allowed in the Bureau, right? That's what I hear when we talk about this."

He massaged his forehead. "You know that's not what I'm saying."

"I'm sorry your, well ..."

"Go ahead. Say it. We both know you're thinking it."

"Fine. I'm sorry about your wife and daughter, but that wasn't your fault. You can't protect everyone you care about twenty-four hours a day. I do understand your concern, and I *love* that you worry about us, but this is who I am. You have to accept that."

He inhaled deeply. "I'll try. Really."

"And promise you won't bring it up when we come to visit?"

"Promise," he said.

"Good. Now, we both need to get to work. Let me know when you get the present I sent, okay?"

"Will do. Kiss Rebecca for me."

He held the phone to his ear for nearly a minute after she hung up, rehashing the conversation in his mind. He hated when she got angry at him, especially when she was right. She *could* take care of herself. But that didn't change the way he thought. Keeping her and Rebecca safe meant everything. He'd failed once, and he couldn't go through that again.

It'd been a dozen years since Holly and Miranda died. His wife and unborn daughter, murdered while he was off playing patriot. He should've been there to protect them.

The killer had never been caught. Twelve years of guilt and fury and frustration.

Anger issues? Yep.

And then he'd met Maggie. Red hair, green eyes, and tough enough to put a man in his place, including her ex-husband. And Rebecca was the spitting image of her mother. He couldn't understand what the two of them saw in him. Once Maggie got the whole story, she'd be gone. He knew it sure as the sun rises in the east.

He traced the crayon tiger's whiskers with his finger and nodded. It'd been a long time since he'd wanted to be part of a family. Did they feel the same way about him? He thought so.

But she didn't know everything about him. Not yet.

And when she did, they'd be gone.

CHAPTER EIGHT

The insurance fraud case was all but closed. It took Jeremy three days, though he could've done it in two. Suspects in jail, awaiting trial. Witness statements documented. The DA's office considering immunity for a couple of lower ranking members of the scam in exchange for further testimony. In six months or so, they'd give Jeremy an update. It seemed a long time to wait, but that suited him just fine. Close the file and forget about it until maybe never. Kind of like what the Bureau had done with him.

It still didn't make sense. They transferred him to Saint Louis with no explanation and no notice. Pack up and go. Good luck and God speed. Don't call us, we'll call you. He'd reached out to a few contacts in HR, but no one seemed to know anything, or if they did, they weren't talking.

His new case involved bogus narcotics prescriptions. Lots of users and one doctor. As with virtually every crime, it all came down to the connections. Somebody knows something. The trick was to find that somebody, then start following the money. Shouldn't be too hard on this one. All he had to do was figure out which of the users would be the most credible to a jury and go from there. Find the right connection and voila, doors opened, and angels sang.

Three quick beeps on his desk phone notified him of an internal call. No need for formalities.

"Yeah?"

"Agent Winter?"

"Uh-huh?"

"This is Scott, down in the mailroom. Got a package in for you."

"Um, okay. Can't you bring it up on the regular run?"

A chuckle. "No can do. You'll have to come get this one yourself."

Jeremy stood and bumped his chair back. "No problem. Need the exercise anyway. Be down in a few."

Incoming deliveries and mail came in on the ground floor at a small loading dock. He opted for the stairs and took his time. No hurry to get back to his computer. His eyes needed a break, and his leg was acting up. Time to stretch it out and give the scar an excuse to flare again.

He walked into the mailroom and stood at the door, waiting to be acknowledged. No sense in interrupting anyone's work, especially since he was in no hurry to return to his own.

"Help you?" a young woman asked.

"I hope so. I'm Jeremy Winter. Scott called and said you guys had a package down here for me."

The woman rolled her eyes, crossed her arms, and frowned. "Yeah, thanks a lot. I'm the one who had to uncrate that thing. Out on the dock, of course, wanding it each step of the way. Took forever. You know how cold it is out there?"

He considered letting her know that according to the weatherman on last night's news, it was unseasonably warm for early April. Her expression warned him not to. "Um, thanks? I'm really not sure—"

She pointed to a corner of the room. "It's over there behind the stacks of mail totes. Enjoy."

"I appreciate it."

"Whatever."

He wandered over, searching his mind for what it could be. No clue. Good surprise or bad? Either way, at least it was something different. And the way things were going, he'd take it. Anything to get out from behind that desk, even for just a—

His chair.

From his old office in D.C. He'd recognize it anywhere. The scraped and scratched brown leather with the stained padded armrests.

Maggie.

He plopped into the chair and smiled. The squeak was audible even over the noise of the mailroom. The left armrest wobbled. The seat leaned slightly to the right.

His chair.

Jeremy couldn't imagine how she'd pulled this off. What kind of effort it must've taken to accomplish this minor miracle. He picked up the seat and one of the wheels clanked to the ground.

My chair.

Maybe this could work after all.

CHAPTER NINE

Jeremy carried a plush stuffed hippo in one hand and a cup of weak, but warm, coffee in the other. He nodded toward Rebecca as she hop-skipped a few steps ahead of them. "I don't know how you do it, Maggie. She hasn't slowed down since we got here. It's like watching a human pinball machine."

"There's some stwiped zebwas over there!" The carrot-topped whirlwind froze, pointed, and looked back over her shoulder, the freckles on her cheeks almost hidden by a pinkish-red glow.

"I see them, honey," Maggie said. "Why don't you run over and get a closer look?"

The girl yanked the green knit cap off her head and handed it to her mother. "Hold this. I'm hot."

"Keep it on. I don't want you to catch a cold."

Too late. Rebecca ran to the zebras, her frizzy hair reflecting the early spring sun while little legs churned, their blurriness implying a speed that wasn't there.

Jeremy laughed. "It's plenty warm. You picked a good time to come. Temps are twenty degrees warmer than normal this time of year. Couldn't ask for a better day." He brushed his finger along her arm. "Of course, I'd have thought the same thing if it was sleeting. It's a good day."

Maggie scooted closer, and the two sat on a bench and watched as Rebecca waved and talked to the zebras.

"So," he said, "you think it's nothing."

Maggie crinkled her eyebrows and parted her lips slightly. "What?"

"The Blackston case. The missing woman."

"Oh. I don't know. There's nothing to indicate anything other than she walked away from her life. It could be something, I suppose, but there are no hits on any of her accounts. Not that she had money in there anyway. Maybe she was depressed or found a new husband. Or maybe something did happen to her. But there's no evidence that points to anything illegal. None. If it hadn't been your friend who asked you to look into her disappearance, what would you think?"

"Yeah, I know. I should drop it unless anything new turns up. It's not like I don't have enough to do without creating work. And he's not my friend. I barely know the guy. He spent a day and a half in the bed next to me at Landstuhl Medical in Germany. I can't even remember what we talked about, except he kept calling me G-man. Drove me crazy."

"Listen. The cops in Indiana have your number. If anything turns up, and they want your help, they'll call. I still think she just left. People get tired of their lives sometimes and drop off the grid, hoping they can be someone different. Haven't you ever wanted to get away from everything and start over?"

Rebecca glanced back to make sure they were still watching, and Jeremy waved before kissing the top of Maggie's head. "Maybe. But not now. Not anymore. Not unless you two are going with me."

A slow breeze moved through bringing a chill and *Parfum d'Elephant*. Maggie inched closer to him, and he did a half-stretch and yawn, landing one arm on the bench behind her. She reached up, pulled his hand onto her shoulder, and scooted until their sides and thighs touched. His chest swelled, and his mouth dried. Good grief. It's like being back in high school.

A family passed behind them, their three boys squawking about which snow cone flavor was the best. Somewhere off to the right, howler monkeys argued with each other, their whoop-whoops echoing from the primate house. A squirrel scurried down a tree and made its way toward them, hopeful for a handout. Jeremy squeezed Maggie's shoulder and ran his hand up and down her arm.

This. A perfect day. He didn't deserve it, but here it was.

Maggie tilted her head up. "Got to go soon. Don't want to miss our flight this afternoon."

"I wish you could stay longer."

"I've got a job too, remember? Corrupt judges don't catch themselves."

"Yeah. They don't. But, you know, if you decided you wanted to maybe put in for a transfer or something ..."

Maggie sighed. "We've discussed this. The divorce agreement is very clear. Unless Rebecca's father agrees to it, which he won't, I can't live outside Virginia, and that's all we're going to say about it. You promised, remember? No talk about changing jobs."

His finger traced circles on her shoulder, and he slowly morphed them into hearts. "It doesn't seem right. After the way he treated you and all."

"He's a much better father than he was a husband."

"He'd better be." Jeremy cleared his throat and stared at the redheaded girl as she carried on a deep conversation with the zebras. "I'm glad. Rebecca deserves that. Being a good husband and dad is about all any man could ask for."

Maggie nodded and looked up at him. "It still hurts, doesn't it? You know you can talk to me anytime. We've been dating ... what? Almost a year now? You don't say much about them. I'm not going to pry, but when you're ready, I'm here."

He drew his lips into his mouth. "I know you are, and yeah, it still hurts. A lot. Sometimes I wonder what it would be like if they hadn't, I mean, if Holly and Miranda ... I wasn't there for them, Maggie. If I'd been home—"

"You'd have been at the office. Same thing would have happened."

"You don't know. You don't. There's a price we pay for the things we do. When I was in Afghanistan, well, maybe they paid for the things I did."

She shifted and turned toward him. "When, Jeremy?"

The question he'd known was coming. He had to tell her. Risk her judgment. But if Maggie didn't understand, he would crumble. Disintegrate. He needed to tell her in person, face-to-face, so he could see her expression. Try to explain.

But not now. He wouldn't ruin this day. "Soon."

"When you're ready," she said. Rebecca glanced back, and Maggie grinned at her. "She likes you. Told me that at the hotel last night. She thinks you're funny."

"Funny, huh? I do like to see her smile." Like? Love.

After a moment, Maggie tapped his knee. "No chance the Bureau will reconsider and bring you back to D.C.?"

"Not likely. At least not for a while. I can't even find out why I got transferred in the first place. Got the 'it'll do you good' speech with a heavy dose of 'we need you there' thrown in for good measure. I'll give it a few more months and then start calling again."

She sighed. "It'd be nice to have you closer."

He squeezed her against him, letting her coconut shampoo and soft floral scent mingle in his memory.

"Close enough?" he asked.

"For now."

A squeaky voice interrupted their peacefulness. "Giwaffes! I see them over there! Come on, guys!"

"Well," Maggie said, "I guess it's time to go see the giraffes. You ready?"

Jeremy closed his eyes, inhaled deeply, and kissed her on top of the head. "I've been ready for a long time."

CHAPTER TEN

Jeremy scanned the database summary for the umpteenth time. The doctor had been a busy man. Seventeen thousand prescriptions spanning a period of three years. Twelve hundred patients. Over two hundred different drugs, yet less than a dozen narcotics made up seventy percent of the total. No question. The doc was nothing more than a drug dealer with a diploma. Unfortunately, proving that would take more than a database.

He stretched and rubbed his eyes. It had to be getting close to lunchtime. A glance at the nemesis clock set him straight. Nine-forty. Great. He tapped a finger on the desk, pretend-wrestling with his desire to make the phone call.

Let someone else figure out what happened to Catherine Mae Blackston. It wasn't his case. Probably not even a crime. Leave it to the locals. Toss the file and forget it.

Can't.

He pulled up his contacts and punched a button. "Officer Obion? Hi. It's Agent Winter with the FBI."

"Yes, sir. How are you?"

"Good. Just thought I'd check in and see if anything new had turned up on Miss Blackston."

"'Fraid not. I went back out to the park a couple of weekends ago to look around. Hoped I'd come up with something we'd missed. Nicer weather, you know, but the wind's been brutal lately. Figured maybe the leaves got blown around and exposed a piece of evidence. Stupid, I know."

"Not stupid at all. I'd call it being thorough."

"Thanks. Didn't find anything though, so for now, we're keeping it an open case. She's in the system, and if anything turns up, we'll get an alert."

"Great. I take it nothing else has happened around there? No one else gone missing?"

"No, sir. Quiet as ever. The NBC station out of Evansville ran a story about Miss Blackston a couple of weeks ago, but nothing came of it. As far as I know, nobody's looking for her other than her ex. He calls every week. Said he was going to put up some flyers around town and in the park."

Jeremy stretched his neck and twisted his head. "What's your gut telling you on this?"

"My gut?"

"Yeah. You're a cop. What's your instinct say?"

He hesitated before saying, "The chief says to drop it and move on. The whole thing doesn't feel right to me, but I couldn't tell you why. No evidence of a crime. No suspects or motives. I figure people who disappear on purpose are either running away from something or running to something. And as far as I can tell, Miss Blackston didn't have any reason to do either."

"You think she was taken."

"Well, if it was some sort of accident, we'd have found her by now. With the warmer weather, there's plenty of hikers and golfers around the park. Something would've turned up. There's a volunteer group up in Indy that's got a cadaver dog, and they're coming down in a week or two. Maybe they'll find something. I'll let you know how it goes."

"I'd appreciate it."

"No problem. I'm looking forward to watching the dog work. They said this is the same German Shepherd that found Sarah Goldman a few years back."

"Sarah Goldman?"

"Yeah. It was big news around here back then. Young girl, around seventeen if I remember right. Disappeared on her way home from high school up in French Lick. They found her body, or at least what was left of it, a year and a half later."

Jeremy's stomach churned. "Where's French Lick?"

"Opposite side of the park, and I know what you're thinking, but it's a dead end. They caught the guy who killed her, and he's still sitting in prison on death row, although he's more likely to die of old age I'd guess, what with the appeals and all."

He exhaled and ran a hand through his hair. "Got it. You'll call me if the dog hits on anything?"

"Yes, sir. Will do."

Jeremy hung up the phone and leaned back in his chair, both hands clasped behind his head. Nine-fifty. An hour and a half until lunch. Enough time to line up a few interviews with the drug doctor's patients.

He sighed and logged back onto his laptop. Twelve hundred names. Sort by number of narcotics prescriptions per patient. Here we go. Start making phone calls. Yep. Any minute now.

His mouth suddenly dry, he closed his office door before minimizing the database and accessing the Internet. Why did he feel like he was doing something wrong? A few minutes to satisfy his curiosity. That's all. Go to Google, search for Sarah Goldman. Can't hurt. A quick distraction to wake him up. That's it.

Six and a half hours later, Jeremy phoned the Indiana State Prison in Michigan City to arrange a meeting with Sarah Goldman's killer.

CHAPTER ELEVEN

Jeremy stifled a yawn and shuddered as a chill sprang on him. Why was he here? It seemed highly unlikely the convicted murderer would provide any helpful information. In the five years since they'd found Sarah Goldman's body, nothing had changed. All the evidence, at least what there was of it, pointed to Lawrence Berkley. Almost four years ago, a jury took less than three hours to determine he was guilty, and two days later the judge handed down the death penalty. They decided who lived and who died by the book. All nice, clean, and legal. Berkley became the thirteenth man on Indiana's death row, and the justice system trudged forward.

Jeremy cleared the prison's security and was escorted into a small room of cinder block walls and metal furniture. Cheery. Berkley would arrive any minute, escorted by at least two guards. The murderer understood, short of an escape, he'd leave prison in a body bag sooner or later. Convicted of killing another inmate during a fight last year, he'd obviously opted for later. Jeremy had to pull a few strings to arrange this meeting, and he'd owe a few favors when it was done. It would be worth the trouble, though, even if peace of mind was all he got out of the brief encounter.

The interrogation room door swung open, and Berkley shuffled in, clad in a khaki prison uniform and hunched over, his hands and feet shackled to the chain circling his waist. The prisoner dropped into the chair opposite Jeremy, yawned elaborately, and held up his handcuffs.

Jeremy shook his head. "Not gonna happen."

Berkley shrugged and slouched into the metal seat. One guard exited the room and the other positioned himself between the killer and the door.

Jeremy studied the man on the opposite side of the table. Twenty-eight years old but looked fifty. Skinny, ash-yellow pockmarked skin, thin lips, and a shaved head. Teeth that showed at least marginal meth use. Neck tattoo. "Only God can judge me." Guess the judge disagreed.

"I'm Special Agent Jeremy Winter with the FBI. I've got a few questions I'd like to ask about the Sarah Goldman case."

"Look, man. I'm not saying nothing without my attorney here."

Jeremy nodded. "Fine. But for the record, what I have to ask can only help you. You're sitting on death row. What could I possibly do to make your situation worse?"

Berkley leaned forward and placed his hands on the metal table. "Help me?" The convict's eyes narrowed. "You people are all the same. Nothing but lies. We both know there's nothing you can do for me. The last time someone said they were going to help, I ended up in these chains. So, you'll excuse me if I tell you to kiss my—"

"Fair enough," Jeremy said. "You're right. I've got nothing to offer you except a chance to tell your side of the story."

"Already did that. You read the transcripts from the trial, right? The story hasn't changed." He leaned back and tried to cross his arms but was hindered by the shackles. "The truth don't change, man. I didn't have nothing to do with that girl."

"A jury of your peers said otherwise."

Berkley laughed, worked up a good spit, and spewed the saliva on the floor. The guard placed a hand on his baton and moved toward the convict, but Jeremy raised his hand and shook his head.

"My peers?" the prisoner said. "Man, I was convicted as soon as they saw me. My picture all over the news saying I did those things to that girl. They couldn't wait to get to me."

Jeremy crossed his arms and allowed his delayed yawn to proceed with full fury. "Mmm hmm. Prisons are full of innocent people."

"I've done a lot of things, but I didn't kill that girl. Wouldn't do that. And wouldn't do none of the other stuff they said about her either."

"Well, Mr. Berkley, let's run through the list, shall we? High school salutatorian turned meth dealer and sometimes user. Breaking and entering. Possession of a stolen gun. And let's not forget about your second murder conviction last year. And that's only the stuff we know about. I'm sure you have other hidden talents. And yet you want me to believe you wouldn't kill Sarah Goldman?"

The felon worked his mouth as if he had a bad taste that wouldn't go away. "Where was the DNA? Wasn't none. Know why? Because I was set up, man, but didn't nobody want to hear it."

Jeremy scratched his cheek. Stubbly. Time to replace the razor. "First of all, the lack of your DNA at the scene means exactly nothing, other than to hurt your whole 'I was set up' claim. Seriously, if anyone wanted to frame you, the first thing they'd do is plant your DNA there. It's not too hard, you know. An old cigarette butt. Maybe some chewing gum. Actually, in your case, probably a needle. Grab it, dump it near the body, and you're done."

"Wasn't like that, man. Yeah, I did some bad things. Got to make a living, right? But kill her? No way. Got nothin' to gain from it. Never seen that girl until the police slapped her picture in front of me."

"Uh-huh. Her body was found in the woods less than a quarter mile from the abandoned trailer where you cooked your meth. Now that could certainly be a coincidence. And when the dogs tracked her clothes to the rotten pine trees fifty feet from your trailer? Maybe that's just your bad luck. But her ID? Come on, Lawrence. Driver's license and credit cards buried under your front steps?"

"Man, how stupid do you think I am?"

Jeremy arched his eyebrows. "You really want me to answer that?"

"If I'd killed that girl, you think I'd up and bring her junk back to my place? Everybody knows to burn stuff that might, uh, burn you. Police can't do nothin' with ashes."

"You might be surprised."

The convict shrugged. "Whatever. And no fingerprints on any of it. Don't make no sense. And then the cops get an anonymous phone call saying I did it? No way, man. Dude set me up. It's not fair."

Heat flashed through Jeremy's face, and he slapped the table. "Not fair, huh? Don't you hate it when bad things happen to good people? I mean, here you are, an upstanding law-abiding citizen, just trying to make an honest living. No problems at all until Sarah Goldman has the nerve to go and get killed nearby. You're not the victim here, Mr. Berkley."

The prisoner slumped and stared into his lap. "I got a good idea who did it. I told them, but they said there wasn't no evidence. That I was lyin'." He leaned forward and reached his hands across the table.

"I'm in the mood for a good story, Mr. Berkley. Fire away."

"Stacks, he did it. Set me up, too. Don't matter now, though. He got what was comin' to him."

"I've seen the file," Jeremy said. "Stacks was your partner. Handled the sales end of the meth business. Funny how none of this came out until after you'd been charged. In fact, you repeatedly told investigators you handled the business by yourself. No one else involved."

"I'm not a snitch."

"Uh-huh. Stacks set you up so he could, what? Take over your little lab of horrors? Sure, sure. I can see that. One problem, though." Jeremy pointed his index finger at Berkley. "Wouldn't it be easier to just kill you? Seems like an awful lot of trouble to go through when a bullet in the back of your skull would have been simpler."

The prisoner nodded. "That's the thing. I don't think he planned to set me up. We were tight. Maybe he found that girl's body. Or maybe he got himself in a situation and tried to make the best of it. Know what I'm sayin'? Kill two birds. Check his file, man. Stacks had a history with chicks, slappin' them around and stuff."

"Well, Mr. Berkley, as I'm quite sure you're aware, your buddy left this life in a blaze of, well, I'm not sure 'glory' is the right word. He should've stayed in sales, I guess. There'll be no more questioning him. And according to the files, he alibied out. Something about sitting in jail on a drunk and disorderly charge if I remember correctly."

The convict worked his mouth again and twisted his head, cracking his neck. "Look, man. Why're you even here? You don't want to hear the truth. You all got what you wanted."

Jeremy pulled a photo from his briefcase and slid it across the table. "Sarah Goldman. Seventeen years old when she was killed. Do you think she deserved to die, Mr. Berkley?"

"I got no idea, man. I don't know nothing about her except what you all told me."

Jeremy rested his elbows on the table. "Really? Because I didn't know her either. In fact, I'm sure I know less about her than you do. But I don't think she deserved to die. And then, to mutilate her like that, well, it takes things to a whole new level of evil, wouldn't you say?"

Berkley fixated on the photo. "She didn't deserve that. Nobody does."

"And her family. Suffering for so long. Wondering what happened to their little girl. Expecting the worst but hoping for the best. Then finding out someone had done that to their daughter. Can you imagine? I can't. It must be horrible. To still be wondering ..."

The felon shook his head slowly and swallowed hard.

Jeremy placed his palms on the cold steel table. "Where are they, Lawrence?"

Berkley's head jerked. "What?"

"Sarah's hands and skull. Where are they?"

The prisoner jumped up, sending his chair flying backwards. The guard yelled for his partner, and each of them grabbed one of the prisoner's arms. Berkley made no effort to resist.

"Told you, man. I didn't have nothing to do with her. Must be the Devil himself to do something like that. Find yourself somebody else to play games with."

Jeremy stood and inclined his head toward the felon. "No games, Mr. Berkley. There's far too much at stake. Thank you for your time."

"So, what was this all about then?"

Jeremy studied the man before him. "I had to know whether I believed you."

Berkley returned the stare, holding his chin high. "And?"

"You, sir, are a threat to society, and I'll do everything I can to make sure you spend the rest of your hopefully very short life in prison. But do I think you murdered the girl? Yeah, I think there's a good chance the jury got it right."

"Knew it. You people only hear what you—"

"Enough with playing the victim." Jeremy scooped up his file and walked around the table until he stood face-to-face with the convict. "I also think there's a possibility, a slight one, that you didn't kill her."

The prisoner shifted on his feet. "So, you're going to reopen the case?"

"No," Jeremy said. "I'm not. You've told me nothing the police didn't already know."

"What's the point then? Waste of my time, man."

Jeremy held up the photo, clenching it so tightly that the picture creased. "The point, Mr. Berkley, is to make sure no one else ends up like Sarah Goldman."

CHAPTER TWELVE

Jeremy held a photo in each hand. Catherine Mae Blackston on the left, Sarah Goldman on the right. Middle-aged brunette and blonde teenager. Meticulously applied makeup versus multiple facial piercings. Moderately overweight and borderline anorexic. Both Caucasian. In other words, nothing.

He placed the pictures on his desk side-by-side and clasped his hands behind his neck, pushing back against them. Was he wasting his time? No other murdered women around the park in the last dozen years. Nothing linked these two together other than Hoosier National Forest, and that was flimsy at best. Certainly not enough to go to his boss with.

Deputy Director Bailey had not been in a good mood since, well, a long time. And if he found out Jeremy was spending part of his day on work that had nothing to do with his assigned white-collar case, his attitude would get a lot worse. Without hard evidence, Jeremy had to keep his suspicions under wraps. Best not to antagonize the boss. Bailey's conversations with Jeremy had become curt, almost terse. Something had changed, but what?

He tapped his finger on the edge of his laptop. The NCIC database showed more than fifty other missing women in Indiana, half of those within the last five years. The National Crime Information Center's data was incredibly useful when it wasn't overwhelming. Not too many to sort through, but probably only the tip of the iceberg. If no one reported them gone, or if the police believed they left of their own accord, they wouldn't be on the list.

Still, it was worth a look. Anything to scratch the nagging itch. He stretched his arms high overhead, shook his hands vigorously, and pulled his computer toward him. Another sip of bitter java from his coffee mug, finally stained the lightest of beige, and then—

His cell phone vibrated, and Jeremy checked the caller ID. Speak of the Devil. Bailey. Doubtless wanting an update on the prescription-pushing doctor. The case would be presented to the prosecutor in a week, maybe less. He had three more interviews set for this afternoon. At this point, he needed to make sure his witnesses, many of them drug abusers, were reliable enough to testify.

Jeremy cleared his throat and answered the phone. "Good morning, sir. How can I help you?"

"Morning, Agent Winter. I'm putting together this month's updates for the powers-that-be. What's going on with your bogus prescriptions case?"

"Wrapping it up now, sir. The prosecutor will have the file within a week or so. I expect it'll be a fairly easy indictment. The doctor's got a passport, so I'm certain they're going to recommend no bail if possible."

"Excellent. Good job on that. What's next?"

Should he take the chance? Mention his suspicion of a serial killer stalking public lands? No. The old expression's true. It's a lot easier to get forgiveness than permission. "Got a couple of options, sir, but it'll probably be a car cloning ring based in central Missouri. They're grabbing sports cars and SUVs out of Saint Louis, switching the VINs, and reselling them on the Internet."

"Hold on, Winter." A scraping noise filtered through the phone as the Director covered the mouthpiece. "Janice! We got any more coffee out there? Okay. I'm back. So, a car cloning ring? That's next?"

"Looks like it."

"Got it. If you could explain something, though. I'm not clear on how either your current case or the auto thefts require a visit to the Indiana State Prison?"

Jeremy tugged at his shirt collar and covered the phone to block his mumbled word selection. "Sir?"

"We're the FBI, Agent Winter. It's our job to know things. Now, what does Lawrence Berkley have to do with these cases?"

"Um, nothing, sir. It's something else I'm working on. At this point, I just have a theory. No point in wasting your time with details."

"I see. It seems to me that your time's being wasted, not mine. Worse, you're throwing away taxpayer dollars. Your priority is to work the cases you're assigned. Hold on." Muttering trickled through the phone, and a short laugh followed. "Thank you, Janice. Okay. Agent Winter, anything else you do cannot and will not detract from your assigned investigation. Clear?"

Uh-oh. The taxpayers. Never good when he went there. "Yes, sir. I understand."

"Okay. Anything else?"

Jeremy took a deep breath. "Sir, I was wondering how much longer I'd be assigned here. In Saint Louis, I mean."

"Is there a problem?"

"Not a problem. It's just that D.C. seemed to be a better fit for me."

"Uh-huh. How so?"

How could he explain without sounding like a whiner? "I feel that my skill set is more attuned to working nationwide cases rather than local issues."

Bailey chuckled. "Your skill set is more attuned? You planning to run for office, Agent Winter? Maybe filling out resumes? I get enough people talking in circles without you doing it too. I think what you mean is you like working the bigger cases. Especially the violent ones. With your history, I suppose that's understandable."

Jeremy grimaced. His history. Holly and Miranda and the nightmare of Afghanistan. The sins of the past, forgotten by most but remembered by the FBI. And himself. Funny. So few people knew the story, and the ones who did thought he was a hero. Still, he was a risk to the Bureau, what with the things he'd seen.

And done.

Was that why they had shipped him off? But why now? "Sir, I believe I've proved myself to be steady and reliable."

"You have. I'm with you on this, but give it a little more time. Listen, I'm running late for a meeting. Let me know when the doctor is indicted. And give Agent Keeley my best."

Jeremy hung up the phone. Agent Maggie Keeley. Was there anything Bailey didn't know? Not likely. Best to stay buried in work, close some cases, and then revisit the possibility of transferring back ... as soon as he checked one more thing.

He turned his focus back to the database of missing women and sorted by the available categories, desperate to find something that stood out. Nothing. A perfectly random sampling of American females. He sorted them by location and plotted each on an online map. A few of the women lived close to the National Forest, but as large as the park was, that could easily be the result of coincidence. He printed the list and circled the names of the three closest to the public land. As good a place to start as any.

He slid the file back into the desk drawer and made himself look away. Like a kid whose parents teased with a wrapped birthday present. Not today, honey. You can open it tomorrow. And no peeking.

He sighed and opened the case file for the prescription-peddling doctor. Get this done, and you can open your gift. Maybe.

Later.

CHAPTER THIRTEEN

The hockey game ended, and Jeremy switched off the TV, effectively casting his bedroom into darkness except for the flashing green light on his cell phone. After a quick check for any urgent emails, he replaced the phone on the nightstand. Fortunately, the game had been a blowout, with the Capitals winning easily. No adrenaline to keep him awake tonight.

He closed his eyes and slowed his breathing, trying to control the images and thoughts that flashed through his mind. Never worked. Bedtime was when he chased the rabbit trails. See where they led him. Replayed the past and pondered the future. One kept him awake at night. The other got him out of bed in the morning.

The buzzing and dinging of his phone jolted his heart, and he squeezed his eyes closed before blinking several times and picking up the device. He didn't recognize the number, but he did know the area code. 202. Washington, D.C.

He cleared his throat to remove any sleepiness from his voice. "Agent Winter."

"Good evening, Winter. Hope I didn't wake you."

Jeremy recognized the voice immediately, though, if you didn't count the dreams, it'd been a dozen years since he'd last heard it in Afghanistan. He'd have been happy to never hear it again. "Colonel Cronfeld."

"Good memory. Been a while."

As if he could forget. "What can I do for you?"

"Son, it's more like what I can do for you."

Son? Cronfeld couldn't have been more than fifty, barely older than Jeremy. "How's that?"

"Let's get together soon. Have a chat about old times."

Absolutely the last thing Jeremy wanted to do. If he needed to talk to someone about Afghanistan, it wouldn't be with Cronfeld. And the colonel knew that. What was going on?

Jeremy sat up and swung his feet to the floor. "Um, I'm not sure—"

"Heard you got transferred. Saint Louis, is it? White-collar investigations now? How's that working out for you?"

And there it was. A not-so-subtle implication that he'd been responsible for Jeremy's relocation. Which meant he could arrange to undo it as well. A retired Marine colonel didn't have that kind of power, but his U.S. Senator wife did. But why?

Jeremy rubbed his forehead. "I go where I'm assigned."

"Of course you do. We're all just soldiers obeying orders. Trying to hold the world together, am I right?"

"I do what I have to do."

"We all do, son. We all do. Now, as it turns out, I'll be in Missouri in the next day or so. How about you and me get together? Dinner on me. Saint Louis has wonderful Italian restaurants. Pick one. I can be reached at this number."

"If it's all the same to—"

"I'm not asking. Tomorrow night. Nineteen thirty. If I need to, I can have Director Bailey arrange things for us."

"That won't be necessary. I'll make the reservations."

"Good. Looking forward to it then. I'll pick you up outside your apartment building. Great to talk to you again, son. Got a lot to catch up on."

Cronfeld knew where he lived. He'd done some digging, but why? Jeremy fell back in the bed and switched on the TV. A west coast hockey game. Not a fan of either team, but that didn't matter. The game was nothing more than background noise to his thoughts.

Colonel Ramsey Cronfeld was back. Why and for how long, Jeremy didn't know. Not yet.

He reached over and grabbed his Glock 19 off the nightstand, then popped the magazine to confirm it was full. Fifteen rounds plus one in the pipe. Backup magazine in the drawer.

Old habits die hard.

Old memories? Even harder.

CHAPTER FOURTEEN

Mason opened the blinds of the kitchen's bay window, allowing the early morning light to saturate the room. The pinkish-orange glow on the horizon highlighted a smattering of clouds, but that would change soon enough. Rain was coming his way. Best to get out and get the work done before the showers hit.

"Mornin', babe." Paula Miller dropped half a slab of bacon into the cast iron skillet and looked over her shoulder at her husband. The sizzling crescendoed, and she scooted the pieces around, letting the fat render and pop. "Get enough sleep? You tossed and turned all night."

"Mornin'," Mason said. He nuzzled his face into her hair and bit her earlobe. "I swear the smell of bacon could wake the dead."

She giggled and swatted his hand. "Too early for that foolishness. Now go on before you make me burn breakfast."

He kissed the back of her neck and took a seat at the yellow dinette table. Everything sat in its proper position. Half a glass of orange juice in front of the plate, a steaming cup of coffee next to it. The newspaper off to the right and opened to the sports page.

"The boys not up yet?" he asked.

"They're stirring. I'll make sure they're ready in time for the school bus. A couple more weeks, and they'll be out for the summer. Seems like this year's flying by." She flipped the bacon and stepped back from the stove. "They'll be down here soon enough once they get a whiff of breakfast cooking."

"True enough." He took a sip of coffee, looked into the mug, and set it back on the table. "Got an email from the bank last night."

She turned toward him. "Turn us down again?"

He grunted. "Yeah. They said we didn't have enough collateral to cover a new loan, what with the other outstanding balances. Said they'd reconsider if I'd be willing to put at least some of the land up to secure the money. Not sure how we're going to get the planter fixed before spring. I can probably rig it good enough to get the cotton in, and a bit of corn in the fall, but after that who knows. Could sell off the cattle, I guess. That's how they do it, you know? They take it away piece by piece until there's nothing left."

"We'll get by. We always do. October's not that far off. We'll bring in enough money on the pumpkins and corn maze to get everything fixed up. And if not, we'll find another way."

"Got no choice, do we?"

"No, we don't. Now, straighten up. I don't want the kids to worry. You'll fix things. You always do." She pivoted back toward the stove, and he swatted her rear. She looked back over her shoulder, and he winked at her.

"You want your eggs scrambled?" she asked.

"Sounds great. Sprinkle a little cheese on there too."

Lucas and Andy shuffled into the kitchen, dressed but looking like they'd been hanging out on the clothesline all night. The red creases on their faces pointed to hair that would need to be drenched before there'd be any hope of it laying down.

Mason chuckled at the pair. "You two look like you had a rough night. Might want to take a look in the mirror before you head off to school."

Both boys grunted their responses and dragged themselves into chairs around the table. Paula brought the eggs, bacon, and biscuits and sat next to her husband. All bowed their heads and held hands while Mason recited grace. As soon as the "Amen" came, forks and knives went to work, clanking against bowls, jelly jars, and butter dishes.

"Supposed to get some rain the next few days," Mason said. "I'll have to hold off on putting out the cotton."

Lucas grabbed his second biscuit and shoved a bite of bacon inside it. "Should be all right as long as you get it in by the end of the month, right Dad? Still got a couple of weeks."

Mason reached over and mussed both boys' hair. "I'll make farmers out of you two yet. We'll be fine. Plenty of time to get the seeds in the ground."

Paula grinned, slathered butter on a biscuit, and placed it on her husband's plate. "They've got a good teacher."

Mason nodded. "Best way to learn is by doing it. My daddy showed me, and his daddy showed him. Supposed to be that way. Book learning is good, but until a man gets the feel of dirt, he can't be a farmer."

"Oh," Paula said, "after a day in the fields, those two have the feel of dirt all right. The look and smell of it too."

"Just boys being boys, Paula. Don't figure I was much different back when we met, was I?"

"That's the hard truth, right there. But I saw through the dirt to the man underneath."

She leaned toward her husband, and he pecked her on the lips. The boys squirmed, poked each other, and scrunched their noses.

"What?" Mason said. "Don't you two have girlfriends yet?"

"Eww," five-year-old Andy said. "Girls are gross."

"We are?" Paula said.

"You're not a girl. You're a mom. That's different."

Mason smiled. "I'm not so sure about that. Now listen up. I need you boys to take care of your mom this weekend. I've got some business to tend to out of town, and since it's going to rain, it'll be a good time to go."

Paula licked her lips and poked at the scrambled eggs on her plate. "How long will you be gone?"

"No more than a couple of days probably. Monsanto's running a seminar up in Cape Girardeau on some of their new weed control sprays. Thought I'd check into it."

She took a deep breath and stared at her plate. "Want me to come keep you company? I'm sure I could get a sitter for the boys."

Mason shook his head. "You'd be bored, honey. Heck, I'll be bored, but I need to keep up on the latest stuff. I'll be home as soon as I can. Promise."

Paula nodded but kept her eyes focused on her food. "Sure. Maybe next time."

"Count on it," he said. "Now, somebody slide the strawberry jelly over this way. A man can't get any work done on an empty belly. Isn't that right, boys?"

Mumbled agreement filtered from food-packed mouths. Andy had apple butter smeared around his mouth, and Lucas reached for what had to be his fifth piece of bacon. Good, strong boys who'd grow into tough farmers. Had to be if they were going to survive everything this life would throw at them.

Weather. Banks. Uncle Sam. Crop prices. All conspiring against him, his family, and his land. They had to be a strong unit, banded together against all threats. Their home had to be a haven from outside forces. A fortress against anything that would dare come against them.

The pressure against them was building, wearing him down, shoving thoughts of giving up. They wouldn't win. Not this time. Not ever.

All he needed was to reset and get a fresh outlook. Clean himself of the doubts and the burdens and remember what it was to enjoy life.

He licked his lips.

Time to go hunting.

CHAPTER FIFTEEN

Mason tossed the collection of herbicide pamphlets, business cards, and freebies into the cracked vinyl passenger seat of his pickup. The new weed killer might be a good thing, but only corporations would be able to afford it. Family farms like his were out of luck.

That's why most of the friends he'd grown up with had sold their farms and moved on. They all said they wanted stability. They got tired of the randomness of the weather and the seed and the pests and the buyers. They were sick of making a fortune one year and losing everything the next, of spending hundreds of thousands of dollars for a single piece of equipment. Times changed, they said, and the smart ones changed with them. They recognized that farming's a business, just like the auto parts store or the Dollar General. Once you understood that, life got simpler and you got stability.

Mason spit out the window and ran the back of his hand along his bottom lip. Forty-plus years he'd been farming. Wasn't even five yet when his daddy showed him how to plant a vegetable garden. Didn't have all the education and science they had nowadays, but got it done. Had to. Wasn't any choice.

He pulled the wire-rimmed glasses from his face and cleaned them with his checkered flannel shirt. Stability. If that's what you want, go work at the frozen food factory in town. Sell off your heritage. Either the farming's in your blood or it's not.

Dad taught him to deal with the stress. The pressure's got to get out one way or another, and if you direct it at your family, things only got worse. Find your outlet and don't be shy about using it.

Dad was a whittler. When things got bad, he'd sit on the porch, part of a thick oak branch in one hand, his old Buck knife in the other. He'd sit out there for hours, shaving that wood down to nothing. No fancy designs or little animals. Just keep going until it's gone. Then he'd go to the barn and sharpen the knife, stick it in his pocket, and get back to work.

You knew not to bother Dad on those days. Let him whittle the worries and anger and stress out of his system so he could focus on farming. He'd passed the knife on to Mason, its woodgrain handle worn to a yellowish tan from years of use. Just as sharp as ever, though. Only one problem.

Mason hated whittling.

....

The first was almost six years ago. Mason had just turned forty, and it was a rough season at the farm. Low yields on the soybeans. The old combine harvester had finally died, and he'd needed to finagle a new one before the winter wheat came in. Money was trickling in and pouring out. Paula even picked up some part-time work as a substitute teacher, but by the time they paid the babysitter to watch Lucas, it was hardly worth it. Just as well. Made him look bad that his wife had to work. A man ought to be able to support his family, and it wasn't happening.

He'd gone hunting to improve both his mood and his food supply. A decent whitetail deer, a hundred seventy pounds or thereabouts, would mean they might make it through the winter without having to butcher one of the cows. They had enough vegetables stored in the chest freezer to last four or five months. As long as they scavenged enough to make at least token payments on their loans, they'd survive until spring. Of course, that'd bring a new set of problems, beginning with convincing someone to lend them money to buy seed.

Duane Forsberg was almost an accident—almost. It takes a special kind of idiot to go hiking through Chickasaw Wildlife Refuge during deer hunting season, especially without wearing bright orange. So what if the zone he was in was posted? Hunters hunt. They go where the prey is. And that morning, the quarry was where Duane Forsberg shouldn't have been.

There are two kinds of hunters. Those that hunt to provide food for family and neighbors, and those that shouldn't be hunting. If it moved, it was fair game whether deer, duck, coon, or squirrel. Nothing topped the thrill of deer hunting, though.

You beat the sun out of bed by hours, donned camos buttoned tight against the cold, and grabbed the Thermos of strong coffee with extra sugar as you eased the back door closed so you wouldn't wake the family. The only other vehicles on the road were likely also hunters, and he always nodded and raised a finger off the steering wheel in greeting. Even though it was dark, he was confident the other drivers returned the gesture.

That morning, he'd tracked alone. A neighbor had offered to join him, but Mason wanted the quiet. He crept through the dark woods, bathed in the pine scent that flowed like streams, and listened to the trees and animals as they whispered and stretched their way to a new day.

He'd stalked the deer for almost an hour and was finally in position. The rush of zeroing in on his target, sixty yards away across a grassy clearing, filled him as everything else faded away. There was just enough light to watch the twelve-point buck as the animal moved along the tree line, grazing and alert for any danger.

Mason's finger rested on the trigger of his old bolt-action Remington 700, given to him on his third birthday by his granddad. Uncountable whitetails had fallen victim to its accuracy, and one more was about to join the club. Perfect setup. And then ... gone. The deer jumped into the woods, spooked by something.

Meat taken from the mouths of his family.

He pivoted the rifle to the right and peered through the scope, seeking the culprit. There. A hiker. There must be a trail back in the woods. Couldn't get a good look, what with all the trees. He swung the weapon to the left and focused on a small opening in a group of pines. At the pace the backpacker moved, he should be there in fifteen seconds or so.

Mason swallowed hard and licked his lips. Heat flared in his ears, and the Remington bounced in time with the pulsing of his heart.

Pretend. That's all it was. Better move your finger away from the trigger.

Ten seconds.

The idiot shouldn't be there. Not safe.

Eight seconds.

A whole morning. Wasted.

Five seconds.

Enough venison to feed his family for at least two months.

Two seconds.

Just another animal.

One.

The shot echoed through the predawn, sending a scattering of birds cawing into the sky. Duane Forsberg would no longer steal from him or anyone else. A blast of tension exploded from the pressure cooker of his chest. His fingers twitched as excess energy struggled to find a release. Mason wanted desperately to run across the clearing and burn off the adrenaline.

Should he go over? See how much damage a .30-06 cartridge did to a human? Explain to someone that it was all an accident? That he didn't realize the area was posted, off-limits to hunters?

No. The risk was far too high. Questions would be asked, and even if they believed him, he might lose his hunting license. Unacceptable. Easier to fade away and hope he wasn't caught. Could always claim he aimed for a deer and missed. Had no idea he'd shot someone. Gosh, are they okay?

Nothing else moved. He turned and crept back into the woods. A few steps, freeze, then a few more. Look, but more importantly, listen. Nothing. A few more steps. Quiet. He was alone.

. . . .

Less than two hours later he was home, showered, and getting ready to work the fields. Another fifty acres of winter wheat needed planting, and rain was forecast for the end of the week. He had to get it done. He grabbed Paula on his way out the door and pulled her to him. "Don't get too tired today," he said. "Maybe see if you can whip up a babysitter, and we'll go out to dinner."

She shushed him away, smiling widely. "Well, what's got into you today? You're in a mighty good mood considering you didn't get a deer this morning."

"Thinking we might have to get to work on a brother for Lucas tonight." Mason winked at her and jogged to his tractor, eager to go about his chores.

He'd found something better than whittling.

CHAPTER SIXTEEN

Ahorn honk brought Mason back to reality, and he waved as the Monsanto rep drove past. It was still early, and Paula didn't expect him home until tomorrow anyway. Could head back and surprise her. Maybe take them all out for some fried catfish and then let the boys play on the four-wheelers until dark. It had been a long winter, and sitting on the front porch swing with his girl and a big glass of sweet iced tea sounded like the perfect Saturday night.

He leaned forward and looked up through the cracked windshield. The skies were overcast but warm, and the threat of a mid-May thunderstorm hovered overhead. Not the best of days to be outside. Still ...

Mason cranked the pickup, pumping the gas pedal until the old truck started, and headed east toward the Trail of Tears State Forest in Illinois, just across the Mississippi. A quick drive through the park wouldn't hurt. Check things out and head on home. Who knows? He might get lucky and, if he hurried, he'd still get to the house at a decent hour.

And sweet tea always tasted better when he was relaxed.

....

He drove along the forest's meandering roads with his windows down, enjoying the sights and smells. Beech and sweetgum trees mingled with oaks and maples to hide the woodland's secrets. The rich soil, darkened by years of decaying foliage and wildlife, oozed a dark, earthy scent. He'd give anything if his land smelled like that. Farming took a toll on the soil and on people too if they let it. He hated turning over the dirt on windy days and seeing the clouds of dust billow off into the atmosphere, but he couldn't afford to let his acreage lie fallow.

He turned left off the main street and followed a side road, twisting and turning onto other paths as the mood hit. A few vehicles clustered around a couple of the fire trails, their occupants hiking, picnicking, or doing who-knows-what. Gotta be careful in places like this. You never knew what trouble lay around the next corner. Like that T-shirt he'd spotted up in Gatlinburg said—*Paddle faster. I hear banjo music.*

Another turn, then a quarter-mile later, a lone car parked near a trail entrance. A later model Toyota. Red with four stick figures on the back window. Dad. Mom. Girl. Boy. No dog? He drove several hundred feet past, pulled over, and stepped out of his truck. The forest was thick, and he'd have to fight through some briars to get very deep. A few scratches wouldn't hurt, though. He hoped the chiggers would leave him alone. Worst things the good Lord ever created. Should've sent them into Egypt at the beginning, and Pharaoh would've begged Moses to leave.

Once under the tree canopy, the world changed. Hunting did that for a man. It made him feel like he was real, like he had a purpose. The tree-huggers and PETA lovers would never appreciate that. Their loss. He moved easily, walking uphill toward a spot where he hoped he could get a better view of the landscape, and more importantly, the trail. A rotting log lay in his path, and he kicked at it. Crumbly slivers of bark peeled off revealing white grubs, ants, and beetles scurrying as the dim light invaded their hiding spot. Doubtless other critters were nearby as well. Maybe a fox or skunk, and surely a snake or two. He'd leave them be, as any respectable outdoorsman would.

A few moments later, and he crested the rise. As feared, there was no sign of the trail. Too many trees. No matter. Hunting required all his senses. If his eyes were of limited use, his ears would make up the difference. He slowed his movement and crept forward, heel pressing firmly into the ground before he lowered his foot and took another step. If the trail ran straight, he'd have hit it by now, but he knew better. Most of the fire trails ran along the ridge tops, meaning he needed to go another hundred yards or so, down then up.

Two or three birds took flight somewhere off to his left, squawking as they flew overhead. He froze in place and hunted with his eyes. There.

His peripheral vision picked up movement down the hill near a small opening. He sidled beside a maple and eased to one knee. This time of day, could be a deer, but not likely. A squirrel clambered up an oak, jabbering at the unseen creature. Patience. Savor the moment. Confirm your target before acting. Safety first.

Gotcha.

A glimpse of a faded blue T-shirt through the trees. Seconds later, a better view.

A lone figure skirted the clearing in the hollow, maybe eighty yards away. A man wearing shorts and hiking boots, a walking stick in one hand, binoculars in the other. Birdwatcher? Nature lover?

Prey.

Mason's fingers stroked the hilt of the combat knife strapped to his leg. No guns today. Too many people around and even with a silencer the echo would bounce around these hills forever and a day. A gunshot would bring attention. The silent slicing of a jugular would not.

People are stupid. Not like animals, always aware of their surroundings. Try sneaking up on any critter and killing it with a knife. Won't happen unless it's already wounded. It'll hear you. Smell you. And assume you're a threat. But not people. Oblivious to what was around them. King of the world. Top of the food chain. Assuming nothing's going to hurt them because nothing's more dangerous than they are.

Stupid.

The hiker looked to be in his early 40s and in decent shape. Good. Toting him the almost half-mile back to the truck wouldn't be too difficult. Not like that overweight girl in Kansas. It'd taken two weeks for his back to recover from her.

Blue Shirt raised his binoculars and turned in a slow semi-circle, scanning the treetops. Twice he paused and jotted something in a notepad. Birdwatcher.

Mason waited and planned his hunt. A quick dash to those two pines, down to the half-dead sweetgum, over toward the redbud, finally to the clearing. Then wait until Blue Shirt reentered the trees to move closer. More ambush options that way.

He flexed his fingers and pulled camouflage hunting gloves from his pocket. Not that he was concerned about being spotted. Blue Shirt either looked up in the trees or down at the trail. Had no idea his life was already over. That he'd never make it back to his foreign red car with the four stick figures. Wonder if his family will peel Dad off the back window?

He pulled the gloves tight until his fingers pressed against the seams.

Had to be careful here.

The knife handle tended to get a bit slippery when wet.

CHAPTER SEVENTEEN

The restaurant was fancy, dark, and expensive. An FBI agent's salary would take a beating at a place like this. Jeremy wasn't worried. Cronfeld would pick up the tab. His invitation, his treat. Not like he couldn't afford it.

The two men sat at a table in the back corner, Cronfeld in a tailor-made black suit and red tie and Jeremy in freshly pressed jeans and an Oxford shirt. Other than a slight belly bulge, the colonel looked just as he had in Afghanistan. Thin, fair-skinned, and dark eyes no longer hidden behind glasses. Contacts or Lasik most likely. His nasally voice defied the Clint Eastwood stereotype of tough Marines, but Jeremy had seen the man in action. Underestimating the colonel would be a dangerous mistake.

"Try the toasted ravioli," Cronfeld said. "Delicious."

"I'm good. Thanks."

Cronfeld shrugged and sipped his wine. "Suit yourself. Sure you don't want a drink?"

"Water's fine."

"The Jeremy Winter I knew would've never turned down—"

"You don't know me. Not then. And especially not now. What's this about?"

Cronfeld placed his empty wine glass on the table and motioned to the sommelier for a refill. "To the point. I like it. Fine. Bailey tells me you're doing a bang-up job. One of his best."

Uh-huh. "And why would my job performance be of interest to you?"

The wine steward approached the table and displayed the bottle to the colonel, who nodded and waited while the dark red liquid filled the bottom third of the glass. The sommelier faded into the background as their server placed their dinner before them and moved off.

Cronfeld studied his plate of shrimp scampi pasta before sampling. "Love this stuff. Too bad it doesn't love me. Terrible indigestion, but one of the benefits of traveling without the wife. No one to remind me what I shouldn't eat."

Jeremy brushed most of the red sauce off his chicken parmigiana before taking a bite. "You talked to Bailey about me. Why?"

"You and I shared an, oh, let's call it an experience, shall we? Isn't that enough reason?"

"Are you responsible for my transfer to Saint Louis?"

The colonel dabbed at his lips with the white cloth napkin. "Responsible. Such a strong word. Who can say who's responsible for what? Things happen all the time, some of them within our control, some not. But you know that, right? The question you need to ask is how do *you* gain control of the situation? That's why I'm here. You do something for me, and I'll do something for you. Quid pro quo."

Jeremy frowned. "And that would be?"

"Certain events transpired during the war. Necessary actions, to be sure, but taken in today's light, they might come across as, shall we say, less than virtuous?"

So that's it. Jeremy took another bite, stared at the man opposite him, and waited.

Cronfeld dropped his napkin and leaned forward. The candle cast dancing shadows across the man's face, making him appear gaunt, almost wraith-like. "Winter, things happened over there. Not saying they were right or wrong, only that they happened. Had to be done."

"I was there. You don't have to explain things to me."

The colonel pointed his fork at Jeremy. "Exactly. You were there. You understand. These days, eh, people forget. They don't want to remember the anger and panic after 9/11. The things that had to be done to keep Americans safe. I don't have to explain all that to you."

"Your point?"

Cronfeld reached inside his jacket, removed a plain white envelope, and handed it to Jeremy. "Read that tonight after dinner. Let me know if you have any questions."

"What is it?"

"A formality. A confidentiality agreement. Simply says that in the interest of national security, you won't discuss certain events with anyone else without official permission."

"Uh-huh. And what if I've already discussed these certain events with others?"

"Have you?"

Jeremy shook his head. "Not a topic I'd prefer to talk about."

"Thought so. Then we agree. Simple enough."

Do we? "Why now? It's been a dozen years. Why the sudden concern?"

Cronfeld waved to the wine steward and motioned to his nearly empty glass. "Closing the loop. Trying to move on, but aren't we all?"

"And the others? Did they sign?"

"The others?"

Jeremy dropped his fork on the plate and ignored the stares from the nearby tables. "Plenty of others were there, Colonel. Can't imagine I'm the only one you're talking to."

"True enough, I suppose. They were all still military, though. It was standard procedure to sign as a condition of discharge."

"Don't believe that's accurate. Easy enough to check out."

The colonel grinned and even in the subdued lighting, Jeremy could see his nicotine-stained teeth. "You got me. Allow me to clarify. For those particular men, it was a condition of discharge. Think of it as our own personal insurance policy. Throw in a few phrases like war crimes or court martial, and everyone was happy enough to forget they were even there."

"Sounds like blackmail."

"Such a dirty word. I assure you, Winter, those men are better off today because of me."

Better off? At what cost? "And if I sign this, what? I get transferred back to D.C.?"

"Oh, I would never interfere with the inner workings of the FBI. I have no control over such issues. But I will say that I hope you can break your apartment lease on short notice. And if not, I'm sure Bailey can work something out."

Jeremy pushed his half-eaten dinner to the side and dropped his napkin on top of the plate. "And if I don't sign? What happens then?"

"Let's not ruin a perfectly good evening. The details are spelled out in the agreement, and I'm sure it's all to your satisfaction. Be a good career move for you too. Trust me, Winter. You'll like having powerful friends. Makes life a whole lot sweeter. Take a week. Think it over. Talk to that redhead of yours if you want."

He's done his research. Knows about Maggie. As for a powerful friend, he'd never be that. There was no trust on either side. If he gave Cronfeld what he wanted, maybe Jeremy's life would get better. Maybe not. And the one card he held, his knowledge of the things that happened in Afghanistan, would be handed over to the only person, other than himself, who could be harmed by it. Yeah, life might get sweeter, but it could leave an awful bad taste in your mouth.

The wine steward edged to the table and refilled Cronfeld's glass. The colonel waited until he left, then took a sip. A small drop of the maroon liquid hung on his upper lip, and his tongue darted out to retrieve it. "An excellent vintage, Winter. You really should try it. Now, tell me. Shall we take a chance on the tiramisu?"

CHAPTER EIGHTEEN

J eremy sat alone in his apartment, a single lamp fighting to hold the two a.m. darkness at bay. The agreement lay on the sofa beside him, waiting for his fourth read.

Official FBI letterhead from the Director. That took some pull. Bailey's boss rarely got involved in personnel matters. Someone with pull must have interceded, and it wasn't hard to figure out who. Cronfeld's wife, Senator Diane Morgans, was the highest-ranking Democrat on the Senate Appropriations Committee. The colonel probably didn't give a rat's hindquarters whether anyone knew about his exploits. Bet he brags about them to his buddies over drinks.

But his wife was a different story. Jeremy didn't know anything about their relationship, but he could make an educated guess. Cronfeld, a retired war hero. Morgans, a lifelong politician from an elite Pennsylvania family. The colonel standing ramrod straight in his dress blues while the senator held her chin high beside him made for a fine photo op. Her access to money, and more importantly, power, gave him all he could ever want.

And for some reason, Jeremy was now a threat to them, or more specifically, to the senator. But how? He'd never met Diane Morgans. Never even spoken to her. And Jeremy had never seemed to be a problem for her before. Was it possible she didn't know her husband's history until recently?

Not likely. Lifetime politicians didn't do anything without considering the impact on future elections. The colonel had surely been vetted heavily before Morgans agreed to marry him. That was, what, three, maybe four years after Jeremy left Afghanistan? Around the time Cronfeld retired? Seemed like ancient history.

He read the agreement again. Short and specific. He, Jeremy Winter, would never discuss the events of Afghanistan with anyone without written permission from the Director of the FBI. Sprinkle in a few terms like "national security" and "public interest" and there you had it. Oh, and if he did speak of his time overseas, well then, it was off to prison to await a trial that would never come.

And his reward for signing the document? Nothing. Cronfeld had hinted that a transfer back to D.C. would happen, but if that were so, it certainly wasn't spelled out here. It was abundantly clear which party had the power in this situation.

And if he chose not to sign it? Again, nothing. But Jeremy held no illusions. There were plenty of other FBI offices much farther away. They'd keep moving him until they found the one that forced him to sign. Dangle ever-growing carrots in front of him. Or worse, drag Maggie into it. Force her to transfer, knowing she couldn't leave the state because of her divorce agreement. She'd have to resign from the Bureau.

He flicked the paper toward the coffee table and watched as it fluttered to the floor. He needed to talk to Maggie. Soon. Get everything out in the open. She had a right to know, even if it meant risking their relationship. She needed to see that part of him. What he was truly capable of.

Outside of a debriefing, he'd never spoken of Afghanistan. What he'd seen. Done. And if he signed that document, he'd never be able to tell her. Couldn't do that. It'd be hard for both of them, but they'd get through it. Assuming, of course, she wanted to.

He flicked off the lamp, laid back on the couch, and told himself not to dream. Not tonight.

It didn't work.

CHAPTER NINETEEN

A million dollars. That was the prescription doctor's bail, and in less than five hours, the money had been posted. No doubt the FBI, U.S. Marshals, and bounty hunters would soon be looking for the good doctor. Sometimes crime did pay, at least for a while. Not the way Jeremy wanted to start his day, especially after the early morning nightmares.

He needed to talk to Maggie and tell her about the dinner with Cronfeld, but she was in some sort of scheduled training all morning. Another productive day at the Bureau. It'd have to wait until tonight when they were off work. He couldn't go into much detail without explaining everything, and that wasn't going to happen on a phone call.

He'd bounce a few things around and try to drive up to Virginia this weekend. Long drive, but it would give him time to think about how to explain Afghanistan. How to ask her for forgiveness. Promise he'd changed.

And hope that she believed him.

The late May sun powered its way through his office window, reflected off the too-white wall behind him, and pinpointed his laptop's screen. He shifted the computer and angled his chair. Should be good for another fifteen minutes before needing to repeat the process.

Thirty-four names still on his list of missing Indiana women. He'd removed fifteen for various reasons, usually something minor that didn't sit right with him. Not a hunch. More of a ... knowing. Like a puzzle piece in the wrong box. He couldn't explain it to anyone, except maybe Maggie, but the women he'd taken off the list didn't belong in the same puzzle as Sarah Goldman and Catherine Mae Blackston. The question was, did any of the others fit? For that matter, were Goldman and Blackston even in the same box?

Jeremy squeezed his eyes shut and tried to force the thoughts and images from his mind. Too much clutter and too many rabbit trails. Which one to chase? Missing women, and what's for lunch, and Maggie, and his next case, and Cronfeld. He knew which one he wanted to run after, but she was a few states away. And if he didn't sign the confidentiality agreement, that distance was going to grow.

He took a deep breath, glanced upward, and pulled the computer closer. It didn't take long for the details beside each name to begin to blur, so he slowed, pausing deliberately as he moved between the columns of data, allowing the information to soak into him. Age. Ethnicity. Height. Weight. Hair color. Eye color. Next row. Jeremy scrolled through the list three times before giving up. If there was a connection, he didn't see it. He could expand his search to surrounding states, make the puzzle bigger, but without knowing what he was looking for, it would be a waste of time. When all else fails, put the pieces back in the box, shake it, and start over.

He clicked to reset the NCIC filters and scrolled to the bottom of the new list. One hundred eleven names. A press of the mouse button, and sixty-two men disappeared, leaving his original list. The white cursor arrow hovered over each option in turn as he debated which to sort by. He'd tried them all multiple times already, so what difference would it make? Doing the same thing over and over and expecting different results. Isn't that what they say the definition of insanity is? Maybe on a T-shirt, but not in real life. Insanity was no motto.

In his two-plus decades with the Bureau, he'd seen the damage broken minds could do. Creating their own versions of reality. Listening to the voices no one else heard. Doing the things normal people found abhorrent.

The Bureau figured that there were between thirty and sixty serial killers at work in the U.S. at any given time. Not as easily identified as the mustached villain tying the girl to the railroad tracks while he waves her house deed in the air, this evil was far more dangerous.

Its face was the bagger at the supermarket or the high school track coach. The city bus driver or the accountant down in the strip mall. Anonymous, deadly, and unstoppable until it was too late for at least some victims. And then the neighbors all gathered on the nightly news saying, "He was such a nice young man. We had no idea."

Jeremy tapped a finger on his cheek and stared at the top name on the list. Patricia Atwater. Twenty-four-year-old blonde who disappeared almost eighteen months ago. Not a peep since then. Worked at a convenience store, still lived with her folks, no kids, couple of boyfriends, neither of whom were considered suspects. Nothing that might connect her with Goldman or Blackston. Sorry, Patricia. Hope you're alive and well wherever you are.

His cell phone vibrated and he glanced at it. Text message from Maggie.

"Hour 2 of this meeting. sleepy. Whatcha doing? :)"

Normally, he preferred texting or emails over phone conversations, but not with Maggie. It robbed him of a chance to hear her voice. Still, this was better than nothing. "Between cases. Staying busy though. How's the meeting?"

"HR stuff. Tolerance in the workplace. If I have to role-play, I'm gonna hurt someone."

Jeremy laughed and ran his hands over tingling arms. "I'd like to see that. And you."

":) me 2. working ur theory on the 2 women?"

"Yeah. Looking at others missing in the state. Not finding anything. One more time thru the list and I'm going to let it go."

"don't get Bailey mad!!!"

"Seems like that's a habit of mine. Better get back to the list before I get a new assignment."

"many names left?"

"Still at the top of the list. Pat Atwater is about to get scratched off I think."

":0 looking at missing men 2?"

Jeremy stared at the message. Men? Serial killers almost always stuck to one sex. Almost. Men or women, they didn't usually cross lines but, on rare occasions, it did happen. Herbert Mullin killed thirteen people—men and women—because he was convinced there was no other way to stop an earthquake in California. His murders were completely random, and he explained his actions to the jury by saying, "A rock doesn't make a decision when falling. It just falls."

Another text came in from Maggie. "u still there?"

"Yeah. Gotta go. And thanks."

"4 what?"

"Give Rebecca a kiss and hug from me. call you tonight."

Jeremy reset his list and added the sixty-two men back into the mix. Several clicks and filters later, nothing stood out. If there was a pattern, he couldn't see it. Maybe he was looking for something that wasn't there. A connection to a killer that didn't exist. That was preferable to the only other option. That they had another Herbert Mullin on their hands, killing at random to appease the voices in their head or stop an earthquake or because they liked watching people die.

He rubbed his eyes and scrolled through the summary of each missing male's case. Fifty minutes later, Jeremy had his answer. Not enough to convince anyone, especially Bailey, but he knew. A killer was at work. Not quite random, but awfully close. Two possible male victims to add to the two females. The death count had doubled to four. Two of the bodies missing, two mutilated. All linked to state or national parks in Indiana.

He needed to expand the search and check bordering states. Dig deeper into the Indiana cases for possible links. Question the detectives who'd investigated the cases of the two men. Find out if—

His computer dinged, the signal that an important email waited in his inbox. Bailey assigning his next case. Top priority. Identity fraud involving dead people connected with millions of dollars in state tax refunds across the Midwest. Briefing scheduled ASAP.

Jeremy pressed his lips together and ran a hand across his chest. Probable serial killer or stolen government money? Death versus taxes. He needed more information on the murders. Something—anything—that would convince Bailey of a connection between the killings. It was there. Jeremy was sure of it. He had to find the connection soon or send his suspicions to the sidelines, working the case as time allowed. He could stall a day, maybe two, but no more. Find something that may not exist and prove it to someone who doesn't believe.

God help him.

CHAPTER TWENTY

Jeremy exhaled a steady stream of frustration and glanced away from the laptop's camera. The computer rested on his lap while he propped his feet on the coffee table. A muted hockey game on TV cast the only other light in his apartment. If he couldn't persuade Maggie, what chance did he have of convincing his boss? "Seriously, Mags, you don't see it?"

She raised her eyebrows. "Uh, Mags?"

"Trying it out."

"Sure, Jer."

"Enough said. So, seriously, *Maggie*, you don't see it?"

"I don't know," she said. "Seems pretty tenuous."

"Maybe. But I think there's something to it. Iffy? Sure. Could be it's all in my head. I need more time."

Maggie scrunched her lips into a frown. "Well, you know if I had the authority, I'd tell you to go for it. But it's—"

A perky voice interrupted. "Dora's over, Mommy. Put the TV on Spider-Man now."

Jeremy's hand hovered near the screen as Maggie turned toward her daughter and smiled.

"Not now, honey. It's bedtime, remember? We agreed you could watch Dora, but then you had to go to sleep."

Rebecca climbed into her mother's lap and burrowed into her arms. Curly red hair surrounded her plump freckled face, and she pointed at the computer. "Hi, Mr. Jewemy!"

His shoulders dropped, and he sighed as the tension flowed from him. "Hey there, sweetie. So, who do you like better, Dora or Spider-Man?"

The little girl sniffled and dragged the sleeve of her Strawberry Shortcake pajamas across her nose.

Maggie rolled her eyes. "Oh, honey. Get a tissue if your nose is running."

"Uh-huh. I like Dora and Spider-Man both. Who do you like the most, Mr. Jewemy?"

He furrowed his eyebrows and pouted his lips. "Well, I'd have to say my favorite is Dora the Spider-Man Explorer."

Rebecca snorted and ran the other sleeve under her nose. "That's not real."

"Not real?" He held both hands out, palms up. "Are you sure?"

"Yeah. I'll show you. Can you come over?"

Jeremy swallowed hard. "Not right now, sweetie. But soon, I hope. Then you'll have to show me. Promise?"

"Promise."

Maggie hugged her daughter. "Okay, now quit stalling. Off to bed. I'll be in to check on you in a few minutes."

Rebecca pushed herself backward and opened her eyes wide. "I love you, Mommy."

"Love you too, baby."

"Please? Just one Spider-Man?"

"Oh, baby. Of course ... not." She poked the girl in her side, inducing a torrent of giggles. "Go on now. Get in the bed."

Rebecca slid onto the floor, waved at the laptop, and took off running. "Night, Mr. Jewemy. Love you!"

Jeremy cleared his throat and slid the back of his hand under his eyes. "Allergies."

Maggie grinned and shifted forward in her seat. "Uh-huh. Tough guy."

"You know it. I've got a reputation to uphold."

"I think you're doing just fine." She inclined her head toward Rebecca's room. "She does too."

"Seems like forever since you two were here."

She nodded. "Five weeks. Your turn. Plan a trip when you can."

"How about this weekend?"

"Taking some time off?"

He shook his head. "Can't. Just up for the day."

"Long way to go for one day. What's up?"

He looked away from the laptop. "Miss you guys. That's all."

Maggie folded her hands in her lap and leaned toward the camera.

"Jeremy, what's going on?"

"Nothing you need to worry about. I'll explain it when I see you."

Wrinkles sprang up on her forehead. "Is it about us? We're not talking about my job again, are we? Did I do something wrong?"

"No and never. It's, um, I need to talk to you. About my past. Afghanistan."

"I'm ready to listen. Don't worry, honey. Nothing you tell me is going to change how I feel about you."

He drew his lips into his mouth and held his breath for a few heartbeats before exhaling. "I hope not."

"Jeremy, listen to me. You know how I feel about you, right? I love you. Whatever you're going to tell me, we'll get through it. That's what love does."

He paused and forced confidence into his voice. "I know. I wish I were closer, Maggie. Back in D.C."

"Well, Bailey is the man who can make that happen. Sell your case to me. Pretend I'm him. Give me your theory on these murders, and make me believe it. Or at least curious enough to want more."

"Role-playing, huh? Thought you hated doing that."

She narrowed her eyes. "The ball's in your corner, and the clock is ticked off. Go."

Jeremy shut his eyes and slowed his breathing. "Okay. Five months ago, I received a call from an acquaintance asking me to look into the disappearance of his ex-wife, Catherine Mae Blackston. The initial investigation by the local police failed to turn up any evidence of foul play. They found her abandoned vehicle in the Hoosier National Forest several weeks later. The forensics team didn't locate any sign of forcible abduction. Barring subsequent information, the assumption is Miss Blackston left of her own accord for unknown reasons."

Maggie yawned. "Is this going somewhere?"

"I later learned of the murder of Sarah Goldman, a seventeen-year-old high school student in French Lick, Indiana. That's on the opposite side of the park from where Miss Blackston's car was found. Goldman disappeared a little over five years ago. A cadaver dog discovered her body a year and a half after she went missing. Her head and hands had been severed and taken in what we assume was an attempt to disguise her identity as long as possible."

She spread her hands and inspected her fingernails. "And her killer now sits in prison waiting to be executed. I've got a meeting in five minutes, Agent Winter. Let's wrap this up."

"Yes, ma'am, uh, sir. I interviewed Lawrence Berkley, the man convicted of killing Miss Goldman. Based on his demeanor and the lack of any solid evidence tying him to the crime, I believe there's a chance he's innocent. Of this murder, at least. On a hunch, I—"

"Don't say hunch," Maggie said. "Sounds like you're guessing."

Jeremy nodded. "Got it. I requested information on other missing and murdered females in Indiana. There was no detectable pattern. Nothing to indicate any link between the two women. I decided to broaden the search to include men, on the off chance that if there was a serial killer, he was random."

"The odds of that happening are extremely low. What made you think to include men?"

"Sir?"

"I mean, it seems like a fantastic idea. Did you come up with it on your own?"

Jeremy grinned. "You're terrible at role-playing, you know?"

She crossed her arms and frowned. "Agent Winter, I don't have time for games."

"Yes, sir. Special Agent Maggie Keeley is actually the one who gave me the idea."

She squinted and cocked her head. "Good agent. One of our best."

"Yes, sir. Anyway, as I was saying—"

"Do you speak with her often? Agent Keeley, I mean."

He held back his smile. "Not as often as I'd like, sir."

Maggie paused and bit her bottom lip. "And why is that?"

"Well, sir, I stay busy with all that's going on arou—"

"Not what I meant. Why would you like to speak with her more often?"

Jeremy scooted forward in his chair, his elbows resting on his knees. "Because I love her, sir."

Maggie glanced toward her lap for a moment before looking back up. Her clear green eyes watered, and her nose had a tinge of redness. "Allergies. Go on, Agent Winter."

"I kind of forgot where I was."

"You broadened your search to include missing and murdered men based on the advice of Special Agent Keeley."

"Yes, sir. Since my initial interest was piqued due to a possible connection between two women at the Hoosier National Forest, I searched for men whose disappearance or death might be linked to other state or national parks in Indiana. I came up with two more names."

"I'm listening."

"Two years ago, Demond Houston, a forty-two-year-old African-American, disappeared while fishing on Cagles Mill Lake in Richard Lieber State Park. That's in the middle-western part of Indiana. Searchers found his boat, and he was presumed drowned, though no body was ever located."

Maggie glanced at a watch-that-wasn't-there on her wrist. "People drown all the time. Bodies get snagged underwater. It happens."

"That's true, sir. Certainly possible. It's a big lake." Jeremy licked his lips and rubbed his fingertips together. "The fourth person I identified as a potential victim is Barry Thornquist, a twenty-eight-year-old white male who disappeared four years ago. Last year, his remains were found by hunters in the Big Oaks National Wildlife Refuge down in the southeast corner of the state."

"Interesting, but not enough to warrant your time. I imagine if I had our statistics people run the data, we'd find that every state has reports of murders and disappearances near public lands. It's a matter of convenience, availability, and population density. Murders happen where there are people, and people are near state and federal parks. Doesn't mean all of them were killed by the same person."

Jeremy took a sip from the warm water bottle on the side table. "Yes, sir, but here's the thing. They found a few bones, but most of the remains were gone."

Maggie shrugged. "Three or four years in the wild'll do that. Animals scavenge. Drag things who knows where. Nothing new about that."

"Animals don't use axes, sir."

"Excuse me?"

"Most of the bones were missing. Like you said, animals probably hauled them away. But the left radius—that's the lower arm bone on the thumb side—was there, and forensics found deep scratches on it. Possible tool marks made by a cutting instrument."

Maggie downed the last of a Diet Coke. "And you think this is related to Sarah Goldman's killer because her head and hands were missing? Did forensics compare the tool marks on the bodies?"

Jeremy glanced downward. "The radius was too damaged by the elements."

"Uh-huh. So, let me ask you, Agent Winter, what's your theory here? Why the cuts, assuming that's what they are, on his bones?"

He focused on the laptop screen. "His hands, sir. The killer took them."

"Hiding the vic's fingerprints?"

"That's my guess. It could also be that he took the bones as his trophy. Maybe to keep with the ones he took from Sarah Goldman."

Maggie leaned back in her chair and tapped her lips. "Let's say there's a serial killer at work here—and I'm not saying that's the case—where are the other two bodies? Why leave Thornquist and Goldman and not the others?"

"It's possible they just haven't been found yet. But I don't think that's what happened. If you look at the timeline of the murders, the two bodies that were located are the oldest of the four. I believe the killer is evolving. Learning. Getting better, if you will. No body, no evidence. He's taking them from the scene."

"And what? Dumping them somewhere else?"

Jeremy pulled his lips into his mouth and shook his head. "Possibly. Honestly, there's not enough data yet to know."

Maggie pointed at the camera. "Exactly. You're asking me to commit to an investigation without enough information. Why would I do that? At this point, all you really have is a cluster of names with no solid connection between them. Not even a tentative one."

He interlaced his fingers. "Because, sir, you believe I might be right."

"Oh, really? And what makes you think so?"

Jeremy tapped his watch. "Your meeting began over six minutes ago, sir, and you're still here."

She squeezed her lips together, but couldn't hide their upturned corners. "What are you asking for, Agent Winter?"

"One week, sir. Give me that much time to try to build a case. If there's something there, that should be enough time for me to find it."

"Three days. No more. Now, as you pointed out, I'm already late for my meeting. Don't make me regret doing this, Agent Winter."

"I won't, sir. Thank you."

Maggie nodded. "Not bad. I'd say you've got a fifty-fifty shot with Bailey."

"Should I request more time? You know he's going to cut whatever I ask for."

"Don't get greedy. Now, there's a little girl who needs to be tucked in for the night. I'd better go check on her. Make sure she said her goodnight prayers."

"Have her say one for me. I could use the help when I talk to Bailey tomorrow."

"Will do. Let me know how it goes."

"Of course. Thanks for your support, Maggie. You're better at role-playing than you pretend."

She leaned in closer and winked. "Oh, you have no idea. Sleep well."

Jeremy took another swallow of the warm water and stared at the blank screen. Sleep well. Right. Too much to think about.

He closed the laptop lid, his heart getting heavier as he did. The end of another day living alone. He needed to see Maggie, to tell her everything about his past, and more importantly, his future. At least the one he wanted. She'd said that no matter what he told her, nothing would change how she felt. Easy enough to say when you don't have the whole story. He wanted to believe her. Knew she was sincere when she said it. But she didn't know yet. Had no idea what he was capable of.

How thin his line was between civilized and savage.

CHAPTER TWENTY-ONE

Maggie had been slightly off in her portrayal of Director Bailey. One day. That's it. Jeremy had twenty-four hours to convince his boss there was something to tie these murders and disappearances together. Bailey didn't buy it, but he was no fool. If evidence did turn up, now or years in the future, he'd be able to say it had been investigated, not ignored. The first rule of politics. CYA.

Jeremy had hit the road early that morning after deciding Barry Thornquist was his best shot. Although more than four years had passed since the murder, at least there was a body. That was more than he had with Catherine Mae Blackston or Demond Houston. The Big Oaks National Wildlife Refuge was five hours from his apartment and had the added benefit of being on the way to Virginia. He'd spend most of his Friday investigating the area where the body was found, then head over to see Maggie and Rebecca.

Trepidation mingled with excitement. He couldn't wait to see his girls but dreaded the coming conversation regarding his past. One thing he'd learned in all of his cases—secrets almost never stayed buried.

He'd emailed the Thornquist case file to Maggie before leaving Saint Louis. She'd volunteered to review it and pull any data she thought he might need. He'd agreed, but insisted she do the analysis only if it didn't impact her other work. The last thing either of them needed was to anger Bailey. Jeremy didn't like the political games, but he understood them. His boss was walking a very fine line and could easily decide to take a detour. If that happened, Jeremy harbored no illusions as to which way Bailey would go.

He was two hours and one bathroom stop into the drive when Maggie called. "You on Bluetooth or speaker?"

"Speaker," Jeremy said. "I'm not sticking those things in my ear. That's how you get brain cancer. And don't roll your eyes at me."

She chuckled. "Turn down your radio. I can't concentrate when Blake Shelton's on. Did you know he's really tall?"

"Um, yeah, I did. Are you stalking him or something?"

"Nah. Just happened to stumble across it on a Google search."

"What were you searching for?"

"Blake Shelton, naturally. And don't roll your eyes at me. I got some info on the wildlife refuge. They used to test bombs and other munitions there back in the Second World War. The National Guard still has a section up in the northern part that they use for practice. Off-limits to the public, of course."

"Interesting. Relevant?"

"Yep. There's probably a lot of unexploded stuff still scattered around parts of the refuge. They cleaned up what they could find, but chances are there's plenty more buried out there. It could be dangerous if someone stumbled across it and didn't know what to do."

Jeremy checked his rearview mirror and changed lanes to pass a slow-moving semi. "I'm surprised they let people in there."

"Yeah, but here's the thing. They only let the public in on certain days. You have to pay a fee and watch a safety video. Then they make you sign a form acknowledging the danger before they'll let you in. Thornquist did all that. The local PD has his signature on the form on the day he disappeared. Handwriting analysis confirmed it was him."

"Assuming the killer played by the rules, he'd have signed the form? I'm sure the local PD would have checked that when Thornquist's body was found."

"They did," Maggie said. "The forms are kept on file indefinitely. Simple matter to find the ones around the time he disappeared. Forty-six people filled out the forms, and all of them were checked. No luck. I pulled the weather data, and they had quite a bit of rain around then. Guess that's why so few people were there."

Jeremy checked his fuel gauge. Quarter of a tank left. About time to grab an early lunch. He stretched his left leg, grimacing as he wiggled his foot. Need to get that checked out. The limp was getting worse, at least from his perspective. "Don't think I'd sign the list either if I were going to kill someone. I assume all the names were valid?"

"Yep. All checked out. It wouldn't be difficult to bypass the guard shack or park office, though."

"Got it. And they're absolutely sure Thornquist wasn't killed where his body was found?"

Maggie sighed. "No, but they're as sure as they can be. Coroner's report indicates probable cause of death as gunshot near the heart. Based that on a partial rib bone they found. If true, and the murder occurred there, small fragments of bone should have been located. Too small for animals to worry with. They sifted the ground but didn't find anything, so the supposition is Thornquist was killed somewhere else in the park."

"Okay. Thanks, Maggie. I should be at Big Oaks in around three hours, depending on traffic around Louisville. Did you let them know I was coming?"

"Yep, but it's been almost a year since they found the body, Jeremy. Not going to be anything to see."

"Got to start somewhere, right? Plus, it's on the way to your place. And listen. No more help on this. Get back to your own case."

"Oh, joy. More hours of wiretaps to review. Seriously, I'm sure this judge is guilty of taking bribes, but if his wife knew about the two mistresses, she'd probably administer justice herself. Save us all a lot of trouble."

Jeremy chuckled. "Maybe you should give the judge a choice. Confess to the bribery charge or you'll tell his missus what he's been up to."

"I wish. I'm pretty sure it'll all come out when he eventually goes to trial. Wouldn't be surprised if he asked to be placed in protective custody once she hears about his affairs."

"I've got to take this exit, Maggie. I'll call you tonight. Be sure and tell Rebecca I said thanks for the prayer. I think it worked."

"Will do. Talk to you later. Love you."

Jeremy's chest tingled, and he scrubbed his hand across it. No matter how many times Maggie said it, his reaction was the same. Like the Grinch in that Christmas show whose heart grew three or five or however many times. "Love you, Maggie. I'll call you later."

He pulled off the interstate and scanned the options. BP settled the issue for him. Two taquitos and a drink for three dollars. The exhilaration of being an FBI agent never ended.

CHAPTER TWENTY-TWO

Jeremy surrendered to the high-pitched whine of kamikaze gnats and moved a few feet to the left. Nothing to see anyway. Some sort of ivy, poison knowing his luck, snaked across the ground between trees. The residue of last autumn's leaves waited patiently to decompose. A mockingbird strutted back and forth on a branch and seemed particularly angry with him. Something to do with the gnats probably.

He checked the diagram in the police report again. Fourteen feet from the road. Far enough to not be seen but close enough to hustle back to a vehicle. Jeremy pointed to his car and drew an imaginary line from there to where the body was found. No direct path. Several trees between here and there, meaning no clear shot. Thornquist wasn't killed here, and the three-year gap between his disappearance and his corpse being found eliminated most hope of finding any evidence. If only it were as simple as kicking a few leaves and magically finding something the CSI team missed.

After one last look to cement the scene in his mind, Jeremy returned to his vehicle. He cranked the engine, switched the air on, and made sure the windows were all the way up in case the gnats came hunting. Why had Thornquist come here? The victim's last known location was near his home in Muncie, a good hundred miles north. His wife thought he was spending the day playing golf with buddies, but that had been checked out. None of his friends were with him.

His car turned up a month after his disappearance behind a Wendy's in Bowling Green, Kentucky, one hundred seventy miles south of here. The vehicle had been there for a while, possibly since the day of the murder. The crime lab found plenty of hairs and fingerprints, none of which provided any leads. In the trunk, they'd discovered a set of Ping golf clubs and specks of Thornquist's blood. Problem was, at least nineteen different people had been in the car at one time or another. Eleven had been identified and cleared. The others were unknown, so the evidence sat bagged and tagged, waiting for a suspect.

The working theory was that the murderer killed Thornquist somewhere else in the park, dumped the body here, drove his car to Kentucky, and either stole another vehicle or simply lived near there. It was a solid explanation with no plausible proof. And it ignored three major issues.

Why did the killer cut off his victim's hands, and if this was a copy of Sarah Goldman's murder, presumably skull? Carjackers don't do that. They may kill to steal, but body mutilation happened only in murder cases. It was personal. Violent. As if a gunshot to the heart wasn't enough. The bigger problem, at least to Jeremy, was Thornquist's car.

The vehicle had been taken from the park. Easy enough to see why. An unoccupied car would be spotted quickly in an area this size. Nowhere to really hide it. From the killer's perspective, best just to get it out of here and leave it somewhere else. Buy some time and put some distance from the crime scene. But that meant that either the perpetrator was on foot when he came here, not likely considering the distance involved, or he wasn't alone. No other vehicle had been located, so two cars had to be driven.

And why had Thornquist come to the park in the first place? None of the other visitors that day remembered seeing him, but after three-plus years, that was no surprise. What Jeremy did know was the victim lied to his wife about where he'd be. That often pointed to an affair or illegal activity, but not always. The local PD had checked into the possibility of a drug deal gone bad, but nothing in the victim's life pointed that way. The man had come here for a specific purpose, one which no one had identified, but possibly the key to solving his murder.

He drove to the Fish and Wildlife Services park headquarters and waited inside for the officer on duty to get off the phone. A wooden counter bisected the office, adorned with two stuffed birds and a map of the refuge taped on top. The officer was an older man, mid-50s maybe, with a deep tan and thinning blond hair. He nodded to Jeremy and held up one finger before finishing his call and walking over.

"You must be the FBI guy." He extended his hand. "Gil Pollock."

"Jeremy Winter. I appreciate you taking the time to let me in the park."

"Hey, no problem. Glad to help out. Find anything?"

"A swarm of hungry gnats, but that's about it."

Pollock chuckled. "You never get used to those little buggers."

"I don't suppose so. Mind if I ask you a couple of questions?"

"Not at all. Don't know that I'll be any help, though."

"Were you here when the body was found?" Jeremy asked.

"I was. Been here almost a year when they found him." Pollock shook his head. "Never forget the look on that hunter's face. Kind of excited and freaked out at the same time, if that makes sense."

"It does. You weren't here when Thornquist was killed?"

"Nope. Not much has changed since then, though. We're staffed pretty thin. That's why the park's only open on certain days. Better for the wildlife too. But if somebody wants to get in here, open or not, they're not going to have much trouble with it."

Jeremy scratched his cheek and looked around the office. "I imagine there were a lot of folks talking about finding the body. Anything stand out to you?"

"Not really. Nobody knew who he was. Kind of made people jittery for a while, like maybe there were more bodies waiting to turn up. A lot of the regulars made sure they never went out alone. After a while, things went back to normal, though."

"The regulars?"

"Yeah. Mostly birdwatchers and hikers. The police talked to the majority of them, but it was a dead end. I mean, well, you know. They didn't get any helpful information."

Jeremy tapped a finger on the counter. "Mind if I take a look at the waivers from four years back when he went missing?"

Pollock shrugged. "Suit yourself. The police took the forms from the day the body was found, and I think a week around the time the guy disappeared. We file by date. Nothing computerized. We're lucky to get enough funding to open the days we do, much less get any decent equipment. Come on back this way."

He escorted Jeremy into a storage room filled with metal shelving. Bankers boxes covered most of them, each with dates written on the end in black marker. Pollock pointed to white labels on the racks.

"Sorted by years," the wildlife officer said. "Each date is in its own manila folder, so you shouldn't have too much trouble. Some days we hardly get anybody, other days we're maxed out. Depends on the season and the weather."

Jeremy placed his hands on his hips and surveyed the boxes. "Thanks. Got a chair I can borrow?"

"Sure thing. Be right back."

Jeremy grabbed the carton marked with the dates around Thornquist's disappearance and set it on the floor.

Pollock returned with two folding chairs and flipped them open. "Figured you might want some company."

"I won't turn you down. Nothing quite as exciting as flipping through page after page of forms."

The officer chuckled. "Such is the life of a government employee, right? Now, what are we looking for?"

"Honestly," Jeremy said, "I don't know. Patterns maybe. Just making sure I cover all my bases. I know the local PD checked it all out, but I'd still feel better giving it the once-over myself." He opened the box and ran his finger along the top of the files. "Looks pretty full. I thought the police took a bunch of them."

"They did." Pollock leaned down and looked at the box's end. "You've got the wrong carton. This one's from 2009. You want 2010, don't you?"

"Yeah, I do." He replaced the lid and bent to pick up the box, but stopped mid-reach. The itch was back. Nagging the back of his brain. A thought creeping in, struggling to form an idea. Jeremy doodled a circle in the dust on the box's top and stared at the shelves of cartons. Year after year after year.

The wildlife officer cleared his throat. "Want me to grab the one from 2010?"

"What? Um, no. Not yet. I think I want to look through this one first."

Pollock tilted his head and parted his lips, but said nothing.

Jeremy pulled a handful of folders from the box and began skimming through the forms. "See if he's in here."

"What? See if who's in here?"

"Thornquist. Maybe he came here more than once."

Pollock grabbed a folder. "Same time every year kind of thing, huh? This one of those hunches you guys always get?"

Jeremy grunted a response.

Twenty minutes and a dozen folders later, he had his answer. Thornquist had been at the park the year before. Same month, different day. Not earth-shattering, but interesting. He grabbed the carton from the same period in 2008. Confirmed. Three years in a row, Barry Thornquist visited the wildlife refuge in the month of April. A bit more interesting.

His pulse quickened as he compared the names of the other visitors with his notes. Other than the victim, only one other person had signed a waiver on the same three days. A woman named Roslyn Martin.

Could be coincidence. Jeremy knew it wasn't. Thornquist had not been alone. More digging in the files needed to be done, but that would have to wait. No time. Witness or murderer, either way he needed to talk to this Ms. Martin. The address on all three of her forms was in Lexington, a little less than two hours away. It would be early evening by the time he arrived. Maybe find a hotel and check in, gather some data on the woman. He hated walking into a situation completely blind. Talk to her in the morning and either continue the investigation or head on to Virginia. He'd make that decision after he heard what she had to say.

He wanted to think that if the woman had information on the murder, she'd have come forward unless she was somehow involved. Or scared. But these days, you never knew. Sometimes people simply didn't want to get involved. Figured it was none of their business that another human being had been killed. Hey, at least it wasn't them, right? Of course, it was entirely possible she knew nothing about it. Just an old girlfriend or something.

This could all be a colossal waste of time, but for the first time, Jeremy felt he was close to something solid. Tangible. Roslyn Martin may not have answers, but she might at least clarify the questions. It was good to finally feel optimistic again.

He called his office to confirm her address was still valid and was put on hold while someone checked. An upbeat country song trickled through the car's speakers, and he turned up the radio's volume. A couple of young women sang about their men treating them right. Or else. Bet Maggie likes this one.

The phone clicked, and Jeremy got his answers. Roslyn Martin had no criminal record, born and raised in Lexington, Kentucky, and was seventeen years older than Barry Thornquist. No known connection between the two, but her address was no longer current. Jeremy sighed and punched the radio knob, turning off the girl duo in mid-lyric.

Roslyn Martin had moved to a new, more permanent location in the Meadow View Cemetery.

CHAPTER TWENTY-THREE

Jeremy bit softly on the inside of his cheek and tried to ignore the cell phone lying in the passenger seat. He'd been driving for a couple of hours, and Lexington was now behind him. Plenty of sunlight left before he had to decide whether to stop for the night or continue the crowded journey along I-64 to Virginia.

He had to let Bailey know he'd hit a dead end but there was still hope. Roslyn Martin was the victim of a horrific auto accident, but her friends and family might know something helpful.

Why did she meet Barry Thornquist every year at the Big Oaks Refuge? Lovers? She was seventeen years older than the murder victim, so a tryst was possible, but not likely. Illegal activity fell more in line with his thinking.

Five-fifteen. Bailey would still be at work. Best to hold off until he stopped for the night, then leave a voicemail. That would eliminate the opportunity for questions and give him the weekend to plan his next steps.

His body had other ideas. The left leg throbbed again, reminding him of times and places and people. Though short-lived, this new pain shooting from his calf to hip could be intense and needed to be checked out by a doctor when he got the chance.

The mental torment created by the pain's reminder, well, that was a different matter entirely. Afghanistan and Cronfeld and death intertwined into a braid of anguish. He gripped the steering wheel and clenched his teeth to the point his jaws ached. Better stop and stretch. Top off the tank, grab a cup of coffee, then make the call to Bailey. Might as well get it over with.

....

The aroma streaming from the truck stop's row of coffee pots beckoned him, and he sampled each variety before settling on a dark Sumatran blend strong enough for the spoon to stand by itself. Elly May Clampett coffee. He grabbed a bag of kettle corn to snack on after dinner, whenever and wherever that might be, before paying and returning to his vehicle.

In the car, he took a sip of the murky mud, closed his eyes, and tried to focus his thoughts before making the call. With any luck, this would be the day his boss went home after only twelve hours of work.

Two rings and "Good evening, Agent Winter. I expected you'd be calling."

Jeremy slumped back into his seat. "Yes, sir. Good evening. Just wanted to update you on what I found today."

"Give me the short version, please."

"Once a year, for the past three years at least, Barry Thornquist met a woman named Roslyn Martin in the national wildlife park where his body was found. The local PD didn't have that information in their reports. We need to follow up and get more details."

"Nothing to tie either Thornquist or Martin to the other three cases on your list?"

Jeremy knew where the conversation would turn next if he didn't deflect Bailey. "Not yet, but this is the first solid lead. Could be the thing that cracks open the door to everything."

"It's thin. Did you talk to this Martin woman yet?"

He sighed and shook his head. The battle was over and he'd barely fired a shot. "No, sir. Roslyn Martin passed away in a car accident a little over a year ago. But she lived with her mother and she—"

"Turn it over to the locals. You get on the identity fraud case."

"With all due respect, sir, I still—"

"Anytime someone starts a sentence 'with all due respect,' I know I'm not going to like what's coming next, so let me save you the trouble. No. You can't have more time." Bailey sighed. "Listen, Agent Winter. Maybe there's something to your theory or hunch or whatever we're calling it. Lord knows you've been right far more often than not. I'd love to have the resources to tell you to run with this, but the fact of the matter is, I don't."

Jeremy swallowed more coffee and let the bitterness wash throughout his body. "I understand completely, sir."

"Yeah, I know you do. Doesn't make it any easier. If one of the local detectives is able to make some sort of connection, we'll readdress it. Until then, you're to have nothing further to do with these murders and disappearances. Agreed?"

"Yes, sir."

"Don't test me on this, Agent Winter. I've done what I can for you."

"Yes, sir."

"Fine. Anything else?"

"Have a good evening, sir."

"Yeah. You too."

Jeremy flipped his phone into the passenger seat. Bailey was wrong. Someone was out there. A killer who claimed victims at will, and now no one would be looking for him. There'd be more disappearances. More deaths. There always were.

He flexed his fingers and drew his lips into a thin line. I've done what I can for you. That's what Bailey had said. As Maggie might say, it didn't take a rocket surgeon to figure that out. Politics trumped everything, at least where he was concerned.

From three hundred fifty miles away, the hollow echo of that wretched plastic office clock burrowed into his brain.

Tick.

No more time to investigate.

Tick.

Identity fraud.

Tick.

Find the money. Forget the murders.

Tick.

Why? Because some government hotshot decided it was more—

Tick.

Heat like a furnace flashed through Jeremy. He snatched the cell phone and threw it at the windshield. A woman exiting the store shuffled her two children toward their minivan, her eyes focused intently on him.

Pieces of the phone lay strewn on the dash. Hopefully just need to pop the battery back in. Or fill out the paperwork to requisition a new one. Again. At least the windshield didn't crack.

Tick.

He buried his face in his hands. What now? Bailey had made it clear enough. Move on. And truthfully, he'd have made the same decision if they swapped places.

Jeremy didn't have the answers, but he believed, even if no one else did.

He'd made his decision.

Tick.

Had to get to Virginia.

Tick.

Let Maggie hear it all. His past. Their future.

Tick.

Hold her hands. See if they trembled, or worse, pulled away.

Tick.

First though, he'd have to try and repair his phone.

Tick.

CHAPTER TWENTY-FOUR

Mason lingered in the rocking chair on his back porch, watching as the pale pink fingers of sunrise darted around the clouds. Wisps of fog sank into the open farmland and moved through the valleys. Water beaded on his forehead, and he brushed the droplets away. It was going to be a hot one, but that was to be expected with summer just around the corner.

No better way to start the day. Coffee in hand and a plate of biscuits cooling on the plastic table next to him. His wife watering the hanging baskets full of ferns and petunias. Birds chirping, dragonflies buzzing, and cattle mooing.

A man couldn't ask for more from his life. Demanding that others sacrifice so he could maintain his slice of heaven, well, that was their problem. Not like any of them had the least inkling about what mattered. Survival of the fittest and all that stuff, although his family would do more than simply survive. They would—

"Want me to get the boys up?" Paula asked.

"Let 'em sleep in. School's out, and not a lot needs doing this week. Besides, they earned it with all the work they put in yesterday. The garden's looking good. You need to see if you can't get rid of some of those tomatoes before they go bad, though."

She chuckled. "The neighbors have been calling me to see if I can take theirs. Everybody's got them coming out of their ears. I'll get them put up this week. Still got to figure out what to do with all the squash and corn, though. Maybe we ought to cut down on the garden next year."

Mason shook his head. "Can't. Sure as we do, it'll be a bad crop. Best to keep it as is. Better too much than not enough."

She emptied the last of her water pitcher into a flowerpot full of daisies. "You're right as rain, as usual. Maybe we can try to sell some of the vegetables this fall when we open the pumpkin patch."

"Speaking of, about time to get to work on a few changes. Got to figure out a better way to do the parking. Had a few folks complain about being blocked in last year."

"Yeah, well, it's not like we don't have the land. I'll get the boys to bush hog a couple of strips down by the corn maze. As long as we don't get too much rain, should be fine."

Mason held his coffee cup to his mouth and let steam condense on his upper lip. "That'll be fine. I swear this thing gets bigger every year. Lot of work."

"You complaining?"

"Not a bit. Folks seem to like it, and the extra money don't hurt none either. Oh, and I've been meaning to tell you that I'm planning on borrowing some horses for the hayride. Give that old tractor a rest."

Paula smiled and patted her husband's shoulder. "Borrow horses? Or buy?"

He cut his eyes toward her. "Borrow. And if it works out, buy."

She winked at him. "Uh-huh. And why am I so sure it'll work out? You've always wanted your own horses. Just never could figure out how to justify the cost."

Mason shrugged and ran the back of his hand across his mouth. "It's about giving the people what they want, honey. Had some customers complain about the tractor fumes last year."

"Oh, and the horses smell soooo much better. Not to mention I've never stepped in a pile of tractor fumes."

"Thinking that if we do get them, come next spring I'll get out some of the old equipment and hitch it up. Train the horses to pull a plow and let the boys see what farming used to be."

"Boys and their toys," she said. "Speaking of, UPS dropped off a package for you yesterday. I put it out in the new barn. The box said it had live insects inside."

He stood, stretched, and yawned. "Appreciate it. More praying mantises and other bugs. I'll take care of them today."

"They helping?"

Hungry little buggers. "Near as I can tell. Not as many flies and other insects in the barns and storm shelter."

"Good, as long as they don't chase all the spiders into the house." She shuddered and a drop of coffee sloshed out of her cup onto her apron.

He waited until she glanced away then trickled his fingers up her arm to her neck. "Spider!"

She jerked away from him and swatted his hand. "Don't do that!"

"I was just having some fun." He leaned over and kissed her, smacking his lips when done. "Mmm. Biscuit crumbs."

Her breathing slowed and she returned the kiss. "I want my biscuit back."

"That's better." He reached behind and squeezed her rear.

She licked her lips and pressed against him. "Somebody's in an awful good mood. Got a big day planned?"

"Not really. Got to clean up a few things in the old barn. Might spend some time this afternoon on the Internet figuring out this year's corn maze. That's about it, though."

"Need any help?"

Mason shook his head. "I can handle it. Barely enough to keep me busy as it is."

She winked and brushed her hand on his thigh. "Well, if you're looking for something to do ..."

He opened his eyes as wide as possible and placed a hand on his chest. "Why, Mrs. Miller. On a weekday?"

A ragged cough echoed from the kitchen. "Mom! Where are you? Any biscuits left?"

Mason stood, stretched, and kissed his wife again. "Best get those boys some breakfast. We'll finish this, um, conversation later."

"I'm gonna hold you to that."

He grinned and arched an eyebrow. "Counting on it."

CHAPTER TWENTY-FIVE

Mason carried the box of insects into the old barn and inched down the creaky ladder into the coolness of the root cellar. He flipped on the light switch, illuminating the mostly dirt room. The musty smell was a pleasant change. When he'd first started his new hobby, a rotting odor had permeated every inch of the space. Unpleasant, but tolerable if you worked quickly. However, like most things in life, the more you practiced, the better you got.

And he *had* gotten better. Much better.

Figuring out how to deal with the blood had been the biggest issue. Most folks had a gallon and a half of the stuff, barely more than a deer. It didn't sound like a lot until he drained his first one down here. The shallow pit he'd dug overflowed, and the sticky fluid spread over the dirt floor and formed an oversize fly trap. Cleaning up the mess convinced him to stick to what he knew next time. Dressing and cleaning a deer was second nature. Only difference was he couldn't prep this prey out by the side of the barn.

The cellar's ceiling was high enough to hang up most folks, and an old tub he'd used for oil changes caught whatever drained after he cut the arteries. As long as he got the organs out quick, there really wasn't any problem. Gutting a person wasn't that much different from gutting a deer, except one you were going to eat and the other you weren't. Didn't mean you couldn't find other uses for them, though.

The oversize Whirlpool chest freezer against the wall kicked on, its orange power light reflecting off the huge pile of dark fertilizer bags beside it. Toting those fifty-pound sacks down here had been a workout, but the diesel fuel drums had been even worse. Had to have them down here though. Just hope there's enough.

He walked to the freezer and brushed the dust and hay from the top, remnants fallen through the cracks of the wooden floor above him. He lifted the lid and inspected the freezer-burned remains of Mr. Blue Shirt, AKA Simon Price.

The torso, pelvis, and right leg remained, each wrapped in that cling film stuff he could never tear straight. The flesh had shrunken around the bones, giving an almost mummy-like appearance to the remains. Over on the workbench, the skull and hands, always the priority, were picked clean and awaited his attention. The fingers still needed to be wired together and connected to the upper hand bones. The phalanges and metacarpals they were called. Funny the things his hobby had taught him. All the other bones had already been worked and lay at the bottom of the freezer, waiting for their turn in the cast iron stove above, the final stop before the grinder.

He moved across the room and slid a plastic tub toward the center so he could get a better view. The green tub had a red lid and was the perfect size to store Christmas trees or body parts, depending on your bent. He tapped the top several times to ensure no bugs clung there, then carefully removed the lid.

The dermestid beetles had done their job with utmost efficiency. They'd eaten Blue Shirt's left leg down to a near spotless femur, tibia, and whatever the other leg bone was named. He'd have to sift through the debris to recover all the toe bones. This beetle colony seemed to still be going strong, but a bit of new blood never hurt.

He dragged another tub next to the first and prepped it by adding shredded newspaper and chunks of Styrofoam. He emptied the box of not-really-praying-mantises into the tub and retrieved the right leg from the freezer. Blue Shirt was shorter than average. Such a considerate man. The beetles would make short work of the appendage.

He used a knife to cut a small piece of the flesh, more like jerky now, and placed it in a corner of the original plastic bin to attract any live insects. Give it an hour and he'd scoop them into the tub with the newest residents. Then he could clean the container and get it ready for the next project. Probably the torso. A quick cut along the sternum and it would be an easy fit. Granddad's old handsaw would make fast work of the job. Of all the tools he'd tried, nothing cut thick bone as good.

Sometimes he'd watch the beetles swarm over the flesh and do their work, but not often. The process was slow, not like those piranhas in the movies. He chuckled. Maybe he should stick an aquarium down here and throw some of those fish into it just to see if they really did work that fast.

After replacing the lids on each tub, he moved over to the workbench and clicked on the desk lamp. A paint-splattered wooden stool, handmade by his grandfather, served as his seat. He reached over the assortment of bones and turned the knob on a decades-old AM/FM radio. Low static crackled through the tinny speaker, accentuated with random bits of chatter from the talk station that managed to find its way to his hiding spot. So much history in this barn.

Wiring the phalanges together was like working a puzzle. Deciding which finger bone went where. Laying it all out so he could evaluate his work before finalizing it. Switching this bone for that one. Comparing it to the pictures he'd downloaded off the Internet. He was no archaeologist and doubtless some of the hands he'd done were a little off. No problem though. It's not like anyone would ever notice.

The hands were his. Intimate. Fragile. Kept stored away for those days when there was no time to hunt but he needed to feel ... better. Hold the reconstructed bones against his own hand. Compare the sizes.

An hour and a half later, he stood and stretched, arching his back to chase the dull ache away. Granddad's stool could use a cushion. He checked the tubs and, sure enough, the original beetle colony had already converged on the small piece of flesh. He used a plastic cup to scoop them into the other container with an ampler food supply. In a couple of days, that leg would be picked clean, and the tub would be full of happy, bloated insects. Such a blessing to enjoy your work.

He retrieved the cleaned left leg bones and placed them in the freezer with the others. In a week and a half, maybe less depending on how hungry the beetles were, Blue Shirt should be finished. Then he could—

A shuffling sound on the floor above froze him in place. He'd forgotten to lock the barn door. Stupid. He held his breath and pressed a palm over his racing heart.

"Mason?"

Paula.

"What's going on down there?"

He glanced at the tubs. "Just doing a little cleaning."

"Need any help?"

"Um, no thanks. About done. I'm heading up there now." He moved toward the ladder.

"Nonsense. I've seen your definition of cleaning." A second later, her legs appeared on the top rung, and his wife began her descent.

Mason stared at the newly formed hands on the workbench. Works of art for his family and farm. Sacrifices made to hold it all together.

Paula finished her descent and turned toward him, her hands planted firmly on her hips while she recovered her breath. She scanned the room slowly, stopping when she saw the bones. Her mouth hung open, her eyebrows furrowed. "Mason? What ..."

"Oh, Paula." He stretched his fingers—phalanges—and moved toward her.

CHAPTER TWENTY-SIX

"Hey, sweetie," Jeremy said. "Why don't you go draw me a picture in your room? Surprise me with something really big?"

Rebecca squished her jaw to the side. "Like what?"

"Well, if I told you, it wouldn't be a surprise, now would it?"

"Elephants are big. So are giraffes and gorillas and whales and—"

"Pick one," Maggie said. "Or draw them all. You choose."

The girl scampered down the hall toward her room and hollered back over her shoulder. "Don't come in here till I'm done."

"We won't," Jeremy said. "Do a good job on it. I need a picture I can show off to everybody at my work."

Maggie sat across from him on the living room sofa, hands clasped in her lap. "Now, what's going on? Is everything okay?"

He forced himself to maintain eye contact. "Um, yeah. I think so. I needed to talk to you. Let you know what's going on."

Her eyes moistened, and she sniffed and hunched forward. "What's happened?"

Best to just come out and say it. "Maggie, I'm quitting the Bureau."

Her eyes narrowed, and she started to speak but paused and pouted her lips. "Wait. What?"

He sighed and rested his elbows on his knees. "I haven't told anyone yet. Just you."

Maggie leaned back and crossed her arms. "Well, on one hand I'm relieved. I thought ... I was afraid this might be about us. On the other hand, I'm confused."

"Twenty-two, almost twenty-three years with the Bureau now. I suppose the politics finally caught up to me. Read this." He handed her the unsigned confidentiality agreement.

She read the letter twice, then exhaled loudly and scrunched her eyes. "What's this about? Why are they so worried?"

He glanced at the ceiling and exhaled. "Things happened in Afghanistan, Maggie. Things that maybe shouldn't have happened. And now, some, uh, important people are concerned the information I have might come out. And that would not be good for anyone involved. Some more than others."

"Including you?"

"Yeah, I suppose so."

"What happens if you sign this?"

He ran a hand down his leg, squeezing and massaging. "Not sure. They implied things will go back to normal."

"Normal?"

"Transferred back to D.C. and freedom to work on my cases."

"That doesn't sound bad, does it? And if you don't sign?"

"I hear Alaska's nice this time of year."

She patted the sofa and waited until Jeremy moved next to her. "How much time do you have before giving an answer?"

"Not enough. Bailey's already backing away from me."

"You're less than three years away from getting your full retirement benefits. You willing to give that up?"

He shook his head. "Willing? No. I don't have a choice, though. Maggie, if I sign that paper, I give away any power I have. They'll own me, and there's no guarantee they won't still ship me off somewhere. If I walk away from the Bureau, at least I'll have control over something I know they want. My silence."

She ran both hands through her shoulder-length hair. "Is this coming from Bailey?"

"No. Far over him. Colonel Ramsey Cronfeld."

"Cronfeld? Diane Morgans' husband? What's he got to do with you?"

"He was the C.O. of the base I was assigned to in Afghanistan. Haven't heard from him since I left there, so I'm guessing this is all about his wife. It seems our shared history may be a threat to the senator."

"A threat? How? And why now?"

"Not sure why now. Maybe she's planning a move up to Pennsylvania Avenue. Certainly has the backing to at least make a run for it. And having a decorated veteran like Cronfeld at her side won't hurt unless ..."

"Unless certain things from the past come to light."

He traced the back of a finger along the side of her face and nodded. "There's more, Maggie. Your name came up."

She leaned away and stared at him. "My name? Why?"

"Don't know for sure, but I'm guessing it's to put more pressure on me to sign. Imply the Bureau might transfer you somewhere else too."

Her hands fidgeted in her lap. "They can't do that. They wouldn't. I can't move from Virginia, not with the custody agreement."

He placed his hand on hers. "I know that. I won't let it happen. If I quit, it puts them on the defensive."

She narrowed her eyes. "How? They could still threaten me to get to you unless ... unless we stop seeing each other. Is that what this is about?"

"What? No. Maggie, the thought never crossed my mind."

"Then what's to keep Cronfeld or his wife from pulling some strings and messing with my job?"

"I'm going to tell him I'll go public if I ever get the slightest hint you're being manipulated. He doesn't want the story out there? Well, I'll make it front page news across the country."

She frowned. "That could be dangerous. Powerful people don't like to be threatened."

"I'm not naive. Cronfeld will understand. I've kept my mouth shut this long, and I'll keep it closed unless he backs me into a corner."

"There are ways to guarantee someone doesn't talk. Thought about that?"

"He's not stupid, Maggie. But just in case, I'll let him know there's a backup plan that'll kick in if anything suspicious happens to me or you."

"And is there?"

He grinned and draped his arm over her shoulder. "Hey, I'm making this up as I go, but there will be. Besides, he won't know one way or the other. The threat is what counts."

She sighed and her shoulders dropped slightly. "This is so sudden, that's all. I mean, what would you do for a living?"

"Yeah, I guess it seems like everything's happening fast, but it's really not. I always expected that, sooner or later, my past was going to catch up with me, and now it has. The only thing I regret is not telling you everything sooner. Got a hundred excuses why the time was never right, but it doesn't matter. I owed it to you. Maybe Cronfeld's doing me a favor by forcing me to get all this out in the open. And the future? I've got a bit of money saved up that will tide me over for a while. And I can move anywhere I want."

Her lips turned up at the corners. "Anywhere? Let me help you out here. From now on, open with the good news. It'll make the rest of the conversation go so much better."

Jeremy didn't return her smile. "Maggie, even with all I've said, if you tell me not to quit, I won't. This can't be something that divides us."

She arched her eyebrows and shook her head. "I could never do that. You know that, right?"

"So we're good?"

She tapped a finger on her bottom lip and grinned. "Good? I don't know. Tell me more about moving anywhere you want."

He took a deep breath and nodded toward his left leg. "Can do. But first, you need to hear it all. I'll be honest. The Bureau's been my life for as long as I can remember. I'd be lying if I said I wasn't a little worried, but that's not what scares me."

Maggie's smile faded. "I told you. I know what I feel, and you're not going to change that. Today, tomorrow, next year, whenever. You'll tell me about Afghanistan when you're ready."

He cleared his throat, slowed his breathing, grabbed her hands, and feigned confidence into his voice. "It was hell, Maggie."

CHAPTER TWENTY-SEVEN

Jeremy looked at his watch. Thirty-seven hours. That's how long it'd been since the Bureau told him to get to Quli Khish, Afghanistan. Handed him a file folder and told him there'd be suspects ready for him to interrogate when he got there. No questions. No limits. Just go. And lose the suit.

"You the guy?" the colonel asked. The man standing in front of Jeremy was far from the tough Marine stereotype. Somewhat thinnish, high-pitched voice, wire-rimmed glasses, and patches of stubble in random locations on his sunburned face. Not what Jeremy expected, but in the five months since 9/11, what was?

Operation Enduring Freedom progressed per plan, which wasn't difficult when the blueprint changed daily. Firefights spread across half the country as U.S. forces hunted for the face of Al-Qaeda. A few weeks ago, most Americans had never heard of the Taliban or Osama bin Laden. Now they lined up to kill anyone in a turban. Soon, the terrorists would collapse back into whatever hole they crawled from, and everybody could go home. Lesson learned on both sides.

"I'm the guy." He extended his hand. "FBI Agent Jeremy Winter."

"Colonel Ramsey Cronfeld. Welcome to Afghanistan." He gave Jeremy a once-over before continuing. "We usually get CIA."

"Yes, sir. As you can imagine, things are a bit of a mess right now. CIA's got their hands full. The rules are in flux since the attacks. Threats to national security fall under our purview, and right now that covers a broad spectrum. Plus, it's not too much of a stretch to make the case that an American soldier getting grabbed by the Taliban constitutes kidnapping under U.S. law. Although I don't think anyone's too concerned about making those kinds of arguments these days."

The colonel spat on the dirt floor of the mud brick home that served as his headquarters. The hut smelled of dirt, cigarette smoke, and machine oil. "Marine. Not soldier. That's one of my men they took. I want him back, whatever it takes. Are we clear?"

Jeremy swatted at a fly and tried to quell the internal argument of which he needed more: sleep or food. "Of course. I'll do what I can, sir. Interrogating is as much an art as it is science. Sometimes no matter what you do, you end up with nothing helpful. But I know what's at stake here. I want that sol—Marine back as much as you do."

Colonel Cronfeld moved closer to Jeremy and squinted, staring directly into his eyes. The officer's head tilted left, then right. After a moment, he spat again. "I seriously doubt that. And as far as you doing your best goes, five months ago these terrorists killed thousands of American citizens. I intend to return the favor several times over. Be my pleasure to rid the world of these vermin. So, son, if your best doesn't get me the information I need, then it ain't worth—"

"Sir, I understand."

"Do you now? We're eighty-five miles from Kabul, as if that matters. Every inch of this loathsome country's behind enemy lines. My men need to believe that if anything happens to them, I'm not going to rest until I get them home, one way or another. And I won't stop, Agent Winter. No matter what I have to do, I won't abandon my men." The colonel leaned in until his face was inches away. "No matter what I have to do."

Jeremy held his shoulders steady as a shudder trickled down his spine. "I'm not the enemy here, Colonel Cronfeld. I'm on your side. Anything I can legally do to help locate your missing man, I will."

The officer straightened and moved to a makeshift desk consisting of two wood planks spanning stacks of olive green crates, each stenciled in white with its contents. Stacked bags of rice served as his seat. "Do you know what bothers me about that statement?"

"Sir?"

"Legally. You said 'legally.' Look around you. We're at war. The United States of America doesn't have time for your stipulations. Was it legal when they crashed those planes into the towers? Killed those people at the Pentagon? Our enemy doesn't care about laws, Agent Winter. Murdering Americans. Civilians on top of that. They'll pay deeply for their mistake, no matter what I have to do. You keep those laws in your pocket and pull them out again when you get home."

Jeremy cleared his throat. "We're not them."

"Thank God for that because when we're through with those—"

A Marine entered the building, his rifle in one hand and a bottled water in the other. His boots and camouflage pants radiated clouds of dust with each step, and his solid green T-shirt had dark patches of sweat under each arm. He took a drink and wiped the back of his hand across his mouth. "Four more, sir. We put 'em with the others."

The colonel nodded. "Good work, Sanders. This gentleman was just telling me about his expertise in interrogating POWs. I expect we'll have a rescue mission underway soon enough. Isn't that right, Agent Winter?"

Jeremy glanced between the two men without responding.

"That'll be all, Sanders," the colonel said. He waited until the Marine was out of earshot. "Do what you have to do to save an American life."

Jeremy swallowed hard. "Sir, there comes a point in an interrogation where you can't be sure whether the information you're getting is reliable or not. Bad info is worse than no info."

"Agreed. That's why we need corroboration." He motioned out the door. "I've got nine suspected Taliban out there. You'll get a shot at each of them. Put enough pressure on them, they'll crack. I figure if we get two or three to tell us the same story, that's good enough."

"It'll take time. I need to build their trust and—"

The colonel jumped up, sending the desk tumbling to the ground. "Time? What do you think the Taliban's doing to my boy right now? We don't have time, Winter. I don't know what fancy tactics they taught you back at Quantico, but this isn't the States. Rules don't apply. You do whatever it takes to get what I need, and you do it fast."

"Sir, you said these men were suspected of being Taliban. You don't know for sure?"

Colonel Cronfeld crossed his arms. "And how would you propose I verify that? Last time I checked, the Taliban wasn't issuing ID cards."

Jeremy licked his lips. "Just to be clear, sir, you're telling me some of the men I'll be interrogating, maybe all of them, will be civilians?"

The officer shrugged. "No such thing as civilians in this country. At least not right now. Somebody shoots at one of my boys, and we round up everybody we can get our hands on. Even if they didn't pull the trigger, they know who did. And if they don't, no problem. There's plenty more of them roaming around."

A bead of sweat sped down the colonel's face and dove to the ground, disappearing in a tiny mushroom cloud of dust. Jeremy's heartbeat resonated in his ears, and he morphed his hands into tight fists. "Then I'd best get started. If you'll point me to the detention area, I'll get set up. I assume you have a translator available?"

"Two-story building on the other side of the camp. They're waiting for you. Translator's there too. I'll be joining you in a few minutes."

Jeremy opened his mouth to speak but closed it without saying anything.

"Problem?" the colonel asked.

"No, sir. Give me fifteen minutes and I'll be ready to start."

"Start now. That Marine they're holding may not have fifteen minutes to spare."

CHAPTER TWENTY-EIGHT

Three Marines stood in the entry room of the two-story home that now served as a brig. One of the men escorted Jeremy to a murky back room that hung thick with diesel fumes. Outside a dark-curtained window, a generator belched noise, exhaust, and electricity. An orange power cord snaked through the window, across the floor, and onto a green plastic table. A lamp spit out enough light to illuminate a photo of the missing Marine and some bottles of water, but not much more.

In a corner sat a pile of soiled white shirts and towels. Even in the dimness, Jeremy could make out large splotches of crimson stains. In the center of the room was a wooden chair, minus one of its back slats. Behind the seat, the dirt floor was noticeably darker. A whiff of gunpowder filtered briefly through the diesel fumes, and he drew the back of his hand across his mouth.

Jeremy turned to his escort. "You've got nine prisoners?"

"Yes, sir. Upstairs."

"Let's go."

Another Marine stood at the top of the steps and led the men to a small room. Jeremy stepped inside and glanced at the turbaned men, each bearded and filthy. They all wore traditional Afghan clothing, a knee-length loose-fitting whitish robe, baggy cotton pants, and a decorated vest. Plastic ties secured their hands behind their backs. These men looked like everyone else he'd seen since he arrived in the country. They could be farmers or teachers or shop owners or terrorists.

Jeremy moved down the line, pausing to stare into the face of each man. They all met his gaze.

"Marine, when was the last time these men had something to drink?"

The guard glanced at Jeremy. "What day is it?"

"They need water. Would one of you bring me some?"

Neither guard moved.

Jeremy sighed, frowned, and stepped out of the room. He turned so he could see the Afghan men over the Marine's shoulder. "Look. I know what I'm doing. If you want to find your friend, then help me."

One of the guards grunted and walked downstairs, returning moments later with nine bottled waters. He thrust them toward Jeremy. "Here. I hope they choke on it."

"Thank you." Jeremy opened one of the bottles and took a drink. Two of the prisoners cut their eyes toward the man on the far right, who nodded almost imperceptibly. *Got you.* Jeremy handed the water back to the Marine. "You give it to them while I get set up downstairs. No games. Let them finish, then pick one and bring him down." He pointed to the man on the end. "Except him. He goes last."

The Afghan's dark eyes seared into Jeremy, belying the brown-toothed smile on his face. There was no mistaking his expression.

What makes a man so angry he'd kill others simply because of where they lived? It wasn't that long ago America had aided these people. Given them the weapons and training that were now being used against U.S. forces. And then came the attacks. They had to know America would respond. Maybe that's what they wanted.

How many innocents had men like this killed? And for what? He flashed to his wife, Holly, now six months pregnant with their first child. A girl. They'd already picked out a name. Miranda. Hard to believe that in a few months, he'd be holding his daughter.

The Afghan still stared at him, his grin even wider now. Daring him to do something.

If the man was trying to be intimidating, it wasn't working. Big and brave when killing civilians. Not so much when the Marines get their hands on you. And now you've gone and really pissed them off by taking one of their men. Bad move. This guy needed to understand the only thing standing between him and death was Jeremy. If he could be reasoned with, there was a chance—

The Afghan spat across the room toward Jeremy. So much for reason. Jeremy smiled and winked. "See you downstairs, buddy."

CHAPTER TWENTY-NINE

Colonel Cronfeld waited for Jeremy in the interrogation room. A younger man stood with him, obviously a local but wearing jeans, a faded red T-shirt emblazoned with a Nike swoosh, and a turban.

"This is Nezam, your translator," the colonel said. "He's on loan from the CIA. Good man. Helped us on a couple of missions already."

"How do you do, sir?" Nezam said. "I am pleased to make your acquaintance."

Jeremy nodded. "Your English is excellent. Spend some time in the States?"

"No, sir. American TV shows." He grinned and looked away from the men. "*Dallas* is my favorite."

"You can pick up American TV here?" Jeremy asked.

Nezam shook his head. "I spend most of my time in Pakistan. Things are not so, um, strict there. I wish the same for my country."

"You have family there?"

The translator grinned and looked toward the window. "A sister. We left Afghanistan almost ten years ago. She was only six but I saw ... things. How the Taliban treated women and girls. Not my sister. Not while I lived. I took her across the border. It was hard, but I had help. Your CIA offered and I accepted. It was a chance to help my sister and change my country. Make things better for other girls."

Jeremy studied the man. "No parents?"

"Both dead. My father died fighting the Russians. The Taliban killed my mother."

"Sorry. Where's your sister now? The Taliban have to know you're working with us. They'll go after her."

Nezam glanced at the colonel. "She stayed here with me for many weeks, but she is far away now. Safe forever."

Colonel Cronfeld patted Nezam's shoulder. "You're a good brother. When all this is over, you'll join her. I promise."

Jeremy arched his back and yawned. So she's back in the States, or at least that's what they want Nezam to believe. Who knows? Maybe she really is. "Okay, let's get going."

"Nezam," the colonel said, "the things that happen in this room must remain in here. You understand?"

"Of course, sir. I will do whatever I can to help find your comrade. I know that—"

One of the prisoners from upstairs shuffled into the room, his arms still bound behind him. The guard hovered inches behind with his rifle held tightly, the barrel pointed at the base of his captive's skull. For a moment, no one moved. The background hum of the generator grew louder as a stifling breeze fanned the heavy curtain into the room.

Jeremy pressed a hand over his gurgling stomach and resisted the urge to shake the surreal feeling from his mind. In less than two days, he'd gone from sorting through pediatricians to a military jet to this room with its weapons and stench. Get to work and get home. He tilted his head toward the chair, and the guard shoved the prisoner into it.

"Thank you, Marine," the colonel said. "That'll be all. Close the door on your way out."

"Yes, sir." The guard paused at the exit to hang a heavy tarp across the doorway.

"You've got fifteen minutes," Colonel Cronfeld said. "Get what you can, then we'll bring down the next one."

Jeremy wiped the sweat off his lip and turned to the officer. "Sir? Fifteen minutes is barely enough time to—"

"The clock is ticking, Winter. Get on with it."

"But if I don't have enough time to do this right, I can't get what you need."

Colonel Cronfeld shrugged. "Do what you can. Our experience is that, um, aggressive interrogation methods work best. I'll be right outside. If this guy doesn't give us any intel on my missing Marine, we'll move on to the next."

"And when we've interrogated all nine of these men?"

"We'll get a dozen more. In case you didn't notice, this country's crawling with them. Fourteen minutes."

Jeremy clenched his jaw and turned to the translator. "Ask him his name."

The prisoner did not respond.

"An American soldier—"

"Marine," the colonel said as he exited the room.

Jeremy cut his eyes toward the officer before turning back to the prisoner. "An American Marine is missing. We're trying to locate him. We have many ways to show our appreciation to our friends."

The Afghan scooted forward in the chair, his eyes wide and his chest rising and falling at an alarming rate. He spoke quickly as if the words had built to an eruption and could no longer be contained. Nearly two minutes of one-way conversation occurred before Jeremy held up his hand.

Nezam cleared his throat and took a sip of water. "He says he knows nothing. The man upstairs, the one on the end, is Taliban. He knows everyone. If any of them help, their families could be killed. He says he doesn't know where your soldier is though. None of them do. He just wants to go home."

Jeremy bent forward, placed his hands on his knees, and smiled at the prisoner. "I understand. But surely there's something you can tell us that will help. Anything. No one will ever know it was you."

The Afghan listened to the translation and shook his head.

"We can protect you and your family," Jeremy said. "We're all on the same side here. All fighting for the same thing."

Nezam and the man spoke rapidly for a moment, each growing more animated as the conversation continued. Finally, the man slumped in the chair, his mouth open and forehead creased.

"He trusts no one," the translator said. "But I don't think he knows anything. He's more worried about his wife and children than anything else. He just wants to go home and take care of them."

Jeremy rested his hand on the prisoner's shoulder. The man shrank away and cowed his head.

"It's okay. Nezam, tell him it's okay. I don't have any more questions. I believe him."

The translator arched an eyebrow before repeating the message.

Jeremy brushed back the tarp and called for the guard. Instead, Colonel Cronfeld entered the room and glanced at the prisoner before turning to

Jeremy.

"Doesn't look any different than he did when he came in here."

"He doesn't know anything. Knocking him around won't change that."

The colonel sighed and crossed his arms. "It may not change anything for him, but it might for the next one. You'd be surprised the effect a few screams can have on a man's willingness to share information."

Jeremy moved closer to the officer. "I don't operate that way. *Sir.*"

"Suit yourself. I'll escort this one to the holding cell personally. You ready for the next one?"

"I am."

"Fine. I'll have him brought down in a minute. Wait here."

Jeremy downed half a bottled water and poured the remainder over his head. He studied the photo of the Marine and wondered if the man's family knew that he was missing. Sometimes the military—

The sharp crack of a gunshot echoed through the building, and Jeremy flinched before pulling his Glock. Nezam hadn't moved. No one was yelling. No more shots. He lowered his weapon and moved out of the room to the front of the home, then stepped outside into the blinding sun.

The colonel stood off to the right, motioning to a pair of Marines. On the ground in front of him lay a body.

Jeremy clenched his throat, refusing to give Cronfeld the satisfaction of seeing him vomit. His finger crept onto the trigger of his semi-automatic.

Cronfeld turned toward him and smiled. "Welcome to Afghanistan, Agent Winter."

CHAPTER THIRTY

Jeremy strode back to the interrogation room, yelling at a guard as he passed. "Bring me the one on the end. Now."

Moments later, the Marine shoved the old Afghan into the chair and secured his hands behind his back. "He's all yours."

"Wait outside."

"You got it. You need anything, I'll be around."

Jeremy ran a hand through his hair. "Okay, Nezam. Tell him what I want to know."

The translator spoke for a moment, then waited as the prisoner spewed an animated tirade in return. "You want word for word?" the translator asked.

"Give me the short version," Jeremy said.

"He says Americans think they can buy the world. Their money is nothing compared to what Allah offers those who stand against the infidels."

Jeremy grabbed the photo of the missing Marine and swung his focus back to the man in the wooden chair. "Tell us what you know about this American. Tell us where he is and you'll live. Go back to your family in peace."

The Afghan glanced at the picture and yawned as Nezam translated.

Jeremy continued, "The man in this photo has a family. A little girl, two years old."

The prisoner squinted at the picture, nodded slightly, and looked up. A broad smile spread across his face, and he spoke slowly, never taking his eyes off Jeremy.

"Nezam, what did he say?"

"He said to thank you."

"For what?"

"For telling him the American had a daughter. It will make his death sweeter."

Jeremy's eyes narrowed and he shook his head. What kind of ...

The man in the chair licked his cracked lips and laughed.

"Does he not understand that I'm trying to save his life? Nezam, tell him."

The translator glanced away and wiped his forehead with the sleeve of his T-shirt. "It won't matter. He doesn't care."

"Everybody wants to live."

Nezam shook his head. "That is not always true. The men flying those planes didn't."

9/11.

Mass murder on an epic scale. Nezam was right. You couldn't reason with some people. Life held no value for them. Death was glory. Especially an American death.

The prisoner held his chin high, glared through narrowed dark eyes at Jeremy, and turned up one corner of his lips.

Jeremy's ears pounded as adrenaline flooded his body. Cowards. Planning their attack to maximize civilian casualties. Rejoicing because mothers and fathers and children were dead. And now young men like this missing Marine were far away from their families in this godforsaken place. Fighting and dying to ensure the nation had its revenge.

And the man before him didn't care. He welcomed the chance to kill others who disobeyed his version of reality. Didn't matter if it was an American half a world away or his next-door neighbor. And if he died in the process, so much the better.

Jeremy grazed the back of his hand across his stubbled cheek as he inhaled the dusty diesel air. Death was a release he wouldn't give the Afghan. Pain, though, was a different story.

The man snarled and displayed brown-stained teeth before launching into a verbal tirade.

Jeremy didn't need a translator to understand. His right fist plowed into the Afghan's jaw. Pain shot across the back of his hand and up his arm. A cut on his middle finger from one of the man's teeth dripped blood. He held up the picture again. "Where is he?"

The man in the chair spat at the photo in Jeremy's hand, dotting the missing Marine's face with crimson specks, then spoke slowly, his tongue dabbing at the blood on his lips.

Jeremy casually wiped the photo on his pants to remove the spots. "Nezam?"

"He regrets that the girl will not know of the suffering of her father. How he screams and begs—"

Jeremy struck him again, this time farther back along the jawline to protect his hand. Euphoria swept through him as the adrenaline did its job. He could do this all day.

He *wanted* to do this all day. Make them pay for what they'd done.

He drew back his fist but froze when the Afghan's sneer erupted into another laugh.

For the first time in his life, Jeremy knew. He'd been trained in self-defense, but this was different. In this room, he had all the control. The Afghan tied to the chair was no threat to him. But Jeremy knew.

He not only could kill another human being, but wanted desperately to do so. Quite easy, really, once you understood that thing in the chair was more animal than man. The photo fluttered to the ground.

Jeremy closed his eyes and forced his breathing to slow. Vengeance. Justice. Murder. Take your pick. He looked at the man before him and made his decision. "Nezam, ask him where the Marine is. One. More. Time."

The prisoner cleared his throat, bringing up as much mucus as possible, and spat on Jeremy's shirt.

The thick wet glob hung there, defying gravity. Jeremy pulled his gun from the shoulder holster and smiled at the Afghan. He wondered if his own face showed the same hatred. He hoped so. He backed a few steps and pointed the pistol toward the prisoner.

The Afghan didn't blink. He thrust his chin higher and began to chant.

Jeremy focused down the length of his arm to his hand. The blurry figure of the prisoner was simply a background to the pistol's sight. So easy to kill a man. Squeeze the trigger and move on. Anything to save an American life. His finger tensed and his breathing slowed as the firearms training kicked in. Don't anticipate. Don't jerk. Squeeze until ...

His weapon fired, sending a 9mm hollow point toward its target. Jeremy's ears rang, but his aim never wavered. The soothing smell of gunpowder covered him, sticking to his sweat. The chanting had stopped.

A crimson stain grew on the right shoulder of the man in the chair. Jeremy knew that the back would be worse. Much worse. The bullet did its job, entering, expanding, shredding. At this range, some of the shrapnel would have exited his body as well. Maybe that's what happened to the missing chair slat.

"Everything okay?"

Jeremy turned to a Marine who had hurried into the room. "Everything's fine. We were just having a discussion."

The Afghan moaned and tried to hold his head steady.

The Marine smiled and turned to leave. "Yes, sir. Let me know if you need more bullets."

Jeremy leaned toward the Afghan and lifted the man's chin. "Now, where were we? Huh? I think you were just about to—"

The man looked over Jeremy's shoulder, blinked slowly, and muttered.

"Nezam, ask him again."

Silence, save for the heavy-pitched remnants of the gunshot still bouncing between his ears.

"Nezam?" Jeremy glanced over his shoulder.

The translator's turban lay on the floor, and his body shook violently. "My mother. They have my mother."

Jeans and T-shirt and scruffy beard. The translator was like any other twenty-something kid. Except for the grenade in his hand.

Jeremy pivoted, fired twice, and spun toward the door as Nezam crumpled to the floor, the grenade bouncing once in the dirt.

Got to get out. Holly and Miranda. Faster.

Too far.

Yell. Warn the others.

Chanting and laughter.

Past the tarp. Turn. Faster. Almost th—

Light and dirt and gunpowder.

Flying and falling.

Left leg. Both ears. Numb. Burning pain.

Screaming and silence and screaming.

Then nothing.

CHAPTER THIRTY-ONE

Rebecca hollered a warning from her room. "Almost done! Don't come in here!"

Jeremy's head was bowed, staring at knees that bounced rapidly without rhythm. Maggie's hands remained in his, steady and warm.

"It's okay, baby," she said. "It's okay."

"I'd have killed him. No question. I can still feel it. How much I wanted to empty my magazine into him. I never hated anybody like that before."

"It was a different time. We were all angry. Desperate to strike back any way we could. The point is that you didn't kill him. You're not Cronfeld."

He released her hands. "But what if I had? I wouldn't have been sorry. Maybe now, but not then. And after I'd killed him, they'd have brought another man into the room. Would I have shot him too?"

She wrapped her arms around his neck and nuzzled against him. "You didn't. In a way, Nazem may have saved you."

"I've thought about that. About him. Wondering if his mother's still alive. If they let her go or if he died for nothing. Lots of people did."

"It's history. What happened, happened, and what didn't, didn't. You're who you are now. Nothing's changed about how I feel about you. It couldn't."

He pulled away and stood. "Killing's not so hard when you think you're right. When you can justify it by saying lives are at stake. I know that now, Maggie. What I don't know is whether I could live with myself after the fact. These people I chase ... these serial killers. It's not that hard for them, you know? The murders, I mean. And they seem to go on with life just fine."

Maggie shifted to face him. "You're not them."

"No. But I can feel it sometimes, especially at night. Afghanistan is there, waiting to come out again. And in case I might forget, I've got something to remind me." He tapped his left leg.

"Is it flaring up again? Seriously, get it checked out. Schedule the doctor and let me know when the appointment is."

He frowned and tapped a finger on his leg. "You don't have to babysit me."

"Just making sure you take care of yourself, that's all. Sure you don't want me to schedule it for you? Or can I trust you?"

He placed his hand on her knee. "I'll do it. Promise. Kind of nice to have someone looking out for me."

"You know, you weren't only wounded physically. The dreams, the night terrors. It's been a long time. Shouldn't it be getting better? I mean, maybe you have PTSD. There's no shame in asking for help, Jeremy."

"It's not just what happened over there."

She looked up at him and ran her hands along his arms, shoulder to wrist and back up.

He stared over the top of her head. "He's still out there. Whoever killed Holly and Miranda. I'm going to find him. And when I do, I'm afraid of what'll happen."

"Okay, first of all, you don't know he's not already dead or in jail. Second, if he is still out there, you'll do the right thing."

"I wish I could be as sure as you are. You know, the Bureau waited almost a week after my family had been killed before they told me. Said they wanted to hold off until my injuries were no longer life-threatening. Make sure I could handle it. Told me by the time I got back to the States, they'd have the killer in custody."

She brushed a tear away and laid her head on his shoulder. "I'm so sorry, honey. I can't imagine what you went through."

He rested his cheek on top of her head. "Time doesn't heal the wounds. It just pushes them deep down inside, and you hope you can keep them there, but you can't. There's always something or someone to drag the memories back to the surface."

"Cronfeld?"

"Yeah. This time. Next time it'll be different."

"Why, Jeremy? Why is he so insistent? Why now?"

He sighed. "If I had to guess, his wife's calling the shots."

"The senator?"

"Yeah. She's putting pressure on him. Maybe she's worried about it coming out during her reelection campaign. Or could be she's set her sights a little higher."

"President?"

He shrugged. "Why not? Worst thing that could happen is she loses and goes back to being a high-ranking member of the Senate. A scandal involving her husband certainly wouldn't help her chances."

Maggie closed her eyes and slowed her breathing. "When did life become so complicated? Sign the agreement. Don't sign the agreement. I don't care. Do whatever you think is best for your future. We want to be a part of that, Jeremy, if you'll let us."

He kissed her forehead. "I'm working on it. Not going to sign the agreement, though. I'll try to talk Bailey into letting me finish out this case. Work out some sort of understanding. I'll tell him I'll play nice, and we'll keep everything status quo before I ride off into the sunset."

She grinned up at him. "Aren't you moving east?"

"Okay, until I ride off into the sunrise. That better?"

"Much. Now, why don't you mosey on down the hall and check on Rebecca? I don't want to spend the afternoon scrubbing crayon off the walls again."

He tipped an imaginary cowboy hat. "Yes, ma'am. And why don't you rustle us up some vittles before we go out and wash my covered wagon?"

She rolled her eyes and headed for the kitchen. "What am I getting myself into?"

CHAPTER THIRTY-TWO

Mason's hands lingered inches from his wife's throat. His root cellar. His workshop. *His bones.*

Paula tilted her head, lips parted, and brow wrinkled. "Honey, I don't ..."

He grabbed her shoulders and bent down, his face inches from hers. The short, warm bursts of her breath pulsed against his lips. He flexed his hands and moved them back toward her neck. Had no choice. Couldn't stop himself even if he wanted to.

She inclined her face and closed her eyes.

His right hand cupped behind her neck, his left brushed against her side. He leaned over and skimmed his lips across hers before pulling her closer and kissing her deeply. "Sorry, babe."

She pushed him away. "You said you were going to teach me. Let me do the next one. That was the deal."

He bit his bottom lip. "I came down to clean up. That's all. But I had to kill some time before I could move the new batch of beetles over."

She squinched her mouth to the side and propped her hands on her hips. "Uh-huh. If you say so."

Mason escorted her to the workbench. "Look. I didn't finish the left hand. You do it. I've got plenty of other stuff to work on anyway."

Paula poked him in the side. "Oh. I get the scraps, huh? Sounds like frozen pizza for dinner tonight then."

"Bleh. Tell you what. I'll grill out burgers and hot dogs. See if the kids want to invite some friends over. Maybe have a movie night or something. Give me an excuse to snuggle with my girlfriend."

She crossed her arms and squinted at him. "You'd better be talking about me."

Mason winked and pulled her to him again. "No one else for me. Ever."

She grinned up at him. "Well, we agree on that at least. Any problem if I invite my boyfriend over?"

He laughed and kissed her forehead. "Been keeping secrets from me?"

"Our secrets are our secrets. Not *mine*. Not *yours*. Ours."

That was certainly true. Within days after his first kill, he'd broken down and confessed to her. Told her everything. In return, she'd nodded and asked only one question. *Does this affect our family?*

It was the same question she asked about any major decision. He understood. He'd seen the toll a fractured family took on her. Not long after they began dating in high school, she'd shared details of her home life. How her dad was an alcoholic and sometimes hit her mom. How her older brother cried at night and had recently started drinking too. And how she'd never, *never*, allow that to happen to her family.

Not long afterward, her parents had died in a drunk driving accident. Less than two years later, her brother, consumed by guilt, had taken his own life. She'd seen the destruction of her family. It would not happen to her children.

He'd assured her that his action did not affect the family. The police had ruled the death an accident by a careless hunter. The Remington now lay buried three feet underground in a spot known only to Mason. The police weren't coming, and even if they did, there was no evidence.

She'd hugged him and told him to be more careful in the future. He said he would.

....

And then he'd killed Sarah Goldman. A random encounter in the woods. She'd been alone, smoking pot. He'd been hunting for the same rush he'd felt after his first kill. It did not go as planned.

He'd smelled the smoke from her joint and had no trouble tracking her. Young and pretty. A twinge of conscience annoyed him and he hesitated. She'd spotted him and stared, her eyes glassy and a smirk on her lips. He'd walked over, still undecided. Or at least that's what he told himself.

She held out the joint. "Want some?"

"No, thanks. You out here by yourself?"

She took a long drag and held it for several seconds before letting the smoke escape her lungs. "What's with the gun?"

"Out doing a little hunting, that's all."

"Yeah? For what?"

The girl was too stoned to even stand, or so he thought. "Anyone I can find."

When he'd raised the rifle, she'd lunged at him, screaming and fighting, leaving scratches and a bite mark on his right arm. Anger and adrenaline easily chased away any conscience remnants. He'd kicked her to the ground, then finished her with a gunshot to the chest.

But his DNA was under her fingernails and in her mouth. Couldn't leave it there. His hunting knife, sharp as ever, sliced through her skin like it was a tomato. The bones took a bit more effort, but his blade didn't chip. At least he didn't have to gut her, though comparing her innards to a deer's might be interesting. Something to look forward to next time. Fifteen tiring minutes later, her hands and head lay separate from the rest of her remains. The abandoned trailer he'd passed on his way in served as a good distraction if—when—what was left of her body was found. Hide her ID, scatter her clothes, and let the police focus on any vagrants in the area. Good enough.

And playing with her bones had been an unexpected bonus. It relaxed him, cleared his mind, and gave him the freedom to daydream about what, or who, he'd do next. The hands were like working a jigsaw puzzle. Some assembly required. The skull was easier, though pulling any cavity-filled teeth had made him squeamish at first.

After that, Paula had insisted on being more involved. Said she had to if she was going to protect her family. Mason had no illusions about her participation. She didn't enjoy it, at least not the way he did. But she tolerated his adventures, making suggestions, even helping lure victims or drive their car when necessary, like that guy up in Big Oaks. She said she'd do anything to keep her family intact, and she proved it over and over.

Best of all, she didn't judge him. Life at home was better with less stress, she said. More laughter, more time together, more of the good stuff. And look at her now. Upset that he hadn't let her wire the bones together. Mason smiled and hugged her again.

He'd picked a good woman.

CHAPTER THIRTY-THREE

The sun's early morning rays bounced off the trunk of Jeremy's freshly washed Taurus, hit the rearview mirror, and reflected into his eyes. He gave up and donned his sunglasses. Monday morning westbound traffic was already building on I-64 as the truckers awakened and started their treks across the nation. Lexington, Kentucky, home of Roslyn Martin's mother, was several hours ahead. Enough time to think about his plans and what-ifs.

He needed to call Bailey. Tell him he had no intention of signing the agreement and would be turning in his resignation. Not that the Director would care much. Another political headache scratched off his list. Still, Jeremy had built up enough goodwill to swing a deal. Or at least he hoped so.

Six-thirty. Bailey's administrative assistant wouldn't be there yet, but the boss would be in the office and working on his second cup of coffee. The man was nothing if not regular. Jeremy turned down the radio and hit the speed dial. He punched the speakerphone button and dropped the phone in the center cup holder.

Half a ring. "Bailey."

"Good morning, sir. Agent Winter. Wondered if you could spare a few minutes?"

"Good weekend?"

Images flooded Jeremy's mind, from thrown soap-soaked sponges to the construction paper grizzly bear, now riding in the passenger seat. "Great weekend. Sir, about the, um, document. I—"

"Scan it and email it to me after you sign. Follow up with the hard copy."

"I'm not going to sign the agreement."

Muttered expletives were followed by a heavy sigh. "Not the way I wanted to start my week, Agent Winter."

"I understand, sir."

"You've thought this through? What it means—could mean for your career?"

"I have."

"This puts me in a very difficult position."

You? What about me? "Can't do it, sir. I know that's not what you wanted to hear. I've done my job. Gone above and beyond more times than I can count."

"Won't disagree with that. And you can keep doing your job. Just realize there are repercussions for the decisions you make."

"No one knows that better than I do, sir. I'd like to propose a resolution that might make things simpler for both of us."

"I'm listening."

Jeremy pushed back against his seat and stretched his leg. Really flaring up today. Too much time in the car. "I'm offering my resignation, effective in two weeks. I believe that solves your problem."

"Won't lie. It would certainly help."

"And in return, I want my full retirement package. All benefits effective on my last day."

Bailey chuckled. "You got any idea how much red tape I'd have to cut through to make that happen?"

"I think I'm owed that much, sir. And you can tell your friends I'll keep my mouth shut. I haven't talked about it before, and I won't start now. Agent Keeley knows, but no one else."

"They're not my friends, Winter. But I do have to keep them happy. You know how this works."

"I do, and it's why I want out. This way, everybody's happy."

"I'm not so sure this'll satisfy certain people, but it's good enough for me. I'll do what I can to make your retirement benefits happen. You email me your resignation today. We can both move on."

"Will do. And while I work out my last two weeks—"

"You'll be digging into your serial killer theory. Alone."

"Thank you, sir."

"Will there be anything else, Agent Winter?"

"Have a great day, sir."

"Yeah. You too."

He turned the radio back up, just in time to catch the end of Reba's latest. Two weeks. It wouldn't be enough, but it was a start. If he could scrounge up enough evidence to at least make his theory plausible, he'd turn what he had over to the Bureau and let them handle it.

Or not.

This was his case. If it meant carrying it into his post-FBI future, then that's what he'd do. Maggie would understand he couldn't turn loose of the chase. Not as long as the guy was still out there. He'd share everything he had with the authorities, of course. But this was his case. All he needed was a push in the right direction. Somewhere to start.

His best chance, possibly his only one, waited a few hours ahead of him. Donna Martin. If she had any information on the meetings between her daughter and Barry Thornquist, that could be the catalyst.

CHAPTER THIRTY-FOUR

Jeremy idled down the street, alternating his view between the houses and the scribbled note in his hand. There. That's the place. Faded green siding, freshly mowed lawn, and a concrete path leading from the sidewalk to an oversize front porch, complete with wicker rocking chairs and a swing. The home Roslyn Martin had shared with her mother epitomized Lexington charm. All that was missing was the pitcher of lemonade.

He gathered his paperwork and organized his thoughts before heading inside. Donna Martin had agreed to talk to him, though she'd seemed hesitant. Her daughter passed away fourteen months ago, the sole victim in a four-car pileup on the interstate. No doubt the hurt was still fresh. Jeremy's hopes hinged on the link between Roslyn and Barry Thornquist. There had to be something—anything—that might open up connections between other disappearances and victims.

He grabbed his suit jacket from the back seat, walked up the path, and rapped lightly on the aluminum screen door. Somewhere in the home a TV was on, blaring *The Price is Right*. Water beaded on his forehead and upper lip, the result of an assault by Kentucky's late May humidity, and he wiped away the sweat before brushing his hand against his gray pants.

An older woman, barefoot and dressed in shorts and a clean blue T-shirt, opened the door. "You must be Mister Winter. I'm glad to meet you. If you don't mind, we'll sit on the porch. It's a bit stuffy inside, and I can't afford to run the air conditioning too much."

"Yes, ma'am. That'll be just fine."

Miss Martin dragged a floor fan onto the porch, pointed it toward the chairs, and switched on its lowest setting. "Too noisy if I turn it all the way up. Now then. You just have a seat. I'll be right back."

"Is there something I can help you with?"

She squinted and looked him over. "For starters, you can take off that coat and tie. Too blamed hot for such foolishness. Now, wait right here."

Jeremy obliged her request and seated himself in one of the rockers, shifting slightly to avoid a piece of wicker that poked into his back. After a moment, Miss Martin returned with two tall glasses of iced tea. She handed him one and eased into the other rocker.

He took a sip and let the sugary cool concoction flow through his body. Condensation dripped off the glass onto his pants, creating dark circles of chill. He raised the tea to eye level and nodded. "Nothing better on a hot day."

"Mmm hmm. Some of my friends use that artificial stuff instead of sugar, but it just don't taste right to me. Gives you cancer too."

"Yes, ma'am."

They spent a few minutes rocking and drinking, commenting occasionally on the weather, a passing car, or a neighbor's flowerbed.

"So Mister Winter, what can I do for you?"

"First off, you can call me Jeremy."

"Well, that'll be fine, Jeremy. And all the folks 'round here just call me Miss Donna."

"Good enough. Miss Donna, as I said on the phone, I'm investigating a murder case, and I was hoping you might have some information that could help me. A man named Barry Thornquist went missing four years ago. We found his body at a wildlife refuge over in Indiana several months back. I started digging into the details and discovered that he'd been coming to the park for several years. And every time he was there, so was your daughter."

Miss Donna's lips turned down at the corners. "Roslyn passed away a bit over a year ago."

"Yes, ma'am. I was real sorry to hear that."

Her rocking stopped, and she took a long drink of the iced tea. "I don't know what you think, but Roslyn was a good girl. She had her problems, but in this world, who doesn't? She didn't kill that man."

"No, ma'am, she didn't. I'm trying to fill in the blanks so I can find who did. There was some sort of, um, relationship between Thornquist and your daughter, wasn't there?"

She nodded slowly. "Roslyn never said much about him till after that last visit. When he disappeared. She was real worried about what might have happened to him."

Jeremy's rocker creaked as he shifted his weight toward the left. "So, she did talk about him?"

"Bits and pieces."

"Yes, ma'am."

Miss Donna reached over and placed a veiny hand on Jeremy's arm. "Young man, there's been enough hurtin'."

"There has, and I'd like to keep any more from happening."

Miss Donna's rocking continued unabated, and she allowed the conversation's pause to stretch to the point of being awkward.

Jeremy swatted at a fly circling his glass. "I know this must be painful for you."

"She was always my baby girl. Made some mistakes. We both did. Didn't matter, though. I loved her no matter what and made sure she knew it."

"Miss Donna, I have one concern here, and that's finding out who murdered Barry Thornquist. Whatever Roslyn was into, whatever she did, I'm only interested insofar as it can help me find a killer. Maybe stop more deaths."

"Roslyn wasn't *into* anything. She got up every day, went to work, and came home. I'd have lost this house a long time ago without her help."

"Yes, ma'am. I didn't mean to imply ... well, it's just that after doing this job for so long, you start to assume the worst about people."

"And are you usually right about that?"

Jeremy watched a large drop of condensation waver at the bottom of his glass before falling. "More often than not, I'm afraid."

"Not much of a way to go through life. There's enough real problems without going out of your way to find new ones."

"I believe you're right about that. So, ma'am, is there anything you can share with me that might help?"

The old woman sighed. "Nothing that'll help with your investigation, I'm afraid. You see, Barry Thornquist was Roslyn's son."

The glass slipped in his hand and he rested it on his thigh. "Her son? I'm not sure I—"

"She was only seventeen. In love, she said. 'Course her boyfriend disappeared right away, and there wasn't any way we could afford to raise a baby. Roslyn did the right thing, though. Gave that little boy up for adoption. Hardest thing either one of us had gone through, but I was so proud of her. Lots of girls her age would've made a different decision. A worse one."

"Yes, ma'am."

"Part of the deal was we didn't know who adopted him. Where they lived or nothin'. And then a few years ago, out of the blue, Roslyn gets a phone call from him. Says he wants to meet her. Well, you can imagine how excited and scared she was. They decided to meet over at that wildlife refuge since it was about halfway. He was real particular about keeping everything all hush-hush. Said he didn't want his folks to know. Didn't want to hurt their feelings."

Jeremy's body felt as if gravity had intensified in the space around the rocking chair, dragging him down to another dead end. "That's it? That's all there was to it?"

"All there was to it? Young man, it may not mean anything to you, but to my Roslyn, it was everything."

"I'm sorry. I didn't mean ..."

She leaned away from him. "I believe you did. There's plenty more in this world besides your investigation. Roslyn was thrilled to get to see her boy once or twice a year. I'm sorry if that doesn't help you, but there it is all the same."

"Yes, ma'am. Sorry for my frustration. I'm kind of on my own here, and I was sure I was on the right trail. Did Roslyn say anything about the last time she saw her son? Anything that might help me figure out what happened?"

"Oh, we talked about it, of course. She was real worried. Said after they met at the park, she headed home like always but didn't feel right. Later on, she called it her mother's intuition. She said she didn't get more than a few miles away from the park before she turned around and went back. Wanted to give him one more hug."

"And did she?"

"Couldn't. He wasn't there no more. She drove around a little but never saw him again. Figured he'd headed on back to his home. She didn't try to call him since that was against their rules. He always contacted her, and always from a pay phone so it wouldn't show up on his cell."

"And she never told any of this to the police, correct?"

Miss Donna shrugged. "What was to tell? She didn't know anything, and there was no point in Barry's folks finding out he'd gone looking for his birth mother. He wouldn't have wanted that."

Jeremy's head tilted forward and his shoulders sagged. "Of course not. I understand."

"A couple days after they last met, she saw on the news that he'd gone missing. She spent her last years worried and wonderin' what happened. Racking her brain for anything else that might help. We didn't talk about it too much."

"Sure. Too painful."

"Yes, it was. She thought if she'd stayed at the park a little longer, maybe it wouldn't have happened. Course, there's no way to know if that's true, but you couldn't tell her that. And she passed just a month before they found him. They're together now, though. Will be for all eternity. She made sure her boy knew about Jesus."

Jeremy squished his eyebrows together and scratched his forehead. "Yes, ma'am. Miss Donna, you said anything *else* that might help. What do you mean?"

"It wasn't enough, she said. Even talked about going to one of those hypnotists to see if they could help her remember. Got killed in the car wreck before that happened, but she'd seen on TV some of the stuff they could do. She thought maybe if she could see a license number ..."

"A license number?"

"On the pickup truck. She didn't think much about it until years later. Said the park wasn't crowded at all that day, but this same pickup truck passed them three or four times while they visited. Didn't get a bad feeling or nothin', and some other cars passed them too. But the truck stuck with her. Couldn't say why."

Jeremy rubbed his hand across his mouth. "Did she give any details about the pickup?"

Miss Donna shook her head and poked out her lips. "Just an old beat up white truck. Had a farm on the license plate."

"A farm?"

"That's what she said. A picture of a barn with the sun coming up behind it."

"Did she see what state it was from?"

"She looked it up on the Internet a couple of years ago and thought it was Tennessee, best she could remember. I'm sorry, but that's all she said. Never told anybody 'cause she figured it wouldn't help any. An old pickup truck with maybe Tennessee tags, and probably didn't have anything to do with Barry's death anyway. She was so frustrated. Reconnecting with her son after all those years, only to lose him again. You can imagine."

Jeremy handed her a business card. "Yes, ma'am. I appreciate your time this morning. You've given me something to consider. That's more than I had yesterday. And thanks for the tea."

"Good luck to you, young man. I hope you find whoever did it."

"Yes, ma'am. So do I."

....

Tennessee. The thinnest of leads, assuming the pickup truck even had anything to do with Barry Thornquist's death. Jeremy drove to a local diner, opened his laptop, and accessed the FBI database through his secure connection. In less than two weeks, he'd have to turn in the computer and, more importantly, his access to the NCIC. He could always call in favors, and certainly Maggie would help if he asked, but that's not what he wanted. Cut ties and start over. A little help from the Bureau now and then might be fine, but not so much that he felt he owed them.

The search confirmed his fear. Thousands of plates with the image, their funds supporting agriculture education, had been distributed in Tennessee over the last few years. Narrowing the list down to only those that were registered to pickup truck owners was pointless. A quick guesstimate put the number at over ninety percent of the plates sold. This probably wasn't the puzzle piece that was going to break open the case, but at least it was a piece. That's more than he had before.

What now? He stared at the screen until it blurred into a hazy blue blob.

Two weeks to find a serial killer. With what he had now, it would be nearly impossible without a major break and, the way this case had gone so far, that wasn't likely. He needed help. Someone from outside the Bureau.

Time to make a phone call.

CHAPTER THIRTY-FIVE

Jeremy perched himself on the edge of the examination table while the doctor studied his left leg. It had only been two days since he'd seen Maggie, but she'd already called half a dozen times to see if he'd scheduled an appointment. He had planned to hold off until his remaining two weeks with the Bureau were up, but time worked against him, and the pain had steadily grown, popping up at random intervals. Enough was enough. "Probably just getting old, huh?"

"Straighten your leg, please." The doctor held Jeremy's foot and pushed the toes backward.

Jeremy gasped and gripped the edge of the bed as a bolt of lightning shot from his calf to his hip. "That's a little painful."

"We need to get an ultrasound on that leg as soon as possible. Could be a blood clot."

"Can't I get a prescription for some blood thinners or something? Not really a good time for me to be away from work, even for a couple of hours."

The doctor tapped a few notes into his tablet computer. "If it is a blood clot, it could break loose and end up anywhere in your body. Maybe cause a heart attack or stroke. You need to get it checked out. I've already transferred the orders over to the hospital. Head on over there now. Stop at the front desk and they'll give you a note for work."

He chuckled and slid off the table. "I don't need a note. I need more hours in the day."

"Can't help you there. I need them too. But the sooner you get the ultrasound done, the sooner you can cross that off your list and get back to work."

Jeremy exhaled loudly. "It never ends. Okay. I'll go on over and let them check out the leg. You think it's serious?"

The doctor peered over his glasses. "No way to know until we see the test results, but if I were you, I'd already be halfway to the hospital."

Jeremy dressed quickly and made the ten-minute drive to the medical complex. The waiting room was semi-crowded, and the woman at triage said she had no idea how long he'd be there. The guy sitting next to him began hacking up a lung, and Jeremy walked to the vending machines, pretending he wanted a snack. After a moment, he shook his head and found a new seat far away from the cougher. Best place in the world to go if you want to get sick.

He pulled out his cell phone and debated calling Maggie. Best not until he knew for sure what was going on. No sense worrying her. Instead, he hit the speed dial for his new sort-of-partner. Huntingburg, Indiana, police officer Troy Obion answered after one ring.

"Hey, Jeremy. What's up?"

"Hi, Troy. Not much. Just wanted to check in and see if you'd had any luck with that information I sent you."

"No, sir. Not yet. I'll be honest. Doesn't seem like much to go on so far."

"Nothing on the Tennessee license plates?"

"No other state has a specialty tag with a barn and sun, so I think Roslyn got that right, assuming that's what she saw. The database you sent over is massive. Without more factors to sort by, not much chance of identifying a suspect. Do you know how many white pickup trucks have the agriculture license plate?"

"Don't tell me. My day's going bad enough as it is. We really need to—"

"Winter. Jeremy Winter." A male nurse in green scrubs stood at the entrance to the imaging department and peered over the waiting room.

"Got to run, Troy. I'll talk to you later. Appreciate all your help on this." He slipped the phone back into his pocket and walked to the nurse. Finally. Another half hour or so and he'd be headed back to the office. He nodded to the nurse. "Let's get this over with."

....

Jeremy clenched his fingers into fists repeatedly. He couldn't take much more. The constant beep-beep-beep. The faintly nauseous scent of filtered air and sickness and bleach. The hard mattress under him, the thin sheet over him, and a pillow shoved under his left leg. An IV running into his right arm. A sensor clipped to his finger. Too much. The blue contraption next to the bed sounded a steady alarm as his blood pressure rose. Third time this hour.

The nurse entered the room, silenced the alarm, and left without speaking. Nothing new to say. She'd vented the last time and threatened to talk to the doctor about sedating him if he didn't calm down. Jeremy had promised he would. That had been nearly twenty minutes ago.

"Knock knock."

He pushed himself up in the bed and grinned. "Hey, Maggie."

She walked to the bed and kissed him. "Hey, yourself. Feeling okay?"

"I'm so tired of this bed. Just give me a pill and let me out of here. I'm no good to anybody laid up like this."

She grabbed his hand. "You're no good to anybody if you're dead, either. Which, according to the nurse at the desk, could happen soon if you don't behave. Nurses know how to make it look like an accident, Jeremy. They have ways."

He massaged Maggie's hand with his thumb. "You didn't have to come, but I'm glad you did."

Her lips turned up the tiniest bit. "Of course I did. Old guy like you in the hospital, well, you never know."

"Old guy? I'm what, eight years older than you? Plus, they say forty-seven is the new forty."

She smiled and pulled his hand to her lips. "Umm, nope. Pretty sure nobody says that. But if it makes you feel better ..."

"Getting out of here would make me feel better. I don't understand why I still—" The machine's alarm sounded again.

Maggie rolled her eyes. "I swear. You're worse than Rebecca sometimes. They want to watch you for another couple of days. Make sure there are no more problems. Why can't you just accept that?"

Jeremy sighed. "Because there's—"

"Because there might be a serial killer out there that nobody's looking for except you."

"You know I'm right."

"What I know is that if you don't do what you're told, you'll end up in here a whole lot longer."

He exhaled loudly and stared at the ceiling. "Fine. Subject change then. Did Rebecca's dad have any problem keeping her this week?"

The nurse entered the room, silenced the alarm, and turned to Maggie. "Can you do anything with him?"

"I'm not sure anyone can."

"We'll take care of that in a little while. The doctor prescribed a sedative so he'll rest, hopefully for the rest of my shift."

Maggie smiled at her. "They don't pay you enough."

"I know that's right." She cut her eyes toward Jeremy before leaving.

He cleared his throat. "I can hear you, you know."

Maggie patted his arm. "Uh-huh. I'm guessing they have a betting pool on how long before one of them snaps."

"And I'm usually such a people person. Must be the drugs. So how's Rebecca?"

"Great. My ex was thrilled to get her for the week."

"How did she feel about going?"

Maggie shrugged. "She said she'd rather come here and go to the zoo again."

"Is that all?"

"Yeah, I think so. Oh. She also said she wanted another chocolate shake from that diner."

Jeremy squeezed her hand. "That was a good day. Nothing else?"

She leaned over and kissed him on the forehead. "She sent that and told me to tell you she missed you and would—let me make sure I get this right— 'tell Jesus to fix you up quick.' You're in the regular rotation for her bedtime prayers. Mine too."

Emptiness swept through his stomach up to his chest, and he sniffled. "I miss that little fireball."

Maggie nuzzled against his face before kissing his cheek. "Somebody needs a shave."

"What I really need is my laptop."

"Uh-uh. No work. Doctor's orders."

"Seriously? I'm not wasting the next two days laid up in here. I'll go insane." He lowered his voice. "It's in my car. I just want to clear out my email. Catch up on a couple of things."

"Can't you do that on your phone?"

Jeremy stroked the back of her hand. "I can do some of it, but I need access to a few files. Please?"

Maggie frowned, shook her head, and lifted a padded black case from behind her chair. "I swear, you're worse than Rebecca. Here. You can use mine, but only for a few minutes. I'm not leaving. And if the doctor asks, you didn't get this from me. Agreed?"

"Yes, ma'am."

"You thought about how this affects your plans? Still going to resign?"

He unzipped the laptop case and handed her the power cord. "Doesn't change anything. Bailey's got it all worked out. The full package—pension and insurance. And now, with all this, it gives the Bureau more ammo to relegate me to a nice, quiet desk in the corner of some tiny FBI satellite office."

She grinned and plugged the power cord into a wall outlet. "Insurance? I figured an old guy like you'd be on Medicare."

"Don't make me call the nurse."

Maggie pulled the sheet higher and placed a blanket across his legs. "They wouldn't come if you called. Besides, there's no need. I'm already here."

CHAPTER THIRTY-SIX

M ason shifted in the tractor's seat and glanced back at the planter. The device had six containers, but only the four in the middle worked properly. They spat out one seed every three and a half inches, a tighter spacing than most farms preferred, but if conditions were right, he'd boost his yield. The two broken containers would have to wait for more money and another year. Hopefully.

It'd take longer to get the seed in the ground, but not enough to be a concern. There was plenty of time and, if the weather cooperated and prices stayed high, he'd turn a decent profit. Not enough to pay off everything, but a good start. By early or mid-October, the fields would be white as snow with the cotton.

Snow. Funny how a word could take you back in time. Sometimes the recollections weren't good ones, but this one was. A little snow, a lot of stress, and a hunt that ended in a clean kill. A memory to be cherished.

. . . .

It had happened a couple of years ago. October was rainy, putting a damper on attendance to the maze. Money was tighter than usual, and it looked like Santa would be skipping their house again this year. By early December, he was ready to explode.

A trip to Arkansas eased his stress. Two or three inches of wet snow covered the ground in Village Creek State Park, and the overcast sky kept most people indoors. Too late in the day to hunt deer, but that wasn't on his agenda anyway.

A lone vehicle, an older white Mercury Marquis with handicap tags, was parked near a trailhead with one set of footprints leading off into the woods. He stopped near it, stepped outside, and glanced casually inside the car. Only two hours from home, Paula would have plenty of time to get here to help move the vehicle if his hunt was successful.

After a last look around, he followed the tracks into the woods. It was too risky to carry his rifle since this clearly was not a hunting area. He did, however, have his pistol and hunting knife, though if the situation seemed safe, he wanted to try something different today. Just his hands.

He quickly spotted the hiker shuffling along not far ahead. The woman had to be in her mid-seventies and leaned heavily on her walking stick, but still managed a decent pace. Not so fast, though, that he'd have any trouble getting ahead of her and planning the attack.

Mason closed the gap between them and, when he was near enough, cleared his throat and coughed so he wouldn't startle her. She stopped and turned around, then pulled her scarf away from her mouth and waved.

"Good morning," she said. "Thought I'd have the place to myself today."

He smiled as he approached her. "Sorry. Was hunting not far from here and, since this is my first time in the area, I thought I'd check this place out in case I want to bring the family sometime."

"Well, this is a wonderful park. You can fish or ride horses, and the campground is very nice. How many children do you have?"

"Two boys, and they're a handful. They love being outside though, so this is just the kind of place they'd like. Let them burn off some energy, you know? Anyway, I won't keep you. Enjoy your walk." He quickened his pace and edged ahead of her.

"I'd love the company if you don't mind listening to the ramblings of an old woman."

Why not? "Be my pleasure. What brings you out here in such dreary weather?"

She tapped her walking stick on the ground and moved forward. "I try to come every day for the exercise. Can't walk if it gets too hot, but the cold doesn't bother me much. I'm Gloria, by the way."

"Nice to meet you, Gloria. None of your friends come along?"

"Not in this weather. Too afraid they'll fall and break something. At our age, a broken bone can be a death sentence."

He arched his eyebrows. "You're not afraid?"

"If it happens, it happens. Just as likely I'll fall going out to the mailbox, and I'm not going to sit on the couch all day. Can't live that way."

"Of course not." He turned to look back, then surveyed the trees on each side of them before studying the woman more closely. Her multiple layers of clothing probably weighed as much as she did. "How far do you usually walk?"

"Depends on how I feel that day. I've probably got another fifteen minutes in me before I'll turn around and head back." Quick, tiny clouds of condensed breath punctuated the air around her mouth.

His heartbeat accelerated, and he gestured toward the scarf around her neck. "You make that?"

"I can't do any knitting because of my arthritis. A friend made it for me. Red and white for the Razorbacks, and it's very soft. Not itchy like a lot of them." She stopped walking, turned to face him, and held out one end of the scarf. "Here, feel for yourself."

His chest muscles tensed as he glanced at her hands. Knobby knuckles and bent fingers. It'll be a challenge piecing them back together. He caressed the edge of the scarf. "Soft and warm." He reached for the other end of the cloth. "This side looks a bit frayed, though."

"Really?" she said. "I hadn't noticed. I'll get my friend to—"

He gripped the scarf and pulled his arms apart, tightening the noose around her neck. A weak gasp escaped her mouth, and he wrapped the cloth around his fists for a tighter grip. Her pale face rapidly turned red, and he bent closer to peer into her blue-gray eyes before tugging harder. Her glare pierced him, and he glanced away, then told himself to be a man and returned her gaze.

He'd thought that even at her age she'd put up more of a fight. Her frail hand grasped for her neck, but the effort was weak. Her mouth moved as though she wanted to say something, or maybe it was simply a fish-out-of-water reaction. There was no challenge, really. It was like wrestling with the boys and not holding anything back. A quick victory was assured. As if on cue, she raised her walking stick and swung it at his legs, but she had neither the leverage nor the strength to cause any damage.

After a moment, the redness in her face transitioned to a bluish-white, and he raised his arms higher to support her weight. Her clear eyes rolled back in her head, and her arms hung limply at her side. He'd heard stories of people regaining consciousness several minutes after being thought dead, and that wasn't going to happen with Gloria. He let her body slump to the ground, then pulled the scarf as tight as he could and tied it into a knot.

When it was over, the expected peace returned to him. Surprisingly, there seemed to be no difference whether he killed from a distance or up close. There was no sense of it being more personal or fulfilling than any of his other hunts. Maybe because this one had been too easy? He'd have to try again with someone stronger.

....

His cellphone rang and yanked him away from his reverie and back to his tractor. He glanced at the caller ID. Unknown number which meant a bill collector or telemarketer. Either way, they'd get no answer. He tossed the phone on the dash. Sounded like it might be time to plan another outing and find a new friend for Gloria.

He turned the tractor and began dropping four more rows of cottonseed.

CHAPTER THIRTY-SEVEN

Jeremy scanned the notes again before slapping his pen on the desk. Three days in the hospital hadn't given him any fresh insights into the case. Director Bailey's "welcome back to work, hope you're feeling better" phone call had been a not-so-subtle reminder that the clock was still ticking on his career, though he'd at least reset the timer. This week and next, then sail off into retirement. Oh, and expect a call from Colonel Cronfeld. Maybe even a visit.

Jeremy suspected that's why his boss had been generous with the extra time. Cronfeld wanted him on the government payroll a bit longer. Sweeten the deal. Talk him out of quitting. Promise whatever as long as the agreement got signed.

He glanced at the clock and realized an hour had passed. Time for a bit of exercise. Doctor's orders and, more importantly, Maggie's. He stood, grabbed his coffee mug, and headed for the break room. People smiled and nodded as he passed them. A few asked how he was feeling. The true answer was that although the blood clot was gone and the leg pain far less common, he was tired and cranky, though the actual response was somewhat less specific.

"Fine."

He was relieved to find the break room empty. He hated making small talk, especially when he was the subject. Funny. He could sit with Maggie for hours, only speaking now and then, and be perfectly happy. Anyone else though, and the awkward gaps in the conversation ate at him.

He dumped his cold coffee in the sink, rinsed his mug, and held the cup higher to get a better look. Could be his imagination, but it looked like the brown tinges inside the mug had darkened. Small victories.

Back in his office, he browsed the get-well cards lining the windowsill.

Most were generically signed by "the 2nd floor gang" or similar. How long was he supposed to leave them out before throwing them away? Greeting card etiquette wasn't his strong suit.

He clicked his tongue against the roof of his mouth, sank into his chair, and scanned his laptop's inbox for anything important. All the messages appeared routine except one near the top. Troy Obion. Maybe he had news.

"Hope you're feeling better. Nothing new. Blackston's ex-husband calls me at least once a week. I don't know what to tell him so I say we're still investigating it. I thought maybe it would help if we got together and brainstormed."

Jeremy propped his elbow on the desk, rested his head on his hand, and reread the email. Couldn't hurt to bounce a few ideas off each other.

He typed a return email. "Hi, Troy. Sounds good. Give me a call when you get a chance and we'll set something up."

Less than a minute after sending the email, Jeremy's cell phone rang. He glanced at the caller ID and smiled. That was fast.

"Hey, Troy. What's up?"

"Not much. Thanks for getting back to me so quick."

"No problem. Good to hear from you."

"Uh-huh. I figured it might do us both some good to get together and talk through the Blackston case. You know, face to face. Seems like nothing else is working at this point."

"Sounds like a plan. The more I try to find some sort of connection between these disappearances and murders, the further away I seem to get. Got anywhere in mind? I'll come to you."

"There's a little diner not too far from here. How about breakfast on Saturday? You pick the time."

"Early. Oh, and I'm going to send you a name to dig into. Duane Forsberg. Accidental death in Chickasaw National Wildlife Refuge. You know where that is?"

"Up in the northwest corner of Tennessee. Who's Duane Forsberg?"

"In December six years ago, he was hiking and was killed with a single shot from a .30-06. The authorities wrote it off as a hunting accident even though he was in a section of the park posted as off-limits for hunters. They never found the shooter. Probably wouldn't have charged him even if they had."

"Hunting accidents happen all the time. What makes you think this one's connected?"

"Pulled some quick data on Tennessee parks, you know, because of the license plate that might have been seen at the Thornquist site. Wondering if our guy killed anyone down that way. Forsberg's death is the only unsolved one in a Tennessee park for the last decade, so I'm hoping there's a link. Kind of thin, I know."

"I'll make some phone calls and get a look at the file and autopsy report. See if they were able to get anything off the bullet and if they've run the details through the database lately."

"I appreciate it. And if you could keep this between us ..."

"Hey, I'm glad to do it. Maybe we'll actually have something to talk about at breakfast. Oh, and come hungry."

....

The plate was huge and entirely too small. Bacon strips hung over the edges, a biscuit held on for dear life, and some of the fried potatoes had already succumbed to gravity and fallen to the table. Jeremy sprinkled the scrambled eggs with pepper and watched as Troy squirted ketchup on his eggs and potatoes.

"You gonna put that on the biscuit too?"

The officer placed his bacon and biscuit on a napkin and mixed his plate's remaining contents with the speed and precision of a hibachi restaurant chef. "Well, that would just be wrong, wouldn't it? Honey or jelly for the biscuit. Sometimes both."

"Whatever gets you through the day, I guess."

Troy leaned forward and lowered his voice. "The waitress has a thing for me. You want extra biscuits, just let me know."

"I'll keep that in mind, but I'm sure this'll be more than enough. I'll probably need a nap if I eat even half of it."

"I've heard that happens to old guys. Naps and whatnot."

"Yeah, I'm starting to get that a lot."

Troy set down his fork and shifted in his seat. "Oh, hey, man. I didn't mean anything by it. Just messin' with you."

Jeremy shook his head. "I know. Don't worry about it. That stuff doesn't bother me. It's like Ronald Reagan once said. 'Don't hold my age against me, and I won't hold your youth and inexperience against you.'"

"Reagan? I think I read about him back in high school. Wasn't he—"

The waitress stopped by the table and topped off their coffee. "Y'all doing okay? Can I get you anything, Troy?"

The officer's tanned round face took on a reddish tint, and he glanced up at the young woman. "Hey, Peggy. I'm good, thanks."

The blonde smiled and placed her hand on the back of the booth's seat. "How about another biscuit?"

"That would be great."

She winked at Jeremy and motioned toward Troy. "Careful. This one will talk your ear off."

"I'm learning that," Jeremy said. "He was just telling me how much he enjoys coming here. Good food and better service. Says you always take such good care of him."

Troy used his fork to remix the eggs and potatoes, moving them from one side of his plate to the other, then focused intently on re-buttering his biscuit.

"Is that right?" Peggy said. She patted the officer on the back. "Well, we do our best. Now, I've got to go take care of my other customers, but I'll be back with that biscuit soon enough. You need anything else, you holler. Okay, Troy?"

His eyes remained fixated on his plate. "Sure thing."

"What did I tell you? Talk your ear off." She laughed and moved off to the next patrons.

Jeremy pushed his plate away and rested his forearms on the table. "Why don't you get it over with and ask her out? You know you want to. And even better, you know she wants you to."

Troy pulled his ball cap lower and pulled a folded piece of paper from his pocket. "Did you come all this way to talk about my love life? Or lack of it?"

"You got something better to discuss?"

Troy shrugged. "I suppose that depends on your definition of 'better.' Let me ask you something. You ever been hunting?"

"Deer hunting? No. I prefer to get my food the way God intended. At the grocery store."

"We should go this winter. I know a place. Sorry. Off topic. Anyway, I do some hunting when I can and I'll tell you this: either Duane Forsberg was the unluckiest man on the planet or he was intentionally shot."

Jeremy leaned forward. "Go on."

"Like we figured, there wasn't much in the file we didn't already know. A hiker shot by a stray bullet. Not enough left of the slug to do any kind of ballistics on, but most likely a .30-06 round. Shell casing never found. The autopsy report was interesting, though."

"How so?"

"The coroner ruled it death by gunshot obviously. Clean hit. Right through the head. Entered through the left cheek and exited by the right ear. The guy most likely died instantly, although the coroner thought he could have hung on for a minute or two. Looking at the photos, I hope it was the former."

"Yeah, me too. Anything else?"

"Yeah, this guy was over six feet tall. Six-two to be exact."

"And?"

"You ever see a six-foot tall deer wandering around? In this part of the country, the white-tails get about three, maybe three and a half feet tall at the shoulders."

Jeremy rocked back in the booth. "Terrain?"

"I looked over the photos but couldn't tell much. Besides the body, there were only a few generic shots of the surrounding area. Nothing against the local cops. They didn't have any reason to suspect anything more than an accident."

"Maybe I can—"

Troy held up his hand. "I already did. Visited the scene, I mean. Is that what you were going to say?"

He's good. "It is. And what did you learn?"

"No hills to amount to anything. The bullet's trajectory at the point of impact was basically flat, possibly slightly upward. No way the shot came from a hunter in a tree stand. And according to the file, this was a clean hit. No tree scrapes found."

"You think Forsberg was targeted?"

"Like I said, if this was an accident, the guy was the unluckiest man in the world. Based on the direction of the impact, the shot came from a stand of trees on the other side of a clearing, minimum distance of around fifty yards, more likely seventy yards at least. Either way, that's close enough to know what you're shooting at. Especially if you're an experienced hunter, which I'm guessing the shooter was."

"Why?"

"Clean shot through the trees. Depending on where the shooter was, there weren't many options available. He'd of had to wait for just the right moment before pulling the trigger."

"That's assuming it was intentional. I've seen freak accidents before. Ten or eleven years ago, there was a case in Florida with a woman driving her car down the interstate and getting shot. Her window was open less than five inches, and the bullet came through that gap and killed her instantly. They were sure they had a sniper on their hands. Turned out to be a hunter. Took a shot at a deer and missed. The bullet ricocheted off a pond's surface and had just enough left to do its damage."

"Occam's razor," Troy said.

"Excuse me?"

"Sorry. Something I learned back in college. Occam's razor is a principle that says in lieu of better evidence, the simplest solution is usually the best. Doesn't mean the answer can't be more complex, but until someone proves otherwise, why not accept the most plausible scenario? See, in this case, the most likely situation was that Duane Forsberg was killed by an errant bullet from a deer hunter, so that's what the police went with. You can't fault them for that. Nothing pointed anywhere else."

Jeremy ran his hand across his scalp. "Yeah, but you think they were wrong. I do too, but I haven't heard anything that sounds like evidence. Could be you're—we're—bending the facts to fit our hypothesis."

"Can't argue with that, but we both know I'm right. What we don't know is whether or not there's any connection between this death and the others. It certainly doesn't fit the profile. The complete body was found. Nothing missing. If this is your serial killer, why didn't he follow his pattern?"

"Don't know. Forsberg was killed six years ago so that would make him the earliest victim we're aware of. The murderer's evolved since then. Maybe he was figuring himself out? Deciding what worked best?"

"Maybe. You're the expert, so where do we go from here?"

"Listen, Troy. I appreciate what you've done, but you don't have to hang around on this. I don't want you to get in any trouble with your chief."

"Eh, won't be any trouble. No way I'm dropping this now. I've had more fun in the last couple of days than I've had in, well, a long time."

"Fun?"

"Maybe that's not the right word. I just feel like I've actually done something that matters, you know? Like I'm doing what I'm supposed to be doing."

"Yeah, I understand exactly how you feel. Anyway, I'll pull the database of licensed hunters in west Tennessee and cross-reference that with the list of people with the agriculture license plates on their pickup trucks."

Troy chuckled. "That'll probably narrow it down to a couple hundred thousand people."

Jeremy stood and stretched. "You got a better idea?"

"Hey, man. You're the boss. I just follow orders."

"You want an order? Call that waitress."

CHAPTER THIRTY-EIGHT

The day dragged as Jeremy's mood staggered between boredom and depression. It'd been days since his meeting with Troy, and nothing had changed. Tennessee's vehicle database provided no clues that would narrow down the search for any potential killer. He'd say the investigation had come to a screeching halt, but it had never been moving to begin with.

His phone rang and he grabbed it, thankful for a break. "Hey, Troy. What's up? You get rid of that cold?"

"Yeah, finally. Calling to give you an update."

Jeremy's heartbeat accelerated. "On what?"

"I called her. Peggy. The waitress you met. We're going out this weekend."

His chest hollowed, and he sank back in his chair. "About time."

"Huh. She said the same thing. Anyway, I wanted to bounce something off you."

"Troy, I'm probably not the guy you want to get relationship advice from."

The officer laughed. "I think I can handle that side of things. But if I do run into problems, I'll be sure to give you a call."

A flash of heat swept through Jeremy's face. "I didn't mean ... forget it. So what's up?"

"I know we're waiting for something to shake loose on the Blackston case. I keep thinking it's got to happen soon. I mean, it's been seven months since she went missing. I drove by her place and there's somebody else living there now. They hired someone to replace her at work less than two weeks after she disappeared or left or whatever. It's like she was never here."

"Maybe that's what she wanted, Troy."

"You believe that?"

"Be nice if I did. I'd get more sleep."

"Right. Me too. So I'm in bed last night, flicking through the TV channels. Infomercials, reruns, and documentaries. I end up watching this show on birdwatching. Exciting stuff, right? People were talking about how much fun it was to spot a bird they'd never seen before. Check it off a list. That kind of thing."

"You're not thinking about taking it up, are you? Can't picture you creeping through the woods for a bird unless you're planning on shooting and cooking the thing."

"Nah. Dove hunting's okay, but hardly worth the effort. Not much meat on them, you know? Turkeys, now that's different. Anyway, I'm kind of half-listening to this show, fading in and out, about to turn off the TV. But at the end of the show, they put up a picture of one of the guys they interviewed. You know, like those 'in memoriam' things they do sometimes. Except this fella wasn't dead. He's missing."

Jeremy stretched his left leg and wiggled his foot. "Missing from where?"

"Trail of Tears State Forest in Illinois."

Jeremy sat upright. "How long?"

"Almost four months. Disappeared back in May. From what I've been able to find out so far, the local news initially covered it as a lost hiker since his car was still there. That didn't make much sense, though, since the guy was experienced and the park's not that big. They searched for a couple of days and didn't find anything. The local PD is treating it as a suspicious missing person case now."

"What's his name?"

"Simon Price. White male, five-foot-ten, one fifty-five. Details are coming your way in a few minutes. Want it to go to your personal or work email?"

"Work. I'll jump on it as soon as I get it."

"You know if you need anything from me ..."

"I appreciate it, Troy. I owe you big time. Next breakfast is on me. Once I do a bit of digging on this and figure out my—our—next move, I'll be in touch."

"Thanks a lot, Jeremy. We'll get this guy. We will."

"Yeah, we will." He hung up and tapped a finger on his laptop, urging the email to come through. His stomach fluttered, and he squeezed his eyes shut in an effort to contain his emotion. He'd been down this road before. The highs and lows. The daydreams and nightmares. And more often than not, he'd been disappointed. Crushed even.

Hope could do that to a man.

CHAPTER THIRTY-NINE

"I'll be in D.C. first thing tomorrow morning." Jeremy turned the laptop slightly to reduce the glare on the screen.

Maggie raised her eyebrows. "You sure this is a good idea?"

"A good idea? Yes. Maybe. I suppose it depends on your point of view. And from mine, I've got nothing to lose."

"Director Bailey is not going to be happy. You at least let him know you're coming, didn't you?"

"He knows. Not all the details, but he knows."

Maggie's shoulders dropped as she sighed and leaned back in her office chair. "And you're one hundred percent positive about this? A serial killer? No doubts? No questions?"

Jeremy intertwined his fingers. "A hundred percent? Of course not. But I'm sure enough that I'm willing to go for it."

"Well, I'd say this was career suicide, but at this point I'm not sure that matters."

He laughed and sipped a Diet Coke. "Yeah, I'm pretty sure I don't have to worry about that. One way or another, I'm done at the Bureau. The only question is whether I go out on my terms or someone else's. I know which I prefer."

"Me too. So, was it hard to get an appointment with Senator Morgans?"

"Not at all. Called her office, left my name, number, and a brief message, and one of her aides phoned me within the hour to set it all up. Guess she just loves meeting with the public."

"Uh-huh. What was the message?"

"I don't remember exactly, but it was something along the lines of 'I know your husband and I can talk to you or I can talk to Fox News. Your choice.' Like I said, she must like sitting down with voters, even ones that aren't from her state. Keep in touch with the common man and all that stuff."

One corner of her mouth turned down. "You're not very good at making new friends. What're you going to say?"

"Not sure. I guess it depends on how she reacts."

Maggie leaned closer to the screen. "Be careful. I don't get the sense that the colonel is going to be too pleased when he finds out you talked to his wife."

"I'm counting on it. But I need you to do me a favor, just in case."

"Anything. What is it?"

"Cronfeld told me the men who reported to him in Afghanistan all signed an agreement to keep quiet. Said it was a term of their release from the military. I need to know if that's true."

"And if it's not?"

Jeremy tapped his finger on the desk. "Then I'm not the only one he's worried about. Could be others who are in the same boat. If so, he's probably playing the same game with them, though he couldn't have as much leverage. Not unless they worked for the government too. He'd have to beg, promise, and threaten. Or worse."

She scrunched her eyebrows. "Worse?"

"Nothing. See what you can find out and we'll go from there."

"You don't think he'd—"

"I think he'd do whatever he had to in order to eliminate anyone he perceived as a threat."

"Including you?"

He shook his head. "No. At least not yet. Too risky. I'm probably getting paranoid. You know I searched the Internet to see if there's a way he could have caused my blood clot?"

"There's not, at least that I could find."

"Great. Now I've got you paranoid too."

"Just covering all the bases. No harm in that, is there?"

"I suppose not. So, you'll check on the other guys in his unit? And keep it as quiet as possible?"

"Yep. I've got a few contacts over at Defense. Shouldn't be too difficult. What're you going to tell Bailey?"

Jeremy stretched and yawned. "If my meeting with Senator Morgans goes well, I won't have to tell him anything."

"And if it doesn't?"

"Been nice working with you."

CHAPTER FORTY

The senator's aide escorted Jeremy into a surprisingly plain office. An American flag stood next to Pennsylvania's square blue one. Dozens of photos, many needing straightening, covered the walls. The room was large but swallowed by an oversize wooden desk covered in stacks of paper. A scattering of mismatched chairs and side tables rounded out the area. Diane Morgans didn't need a fancy office. People fought to impress her, not the other way around.

"Senator Morgans will be with you shortly," the aide said. "Please make yourself comfortable. Can I get you anything?"

"No, thank you. I'm fine."

"Very well. The senator has allotted ten minutes to speak with you. Please respect her time."

"You got it."

Jeremy dragged one of the chairs closer to the desk, sat, and pulled out his phone to sort through emails. He still hadn't decided what to say, or perhaps more importantly, how to say it. He knew what he wanted, and he thought he understood what she wanted, but bringing the two concerns together could be tricky. To make matters worse, the senator had made a career out of successful one-sided compromises. She tended to get her way.

Voices outside the door alerted him that his waiting time was over. Senator Morgans, her brunette hair slightly disheveled, strode into the room. She wore a dark dress rather than the pantsuit many women in politics seemed to favor. A silver chain dangled around her neck, complementing her diamond earrings and the obligatory American flag pin. Overly red lipstick seemed to be the only makeup she wore. Somehow, the outfit didn't clash with the black running shoes on her feet. The woman was in her mid-fifties but looked a dozen years younger. Politics and power treated her well.

She extended her hand. "Special Agent Winter. Diane Morgans. Nice of you to meet with me."

Jeremy ignored the urge to tell her it was he who'd called the meeting. "Senator. A pleasure."

"Now then. What's this all about? How can I help you?"

"Actually, it's more about how we can help each other. Compromise. That's what happens in Washington, right?"

The senator laughed and settled into her chair. "You no more believe that than I do, Agent Winter. Arm-twisting, yelling, and threatening. And that's on a good day."

"Yes, ma'am. And I'm here to make sure today is a good day for both of us. Perhaps a very good day."

Morgans leaned forward. "You have my attention for the next eight minutes."

Jeremy cleared his throat. "I'll only need two."

She nodded for him to continue.

"First, I'll assume you're recording this conversation. I've got no problem with that. I'm confident you're assuming the same thing."

The senator pulled a mirror from her desk and inspected her lipstick.

"Fine," he said. "I'm certain you're unaware, but your husband has paid me a few visits lately. Wants to talk about some things that happened in Afghanistan which, again, I'm sure you have no knowledge of."

Morgans held the mirror up to get a look at her hair, frowned, and dropped it back into the drawer.

He dropped his voice a notch and kept his face expressionless. "Senator, I'm on the verge of early retirement. That's all I want. To go away peacefully and quietly. No problems. No rocking the boat. I'm not into the political side of things. Don't want to be. But at the point my girlfriend gets dragged into the situation, I start to get upset. Can't control myself. Maybe you've seen my file? Anger management issues, it says."

"Agent Winter, let me assure you that I hold the members of our law enforcement community in the highest regard. The highest. I have no patience for those who seek to make a difficult job even harder."

He scooted to the edge of his chair. "Thank you, Senator. Sometimes, when I get all worked up about something, I do things I'd rather not.

Understand? Won't have that problem once I retire, I'm sure. I'll leave the politics to the folks who know how to handle things. Like yourself."

Senator Morgans stood and smiled. "Thank you for stopping by, Agent Winter. Always a pleasure to meet the people we're working so hard to serve."

"Yes, ma'am. Thanks for your time. I wonder, if it's not too much trouble, if you could do one thing for me."

"Certainly, if I can."

He passed her a piece of paper. "Just need you to make a phone call."

She scanned the note quickly. "Have a pleasant day, Agent Winter."

....

As he'd expected, Director Bailey was not happy. It had been less than an hour since Jeremy's meeting with Senator Morgans, and he'd been standing before his boss for the last ten minutes, silent and weathering the verbal storm. Finally, Bailey motioned to one of the burgundy leather armchairs and Jeremy sat.

The director made brief eye contact, then turned back to his computer monitor. "Now then, Agent Winter, would you care to share the details of your visit to the senator?"

"Sir, Senator Morgans made it very clear that our meeting was to remain confidential. I can't discuss it."

"So you go behind my back and—"

"I wasn't trying to circumvent you, sir. It's just that—"

"Don't interrupt me again. You went behind my back. Plopped me right in the middle of your little firestorm."

Jeremy shifted in his seat. "That wasn't my intention, sir. I wanted to find a solution that worked for everyone."

"Really? The most important senator on the Appropriations Committee calls and tells me what I'm going to do, and you think that works for me?"

"Well, I'm no longer your problem, sir. You've got a free pass on me. Anything goes wrong, you can tell everyone you had no choice. Just doing what you were told."

"Agent Winter, you still report to me. That means no matter what, you're my problem. Just so we're on the same page here, let me clarify a few things. First, you will remain an FBI employee until your serial killer theory is resolved. Second, I'm the one who will determine when that is.

No progress means no case. Lastly, you work alone. No support from the Bureau."

"Fair enough. When I do confirm we've got a killer on the loose, can I assume I'll get some assistance at that point?"

Bailey's lips formed a thin line. "I wouldn't assume anything if I were you."

Great. "Understood. I did want to let you know that we've come across a new disappearance at a state park in Illinois two months ago."

"Physical evidence of a connection to the other cases?"

"None."

"Then I'm not interested."

"Sir, I truly am sorry for putting you in this situation. If I'd thought there was any other way ..."

Bailey took a heavy breath and punched a few keys on his computer. "Three days ago, you were on the phone with a police officer in Indiana. Care to tell me what that call was about?"

Jeremy stretched his legs and wiggled his feet. "You're monitoring my phone calls?"

Bailey shrugged. "We monitor all calls going in and out. You know that."

"I've been with the Bureau for more than two decades and it's never come up before. The timing seems odd."

The Director walked over and sat in the chair next to Jeremy. "You know, there are days I wish I was back on this side of the desk. Then I think about your paycheck and remember why I put up with the politics. You were—are—a good agent. Finish strong and I'll do what I can for you."

Jeremy held back a smile. "There's one more thing, sir."

"Don't press your luck."

"It's not for me. I've got a friend who'd make an excellent agent. I was hoping you could arrange an interview for him."

"Let me guess. Your police officer buddy in Indiana?"

"Yes, sir. You'd be doing the Bureau a favor if you took a look at him."

Bailey stood and moved back to his desk. "Uh-huh. Send me his resume. No promises, though. You know how tight the budget is these days."

Jeremy nodded. "Yes, sir, but I also know there'll be an opening soon."

The director held out his hand and Jeremy took it. "Yes, there will be, Agent Winter. For better or worse, there will be."

CHAPTER FORTY-ONE

Mason's boys walked with him through the corn maze to check that everything was ready. The crop looked good and thick. He'd planted twice, first north-south, then east-west. This was the fourth year for the maze, and each time the design became more intricate. GPS units allowed him to stake out the paths and then mow through when the corn was less than a foot tall. From that point, regular cutting and trimming was all the upkeep needed. Shouldn't be any problem maintaining the six-acre attraction until Halloween.

This year they'd gone all out and purchased two hundred flashlights so they could operate well past dark. Paula thought they should charge extra at night, but he hadn't decided yet. This was as much a project for the community as it was a way to generate additional income for the farm. Still, his wife had a point. It would be mostly teenagers at night, and if they spooked the maze up a bit, an extra dollar or two per person would be justified.

"Probably ought to put a stack of hay bales there," Lucas said. "Add a ghost or scarecrow."

The boy would be eleven in another month and had a knack for life around the farm. His younger brother worshiped the ground he walked on, so no doubt he'd develop the same traits. Good boys make good farmers. "Agreed," Mason said as he made a note on his sketch. "We can put a guide there too."

Each year, half a dozen of the local kids signed up to work in the maze as helpers for lost wanderers. Most people took a little over an hour to get through the whole thing, but it wasn't unusual for some folks to spend twice that long in there. Especially the teenagers who sought out dark corners to pursue other activities, though the guides were told not to let things get too serious. Mason didn't mind since the longer people wandered about, the more it increased business at the cold drink stand set up at the maze's exit.

"Dad," Andy said. "We shouldn't call them scarecrows."

"No?"

"Uh-uh," the boy said. "They're skelcrows."

Skelcrow. Part scarecrow. Part skeleton. "I love it. Skelcrows it is. Now, let's get finished out here. I'm about to get hungry and your mom's fixing—"

"Betcha can't find me!"

Andy had run ahead—again—and hidden himself somewhere around a corner.

Mason squatted next to Lucas and placed a hand on his shoulder. "Shhh. Let's just stay quiet and wait here."

His son grinned, nodded, and loud-whispered. "How long do you think it'll take?"

"Couple of minutes. Probably less."

A gust of wind, still quite warm for early September, rustled the corn stalks and caused their long shadows to dance along the path.

Andy hollered from up ahead. "Are y'all looking for me?"

Lucas stifled a giggle, and Mason winked at him.

"Guys?"

A cloud passed in front of the low sun and its shadow covered the fields.

Lucas cupped his hands around his mouth. "Ooooo. Aaandy. Ooooo."

Two seconds later, the younger boy barreled around the corner. "I knew it was you."

"Did not."

"Uh-huh," Andy said. "There's no such thing as ghosts. Is there, Dad?"

Mason stood and tapped a finger on his chin. "Well, that's a good question. I think—" He grabbed his youngest son and scooped him up, planting kisses on his neck and cheeks. The boy's ever-present camouflage ball cap tumbled to the ground. "I think we need to get finished before the sun sets. Your mama's not going to be real happy if we're late for dinner."

The trek through the maze took another hour. A few more areas would need hay bales and additional cutting. Mason agreed to let Lucas use the tractor tomorrow to move the straw to the attraction's entrance before using the small mower to place them in the final positions. His younger brother begged to help, but distractions were dangerous when heavy equipment was involved. Safety first. Instead, Andy would spend the day with his mother at the thrift store shopping for clothes.

Four new skelcrows would make their debut this Halloween. The bigger the maze, the more decorations were needed. Each had to be dressed just right, though Paula had kidded him—once—about the time he spent primping them. Back then, she hadn't understood yet.

It wouldn't do to have his friends hanging out all month without proper attire.

CHAPTER FORTY-TWO

The old storm cellar had a bit of a chill, and Mason cranked up the space heater. Normally, he'd leave it off so things didn't rot too fast, but the warmth wouldn't be a problem now. Blue Shirt was done, the beetles fat and happy. The only bad thing about this time of year was how busy he got. No time to gather more decorations.

Most of the insects would die off before they'd be fed again, and he'd need to replace them. Cost of doing business. Besides, he had enough skelcrows for this year. Didn't want to be like the neighbor who already had up half a dozen Christmas trees in her home. Overkill.

Such a great word.

He and Paula had already decided to expand the maze by a couple of acres next Halloween, so he'd need to increase the inventory before then. But not now. Have to wait until Halloween is over. The sacrifices one makes.

Sarah Goldman got dibs on the clothes. First come, first served. He pulled the box containing her skull from a shelf, brushed the dust from the lid, and opened it. Sarah looked good. Hadn't aged a bit. His design process was holding up well. He'd stumbled across a video on the Internet, made a few adaptations, and voila! An actual skeleton that looked like a fake plastic one from Dollar General.

Simple, really. After the dermestid beetles finished their work, he sprayed the skull with several thin coats of polyurethane. The resin gave the bone a sheen but, more importantly, it offered some protection. Next, he wrapped the skull in cheap, wafer-thin plastic drop cloths from the hardware store. A heat gun shrunk the plastic onto the bone. He'd debated using stains to spook up the appearance, but in the end decided to leave it bleached white. So much purer. The result was a plasticky-looking skull that looked fake but real enough, and it was protected from the weather.

He toted the box upstairs and placed it on the workbench. Sarah had been a petite girl. Last year they'd actually used junior misses' clothes for her skelcrow. She needed to grow up this Halloween. He glanced at the skull and shook his head. Five teeth missing. He'd had no choice. Store-bought skeletons didn't have fillings in their teeth.

Paula had left the boxes from the thrift store shopping expedition by the barn door, and he ruffled through them. Couldn't throw any old thing on his Sarah. She wouldn't like that. He pieced several outfits together before settling on one. A black long-sleeved T-shirt with some sort of Asian design on the back, ripped jeans, and an Atlanta Braves cap.

He tied the bottoms of the pants legs, cut a hole in the seat, and fed a ten-foot piece of 2x2 pressure-treated lumber through the jeans. He partially stuffed the pants with hay, making sure not to overdo it so she wouldn't look fat. About a foot down from the top of the pole, he nailed a crossbeam and pulled the T-shirt over it. Safety pins attached the jeans to the shirt. This was easier with the men, but his girls didn't wear suspenders. He stuffed her to chest-high, propped the skelcrow against the barn wall, and stepped back to admire his work.

So far, so good. Her outfit looked appropriately youthful, like something she'd really wear to school if she was still alive. Years of displaying them and no one had shown any concern that they might be real. Nor would they. Still, he had his answer ready if the question ever came up. A chuckle, then explain his skeletons are a little pricier than the ones you get at the dollar store. Had to order them off the Internet from a specialty Halloween supplier. Maybe even let the curious guest touch one of them just to feel the plastic. That would satisfy anyone.

He'd keep his friends' heads out of reach, around eight feet off the ground. The posts would set in concrete about a foot deep, then he'd yank them up with the tractor when the season ended. Until then, he'd make sure the guides kept an eye on the decorations. No vandalism would be tolerated.

He finished stuffing the shirt and looped a piece of wire at the end of each sleeve, being sure to leave some hay sticking out. Back at the bench, he measured the hole at the base of Sarah's skull. Funny how that opening on everybody's head was different. Wonder if they're like fingerprints? Have to look that up.

After trimming the top of the 2x2 with a jigsaw, he wrapped the wood with a generous amount of duct tape. This was always the trickiest part. The fit had to be tight enough that the wind wouldn't move the skull and possibly crack it, but loose enough that he could get it off as needed. They were trying something new this year. Battery-operated LEDs inside the skull would light it up from the inside, and the batteries would need to be replaced each morning. They'd briefly considered getting red lights but decided to just use white. Red seemed too demonic.

Once he got the fit right, he placed the Braves hat on Sarah and tilted it so the brim was a bit cockeyed. Mason tightened the cap as best he could, but if the wind blew it off, so be it. Hats were cheap. Skulls were not. No way was he going to risk damaging Sarah by gluing, taping, or stapling it to her.

All-in-all, she looked good. The shirt was iffy, but he'd let Paula make the final call on that. He headed back to the storm cellar for the next box. Less than two weeks until the pumpkin patch officially opened. Had to pick up the pace.

He grabbed one of the newer containers off the shelf, peeked inside, then climbed back into the barn. Catherine Mae Blackston. Let's see. Her first Halloween at the farm. What to dress her in? She'd seemed a bit plain. Boring middle-aged woman. Couldn't wear a dress. No way to stuff it properly. A nice pant suit, maybe some dark glasses, and, oh! a string of pearls. Perfect.

He could almost see the excitement in Catherine's smile.

CHAPTER FORTY-THREE

No matter how long Jeremy stared at it, the calendar didn't change things. Nothing new since he came to Memphis a month ago except the additional pressure on his belt, compliments of a few extra pounds from the local pulled pork barbecue. Troy had stopped by the last couple of weekends, but no progress was made. Maggie checked in at least twice a day to encourage him. On one especially bad day, she'd hung up on him after he mentioned a new job posting for a D.C.-based fixed surveillance specialist. He'd fretted for half an hour before calling her back to apologize.

At least Cronfeld had disappeared, and Bailey had left him alone, but that wouldn't continue much longer. At some point, the FBI had to make the call. Case closed. Thanks for your service. Don't let the door smack you on the way out.

He sighed and opened the vehicle database for the umpteenth time, more from habit than anything else. But at this point what—

His phone vibrated and he debated throwing it across the room. Not in the mood to talk this morning. He glanced at the caller ID. Maggie. After a deep breath, he put on his best happy face and answered the call.

"Hey, Maggie. What's up?"

A male voice, high-pitched and angry, responded. "Oh, not much. What's up with you, Agent Winter?"

Cronfeld. Was he with Maggie? Why was he on her cell? Jeremy bit his lip and gripped the phone. "Colonel."

"Wasn't sure you'd answer if you saw who was calling so I spoofed your girlfriend's number. Neat little trick. Telemarketers do it all the time."

"What do you want?"

"For starters, answers. Been a while since you met with my wife. A meeting I do not approve of, by the way. I played nice. Figured I'd let you two work it out. But here we are and nothing's changed. You're still collecting a government paycheck for doing ... what, exactly? Doesn't seem like much is happening down there. Don't you feel guilty? Ripping off the taxpayers like that? I swear. I don't know how you sleep at night."

"Again, what do you want?"

"Tell me what you discussed with my wife."

His own spouse doesn't trust him. No surprise there. "Have a good day, Colonel."

"Listen to me, Winter. If I have to come to Memphis to deal with—"

"Uh, uh, uh! Play nice or I'll have to call a certain senator again."

"I don't know what you think is going on here, but you're in no position to make threats. You want to call my wife? Call her. Go ahead. I don't care. Need her number?"

"Nope. Got it."

"You have some sort of agreement with her. So what? One word from me, and I guarantee your deal would go straight into the trash. You've misread the situation rather badly."

"If you say so."

Cronfeld's voice rose. "I do say so. Now listen closely. I'm going to spell out exactly what you're going to do, starting with signing that confidentiality agreement."

Jeremy yawned, making sure it could be heard over the phone. "Not happening."

"No? I think it's time I upped the ante. Your girlfriend ... Margaret Keeley, is it?"

He bolted upright and breathed hard. "Leave her out of this."

"I hear she's a fine agent. A real asset to the Bureau. In fact, I understand she's being considered for a transfer somewhere out of state. *Far* out of state."

"You son of a—"

A click ended the discussion, and Jeremy tossed the phone on his desk. Cronfeld had the ability to make good on his threats. Maggie would have to quit the FBI if they forced her to transfer. No way her ex would allow Rebecca to move out of state.

He needed to clear his thoughts, and nothing did that like some extended therapy at the shooting range. No aiming for center mass this time, though. Head shots fit his mood much better.

CHAPTER FORTY-FOUR

Mason stood in front of his house and pointed to an area off to the left and down a rise. "The boys need to get out there this weekend and bush hog all the way to the road. Don't want to run out of parking again this year."

Paula scribbled a note. "Got it. Everything else going to be same out front?"

"Yeah, I think so. Pumpkins, hay bales, gourds, that kind of stuff. I was thinking if we could find some cheap wagons, we'd throw a few out there for the parents to haul around their kids."

"I'll check, but don't count on it. I think they're fairly expensive. Yard sales are probably our best bet. Oh, and the pumpkins are ordered and should be here within a week."

"Good. Already had a bunch of folks asking when we're opening."

"The maze ready?"

"Pretty near. Still need to put a few ghosts out, hire a few more guides, stuff like that. Won't take more than a day or two. The concession stand could use a coat of paint, but I suppose it'll make it another season without it."

"Uh-huh. I believe that's the same thing you said last year. I'll have the boys throw on some old clothes and spruce it up. What about the hayride?"

"Picking up the horses tomorrow. We'll do a few trial runs to make sure they'll work out. Wouldn't mind handling them myself every day, but that's not likely. Too much else going on."

"You can play with your toys this winter after things settle down. See about getting somebody to do it for you. The boys don't know anything about handling horses, and until they do, I don't want them hauling around a wagon full of people."

Mason rolled his eyes. "Yes, dear. I'll take care of it."

"Opening next week then?"

"I'll be ready if you will. Just got to put the signs out on the road and let the bank know to build a bigger vault to hold all the money."

Paula planted her hands on her hips. "Sure. We'll be lucky to clear enough to pay for those horses."

He leaned over and kissed her. "Keep the faith, baby."

"The scarecrows all done?"

"Skelcrows. Yep, done as they're gonna be. Next time you're over that way, stop in the thrift shop and get a few extra shirts. If we get much rain, might have to replace some of their clothes."

"Mason, are you sure it's a good idea? Putting them out in the open like that?"

He lightly dragged his fingers up and down her back. "We're not having this conversation again this year."

"I know, but it seems like the more of them you put out, the more likely it is—"

"Nobody's looking. And if they are, we'll follow the plan. We both know that sooner or later, my part in this is going to end, right? What's done is done, and we can't change it. All we can do is enjoy what we have. No matter what, you and the boys are protected."

"Doesn't mean I don't worry about it."

He laughed and mussed her hair. "You wouldn't be the woman I married if you didn't. Now, best get to work. Both of us. This farm's not going to run itself. And if it'll make you feel better, I'll double-check the old barn. Make sure everything's ready, just in case."

She kissed his chest. "You don't have to do that ... but I wouldn't mind it if you did."

He let his fingers dance on her back again. "That's my girl."

CHAPTER FORTY-FIVE

ay three of the pumpkin patch festivities, and things were going off without a hitch. Borrowing the horses from the neighbor proved to be a huge hit on the hayride, although the realism could be a bit smelly at times. Paula had already ordered a second truckload of pumpkins, and the weather had turned breezy and brisk with no rain in the forecast.

The sun crept toward the west, and in another three hours it would be dark enough to start charging extra for the corn maze. A few families meandered through it now, but the real crowds came out once the sun set. That's when the fun began.

The guides dressed up as zombies or some other creature of the night and wandered in their assigned areas. Mason had strict rules regarding their behavior and had fired the Palmer kid on the first night for getting too close to a guest and then mouthing off about it. The safety of everyone on the farm was paramount. These were his friends and neighbors. Sure, he wanted—needed—to make money, but not at the expense of damaging relationships in the community.

He patted his pocket to make sure his cell phone was there and climbed onto his John Deere lawn tractor. Last year he'd run out of gas in the middle of the maze and had to walk back to the new barn for more. Not a mistake he wanted to repeat. A box of AAA batteries and other supplies sat in the tow-behind trailer. The LEDs in the skulls needed to be replaced, and no one touched the skelcrows except him or, on occasion, Paula. Rule number one.

The maze's entrance sign was starting to look a little worse for the wear. He'd have the boys touch it up a bit tomorrow. Next to the sign was an overhead photo of the maze taken by a crop duster, blown up to poster size for easier viewing. Each year, the design became more involved as Mason and the boys progressed in their skills. This Halloween, they'd opted for a clown's head, complete with bulbous nose and wild hair. Enter through the left ear, eventually exit through the right.

Ten yards in came the first decision for guests. Left or right? Mason could run through it blindfolded, but he had to check out all the dead ends and twists anyway. Skelcrows, pumpkins, ghosts, and all manner of eerie things were spread throughout. Even on the tractor, it would take him a good hour and a half to get through the whole thing with all the stops he had to make.

The corn was dry and dark, and the roughness of the brown stalks rubbing against each other in the wind only heightened the spookiness. The decorations seemed to be in good shape, save one pumpkin that someone, probably a teenager, had decided to bust. Boys will be boys.

As he approached the clown's right eye, a flash of red off to the left caught his attention. He climbed off the tractor and walked back to check it out. An Atlanta Braves baseball cap. Poor Sarah must've lost it last night. He picked up the hat, tossed it in the trailer, and motored off to return it to its proper location just around the next turn. Even with the polyurethane and plastic, Mason didn't like leaving the skulls exposed to the sun for too long. They needed to last a lifetime.

He rounded the corner and smiled at—

Nothing.

Sarah was gone.

Mason's scalp tingled and ice flowed through his chest. He sat, staring and unbelieving, at the wooden cross before him. Her jeans had fallen to the ground. The unstuffed shirt still hung on the crossbeam and fluttered in the breeze. The dull gray duct tape atop the 2x2 pointed upward as if Sarah had somehow gone there. Hay bales had been dragged over and stacked, forming steps to what remained of the skelcrow.

Paula needed to know. He pulled the phone from his pocket, paused, and replaced it. Not yet. Don't panic. Sarah's here somewhere. Just a prank. That's it. Someone hid her in the corn. Probably the same boy who busted the pumpkin.

His body shuddered as a chill raced down his spine. He stepped off the John Deere and brushed his palm across his forehead. She's here. She has to be here.

He patrolled the clown eye's perimeter, searching for any sign that the corn had been disturbed. Nothing. She could have been tossed back in there, though. A sudden wave of heat exploded from his chest into his face. Thrown. Like trash. Unwanted. Who could do such a thing to his Sarah? He'd find out, and when he did ...

"Hi, Mr. Miller!"

Mason swung around. The Kelly family. Dad, Mom, and Amy. He swallowed hard and forced a smile. "Well, hello there, Amy. Are you having fun?"

"Yeah."

Mrs. Kelly whispered to her daughter, and the little girl frowned before speaking again.

"I mean, yessir."

"I'm glad. Are you showing your mom and dad the way through the maze?"

"I'm trying, but it's hard and my legs hurt. Daddy said he'd carry me in a minute."

Amy's dad rolled his eyes and shook his head.

Mason glanced back at the lonely cross. "You don't have too much farther to go."

Mrs. Kelly nodded toward the vacant wooden structure. "Problem?"

Mason rocked on his feet, one hand behind his back clenched into a fist. "Naw. Just doing some maintenance. Changing batteries, things like that."

"We won't keep you then," she said. "And thank you for doing this every year. I know the kids really enjoy it."

"Yes, ma'am. My pleasure." His heart's pounding reverberated through his ears.

Amy turned to her dad and stretched her arms upward. "Carry me, Daddy."

Mr. Kelly picked up his daughter and slung her over his shoulder. "Okay, Munchkin. Which way next?"

Mason waited until he could no longer hear them and moved into the corn. He made several passes, each time moving the arc farther out, doing his best not to disturb the stalks. No one else had traipsed through here. He was sure of that. No sign of Sarah.

Who?

Why?

Calm. Keep it together. He dialed Paula and gave her the news. Not good. Not good at all.

Tidy up the area, she'd said. Put the clothes back together and stuff them with hay. Make it look like it was supposed to be that way. They'd figure it out. Just stay calm.

Easier said than done. When he caught whoever'd taken his Sarah, he'd show them what it meant to steal from Mason Miller.

CHAPTER FORTY-SIX

Mason couldn't stop moving. Kitchen sink to living room sofa to bathroom. He'd already thrown up twice. Sarah was out there. Alone.

Paula patted the couch. "Honey, will you please sit down?"

"What are we going to do?"

She walked to him and squeezed his hands in hers. "You're shaking, baby. Let me get you something that'll help you relax."

He jerked his hands away. "No. No drugs. I've got to focus. Think."

"It's just some kids playing a prank. We'll find her. I promise. But we've got to keep going like nothing's happened. Mason, do you hear me? Like nothing's happened."

He stretched and yawned violently, forcing as much tension as possible from his body. "How do we do that? What if the police have her?"

Paula pointed at his recliner. "Sit."

"Baby, I don't—"

"Sit. Now. I mean it."

He trudged to the worn leather chair and sank into it, the seat's padding long ago having conformed to his body. Paula reached down and pulled the lever to raise the footrest, then moved behind him.

"Close your eyes." She rubbed her fingers across his temples, massaging tiny circles one way, then the other. "We'll get through this. We always do."

Mason grabbed her hand. "We always do? Nothing like this has happened. It's bad, Paula. Bad."

"Yeah, I know it is. We'll find her, baby. I promise."

He took a series of deep breaths, holding each before slowly blowing out. "You say that, but you can't know. Not for sure. She's out there somewhere. No family around her. Wishing she was home."

"Well, let's think about this for a minute. We can be sure the police don't have it, I mean, her."

"We can?"

"Well, they couldn't have taken her without a warrant, right? And if someone had given Sarah to them, don't you think they'd have been here by now?"

He turned to look at her. "Probably."

"So isn't it more likely some kids took her?"

"Maybe. I know some of the boys around here got no respect for other folks' property."

Paula kissed the top of his head. "Oh, honey. Has it been that long since you were a boy? I'm sure you never did anything like that around Halloween, now did you?"

He chuckled. "Did I ever tell you about the time me and Johnny Orsteen snuck into old man Smithson's barn?"

She leaned close to his ear. "At least a dozen times."

"I can't just sit around waiting, Paula."

"I know you can't. We'll find her, but we need to be smart about it. First things first, though. What are we going to do to protect the others?"

Mason stood, placed his hands on his hips, and arched his back. The chair might be comfortable, but its back support had become sorely lacking over the years. "I'll get with the guides and station one of them next to each skelcrow. Let them know one is missing and to keep their eyes open."

"How about dangling some cash in front of them? Tell everyone there's a reward for the safe return of the, um, decoration."

"Good idea. Wouldn't surprise me if they know who took it. Kids like to brag about stuff like that. And we've got a good group this year. Except for that ..."

"What is it, Mason?"

He stared off into space, his mind churning. "The Palmer kid. What's his name? Lanny."

"What about him?"

"I fired him, remember? He got too close to some of the customers, girls from the high school, then smarted off to me when I talked to him about it."

"And you think he took Sarah?"

"Wouldn't put it past him, that's for sure."

"Well, maybe he did, and maybe he didn't. The important thing is to act like it's no big deal. Show too much concern, and people will start to wonder. Can't have that now, can we? Every family has secrets and ours are, well, a little more dangerous than others, I suppose."

"I know that. Everything I do is for this family and our farm. I'm not going to risk anything."

She smiled at him. "You'd better not. I don't know what I'd do without you. Find somebody better, probably."

Mason wrapped his arms around her waist and pulled her to him. "Love you, baby."

She glanced up, grinned, and rolled her eyes. "Love you, too, though for the life of me I can't imagine why."

He'd get through the night. Keep a smile on his face. Thank the customers for coming. Make sure no one else went missing. But tomorrow morning he'd take a little drive.

Lanny Palmer needed a stern talking-to.

And maybe something more.

CHAPTER FORTY-SEVEN

The Palmer's house sat alone on a back road about three miles from Mason's farm. It was a school morning, so the boy would be heading to the end of the road to catch the bus soon. Mason parked at the intersection and waited. Paula had wrapped up a hot sausage and biscuit to give Lanny as a peace offering. She knew boys.

Just talk. That's the plan. Tell him he can have his job back as long as he behaves. The boy's fourteen, probably going on fifteen soon. He needs to learn respect. Follow the rules. If his own daddy couldn't teach him that, it was Mason's duty to step up and do the neighborly thing.

A foggy mist hung low over the fields along the dirt road. Likely some deer moving around, though he didn't see any. Another couple of months, though, it'd be a different story. Hunting season would open again.

After a few minutes, Mason spotted the boy heading his way. He got out of his truck, leaned against the hood, and waved. Lanny slowed for a moment before returning the wave and walking toward the vehicle.

"Mornin', Lanny. Brought you some breakfast. Paula fixed it up fresh a bit ago."

The boy glanced around before taking the biscuit and biting into it. "Thanks, Mr. Miller."

Mason crossed his arms. "Sure. Listen, I've been thinking, and I'm real sorry about how things happened back at the maze. Now, don't get me wrong here. You should've never got that close to those people, and you sure shouldn't have mouthed off to me. But Paula reminded me what I was like when I was your age and, well, let's just say I was reminded of a few times I stepped out of line too."

Lanny cocked his head and started to respond, then looked down at the ground without speaking.

Mason patted him on the shoulder. "Tell you what. How about we both chalk it up as a lesson learned? I could sure use some more help back at the maze if you're willing."

The boy shrugged. "I dunno. Maybe, I guess."

"Of course, you'd have to follow the rules. Think you can do that?"

Lanny nodded slightly.

"Well then. Consider yourself rehired. Can you be there tonight? Always big crowds on Fridays and we can use all the help we can get."

"Yeah, I'll be there, Mr. Miller."

Mason smiled. "Great. I'm glad we cleared that up. Don't want any bad blood between us. You're a good kid, Lanny."

The boy shuffled his feet, and his lips turned up slightly. "Thanks, Mr. Miller."

"I mean every word of it. Start with a clean slate, I say. Now, is there anything you want to tell me?"

"Uh, I'm sorry?"

"For?"

"Not following the rules?"

"And?"

"And ... what else?"

Mason twisted his head as tension built in his neck. "Well, I thought you might know something about one of our, um, decorations going missing?"

Lanny licked his lips, and his eyes shifted left-right. "I don't know anything about that, Mr. Miller."

"No? Are you sure?"

"Yes, sir."

Mason took a deep breath. Stay calm. Don't scare the boy. "Do the right thing, Lanny. I won't be mad. Just tell me where she is."

The youth scrunched his face and took a step back. "Who?"

"No more games, Lanny. Where is Sarah?"

"I don't know anybody named Sarah, Mr. Miller. Honest."

Mason placed a hand on each of the boy's shoulders. "I want you to listen to me very carefully, Lanny. Where. Is. Sarah?"

The young man's eyes widened. "I told you. I don't know—"

"Enough! Tell you what. Hop in and I'll take you to school. We can talk about it on the way."

"I don't know. Maybe I should let my mom know or something?"

Mason shrugged. "Up to you. I've got one more biscuit in the truck, though. Split it with you?"

The boy glanced over his shoulder toward home, then opened the truck door. "Can't be late, though."

"We'll make it in plenty of time. You can bet the farm on it."

CHAPTER FORTY-EIGHT

The kerosene lantern sputtered, and Mason switched it off and flipped on the fluorescents. Didn't need the lamp's smells down in the storm cellar anyhow. The room kept its musty silence, save for the humming and sporadic shudder of the old chest freezer. The boy slumped on the floor, his back resting against a wooden corner post. His hands were tied behind the beam, but his legs remained free, and Mason paused to examine the new scrapes on the dirt floor. The boy had struggled before giving in to exhaustion and falling asleep. Mason hovered over him and lifted the youngster's chin.

"Time to wake up, Lanny."

The youngster licked his lips and squinted into the light. Tear streaks scarred his filthy face, and he stammered when he spoke. "D-don't know her."

Mason leaned and checked the knots on the nylon rope that held the boy's hands together, then dragged a stool over and sat in front of the boy. "We'll get to that in a minute. You feeling okay? Ropes not too tight? Don't want to cut off the circulation."

"Thirsty."

"Sure, sure. Thought you might be. Got you some water right here." He held a straw to Lanny's mouth and waited until the drink was gone.

"Why you doing this, Mr. Miller?"

In the two days of confinement, the bravado of a young man had given way to the fear of a boy. "Need to go to the bathroom? I brought the bucket."

The youth sniffled, and a tear rolled down his face. "I-I don't know her. I'd tell you if I did. You know I would."

Mason scooted the stool closer. "Shh ... shh. It's okay. I know you would, son. I know you would. But see, Sarah's special to me. Right now, nothing's more important than finding her. I need you to think really hard. Focus."

"Wh-what does she look like?"

Mason patted the young man's shoulder. "I'm tired, Lanny. Really tired. Listen very closely. The skull. You took it. I know you did. Tell me where she is and all this ends. I just want her back. That's all. No hard feelings."

"Skull? One of the decorations? I didn't do nothin' with them. Honest, Mr. Miller. All this is about one of those toys? I-I don't under—"

Mason stood and grabbed the lantern. "She's not a *toy*. You took her, and I want her back. I'll be back in a little while, and then we'll finish up."

"I can go h-home then?"

"That all depends on what you have to tell me. I need you to think real hard, Lanny. I'm gonna take the lantern because a man does his best remembering in the dark. Besides, I've always wondered about something, and maybe you can clear it up for me. Those green and red tubs over there. See 'em? When it's all dark and quiet down here, you ever hear any noise from them? Maybe scratching sounds? Or chewing? See you soon, Lanny. Be ready."

CHAPTER FORTY-NINE

"Wind's picking up again. Coming out of the north. Gonna be a cold one." Mason stared out the kitchen window, snacking on cornbread left over from last night's dinner.

Paula stood beside him and gestured toward his coffee mug. "Need some more?"

"No thanks. Too much caffeine already today."

"You check on the boy?"

Mason nodded. "Nothing new. Probably needs another day or two to think about it."

"Have you thought about where this ends?"

"What do you mean?"

"With Lanny. What happens after you're, um, done with him? Maybe he knows where Sarah is. Maybe he doesn't. Either way, at some point you'll have to make a decision about him. Been two days already, and the county's crawling with police. Sooner or later one of them will stop by here. Can't keep a man in the cellar forever."

"He's a kid, Paula."

She scratched her hand across his back. "He is. But you know he's barely two years younger than Sarah was, right?"

"Yeah. But fourteen years old ..."

She leaned closer and lowered her voice. "Almost fifteen."

He sighed and sat his coffee on the counter. "I know, but—"

"No buts. I've never once complained about your activities. Even helped when you asked. But no matter how this turns out, that boy's a threat to this family. We both know it."

"He said he wouldn't tell anyone."

"You believe that?"

He shook his head. "Maybe for a while, but sooner or later, he'll talk."

"Yep. He will. Then they'll come take you away. Me too, probably. The boys will end up in some foster home. The state might even separate them. Is that what you want, Mason? Your boys raised by strangers? Your farm sold off to some foreign company?"

He pressed his lips together. "I'm not gonna let that happen. I'll take care of Lanny. No need in you worrying about it."

"What does that mean? Take care of him how?"

He caressed her chin and lifted her face toward him. "It means I know what I have to do."

She wrapped her arms around him and pulled. "You take such good care of us."

"Better or worse, death till us part, and whatever else you tricked me into saying."

She snuggled her head under his chin. "I'm pretty sure it was you who chased me, but you can believe whatever you want to believe."

They stood for a moment, staring out the window as the wind gusts moved across the corn maze like ocean waves. Such tranquility came at a price, but it was worth every penny, every bead of sweat, and every drop of blood, his and others'. His land was worth protecting no matter the cost.

He hugged Paula before heading for the door. "Tell the boys to check the maze good. Saturday night this close to Halloween, we'll have a big crowd. And tell Andy to make sure the four-wheeler's full of gas. He'll be running heated water out to you all night. I reckon you might have your hands full making hot chocolate. Want me to get you some help out there?"

"And share my tips? I don't think so, mister. I work hard for my money."

"I know you do, babe." He grabbed another piece of cornbread, pulled on his denim jacket, and yanked his cap down low. "I'll be in the storm cellar if you need me."

Paula glanced at the clock. "Lunch at noon. Don't be late."

"Yes, ma'am." Mason winked at her and headed for the barn.

CHAPTER FIFTY

Mason sat on the floor next to Lanny. "I bet you're hungry, huh? Brought you some cornbread. Nobody makes it like Paula does. Cast iron skillet, extra butter. Better'n birthday cake. We'll get to that in a minute, though. Wanted to see if you'd remembered anything yet."

The boy shifted on the floor. "What's in those tubs, Mr. Miller? I thought I heard scratching this time. I swear I did."

"Nothing you need to worry about. I was just messin' with you. Trying to spook you a little so you'd loosen up and tell me what you did with Sarah."

The boy's chin quivered, and he fixed his gaze on the ground between his legs. "I can't feel my arms and legs any more, Mr. Miller."

Getting tired of his whining. "I'm sorry, son. I should have thought of that. They fell asleep, that's all. I'm going to untie you in a minute and let you get up and stretch. You've got to promise not to leave until you tell me where she is, though. Agreed?"

Lanny sniffled. "I don't know. I swear it. I'll help you find her, though. P-promise I will. I'll ask around at school. Somebody'll tell me. They always do."

Mason pulled out his pocketknife, examined the blade, and began scratching lines in the dirt. "Don't have much tolerance for thieves. Never have. I remember the time someone cheated me out of a deer. I'd been stalking that thing all morning and then, bam! Some idiot spooked it. All I saw was a whitetail bouncing into the trees. Gone. Taken from me."

The boy tried to push his back deeper into the beam. "W-what're you gonna do with that knife, Mr. Miller?"

Mason etched the ground closer to the boy. "I haven't decided yet.

That's up to you, I suppose."

"But I told you I don't—"

"You've gutted a deer before, right?"

Lanny tried to inhale the snot dripping from his nose. "Y-yeah."

Mason held up his knife. "Of course, you wouldn't use something like this. Too small. It might slip in your hands, not to mention make it tough to cut through some of the skin and muscle. Yeah, there's nothing like making that thin slice through the skin, then—" He flicked the blade within millimeters of the boy's stomach.

Lanny screamed and tried to jerk back, but couldn't move. He might have said something, but it was hard to tell with all his yelling and crying.

Mason scooted closer. "Then you peel that skin back and cut through the muscle. Got to be careful, though, right? You ever puncture the stomach or intestines? That'll ruin your day, for sure."

The boy's swollen eyes looked desperately around the room, and a strong odor of urine soaked the air.

"Lanny, did you wet your pants? Now why would you go and do something like that? Word of it gets out, you'll never hear the end of it. You hear what I'm telling you? This will be our secret, okay? You keep your mouth shut about all this, and I'll keep your secret too."

His whimpering slowed, and he looked at Mason. "Y-you're gonna let me go?"

"I told you I would, didn't I? Just wanted to make sure you were telling the truth, that's all. I'll drop you off somewhere, and you can walk home. Tell everybody you've been hiding in the woods this whole time. I bet you've got plenty of good hiding spots, don't you?"

"S-some."

"Good. Make up a story like you didn't want to go to school or were mad at your parents. Stick to it, and no one will be the wiser. Do we have a deal?"

"Yes, sir."

Mason leaned behind the boy and cut the rope binding his wrists. "I'm sorry all this had to happen, but you understand. Here, let me help you up."

Mason dragged a stool over and helped Lanny onto it. "Sit there for a minute until you get the feeling back in your legs. Don't want you falling off the ladder, do we?"

Lanny dragged his arm under his nose. "No, sir. I won't tell nobody. I swear it."

"I believe you, son. You ready to go home?"

He pushed himself off the stool. "Yes, sir."

"Good, good. Head on up that ladder then."

The boy was on the second rung when the shovel struck the back of his head. Mason tried to judge the impact needed to kill, or at least stun Lanny without damaging his skull. He bent over the fallen body to inspect his work.

Blood matted the teenager's hair, and the boy wasn't breathing. Mason squatted and caressed the back of Lanny's head, grimacing when he felt the flattened section. He'd hit too hard. Still, the damage was in the back. The recognizable parts, the eye sockets, jaw, and so on, would be fine.

He grabbed a bottled water off the shelf and guzzled half of it. Paula's cornbread sure did make him thirsty.

CHAPTER FIFTY-ONE

Mason stood a couple of feet inside the tree line and scanned for any signs of movement. Off to the left, his pickup truck sat parked next to the Forked Deer River. Just another guy out fishing on a crisp October morning, or maybe scouting out a spot for his deer stand. Ahead, an opening in the woods allowed high power lines through. To his right, more trees.

Getting here had been easier than he'd expected. No neighbors flagged him down to talk about the weather or the boy or politics. State Road 188 did have more traffic than usual, though, doubtless folks headed to help in the search for Lanny Palmer. Mason knew better than to show up with the crowd. Returning to the scene of the crime was never a good idea, and besides, he had a good excuse if anyone asked. Keeping the pumpkin patch up and running took all his time, and folks insisted he keep it open.

Law enforcement had focused their search in the area around Lanny's home. On the record, the police said the boy's parents were not suspects, but some of Mason's neighbors were starting to whisper. Things like this didn't happen around here.

Off 188, a dirt road paralleled the Forked Deer to the northwest. Mason and his boys had been fishing near here many times. Cane pole and a red-white bobber. The same way his father taught him. The best way for kids to learn. He'd considered leaving Lanny's body in the river but couldn't do it. The boy may be a thief and a liar, but he still deserved a decent burial. The thought of leaving him in the water, where all kinds of critters could get to him, was too much.

He carried the corpse a few feet into the woods and chose a spot under a mid-sized oak. With no time for the usual process, the boy would get a traditional burial. Minus the skull and hands, of course. The ground was soft due to years of decomposition, and he dug the hole without much effort. Around two feet deep, so no animals would smell him and try to dig him up. He rested the shovel against the oak and debated saying a prayer before covering the body. No need. Plenty of prayers being said already. Besides, it's not like Lanny was really gone.

In a few weeks, there he'd be, dressed in garb from the local thrift store, hanging around in the cellar. Well, part of him anyway. A companion for Mason. Someone to talk to while he worked down there.

A touch of sadness closed around his heart. He and Paula had agreed the boy could never come out again. Too risky to put him in the corn maze, as if anyone would recognize him from a skull. Fourteen years old. No hope of going outside and watching as friends and neighbors wandered around him in the maze. Didn't seem right.

They may need to revisit that decision next Halloween.

CHAPTER FIFTY-TWO

"Where ya been, Dad?" Andy clambered into the bed of the truck.

Mason scooped up his son and kissed his cheek. "Had to make a run to the dump."

Lucas stood on the pickup's bumper and peered into the vehicle's bed. "Aw, man. Why didn't you take us?"

"I should've. Need to get even with you boys. If I remember right, last time Lucas tossed the trash the farthest."

Andy wriggled down from his father's arms. "No way, Dad! I won, remember?"

Mason winked at Lucas. "Hmm. You might be right. We'll call it a tie. How's that?"

Andy crossed his arms and frowned.

Lucas winked back at his dad. "No, Andy beat me. Just barely, though. Even a blind hog finds an acorn once in a while, right Dad?"

"Sure enough. You boys got everything ready for tonight?"

"Yes, sir," Andy said. "The four-wheeler's full, and I checked the maze. Still got to put new batteries in a bunch of flashlights, though."

"Better get on that," Mason said. "How about out front in the pumpkin patch?"

Lucas motioned toward the field. "It's pretty full. I put some more big ones out, but we've probably got enough to get us through another week at least."

"Great. Anything else?"

Lucas jumped off the truck. "Dad, can I talk to you?"

"Sure. What's up?"

The boy cut his eyes toward his younger brother. "Um, I need to, uh—"

"Andy, run and tell your mom we'll be ready for lunch in a few minutes," Mason said.

Lucas waited until his brother left, then continued, "All this stuff that's going on now. Some of the kids were talking. I mean, about what might have happened to Lanny. Everybody at school's kind of freaked out."

"Well, they should be. Listen, you boys need to watch out for each other. Like your mom and I said, don't go anywhere alone for a while, at least not until they find Lanny. I'm counting on you to keep an eye on Andy."

"Yeah, I know, Dad. But what if they don't find him?"

Mason squatted and placed his hands on his son's shoulders. "We need to pray they will. But if they don't, if something bad happened to him, they'll get whoever did it. They always do."

"Always?"

"Of course. Listen, the point here is to be careful, but not afraid. You can't go through life scared. That's no way to live. There's plenty of police around and, if someone did take him, he'd be an idiot to try it again." He pulled Lucas to his chest and embraced him.

"Thanks, Dad. I was just worried for Andy."

Mason stood and straightened Lucas's ball cap. "Of course. That's what brothers are for. Now then, what say we go see what your mother's got going for lunch? I'm hungry as a horse. You?"

"Starvin'."

Mason laughed. "Now that's no surprise. I swear, you boys can eat like nobody's business, and I still see your ribs poking through. Need to put some meat on those bones. Either that or use you for skelcrows."

"Oh, Dad? I think I know who took the one that's missing from the maze."

Mason's stomach tensed. "What? Who?"

"One of the boys in eighth grade. Carson something, but everybody calls him Fishy. I don't know him, but a couple of kids told me he was showing them pictures of a skull on his phone. He said it was Lanny, but everybody knows it's not. They said it looks like plastic, and it's just the head."

Mason bit the inside of his cheek. All that time wasted on the Palmer boy. "Appreciate you telling me, Lucas. I'll check it out. If Carson did take the decoration, I'm sure it's just a prank. No harm done, long as I get it back."

"Want me to ask him at school on Monday?"

"Um, I really don't want to wait that long. I reckon we'll have a big crowd tonight, and I'd sure enough like to have the maze looking perfect. Tell you what. Think you can call around? Find out the boy's last name for me?"

"Sure."

"Then I'll track him down from that. With all the police around, I'm certain he'll be happy to give it back. Let bygones be bygones."

"I can probably find out his phone number. If you want, I'll call him and tell him to bring it back before he gets in trouble."

"No, that's all right. You've got enough to do to get ready for tonight. I'll handle it myself. Now then, race you to lunch?"

The boy sprinted away, laughing and yelling as his father fell farther behind. "You're not even trying, Dad! Bet you can't catch me!"

Catch him. If there was one thing he was good at, that was it. Catching people. Fishy would learn soon enough.

CHAPTER FIFTY-THREE

Mason knocked on the door of the brick ranch-style home. Carson Andrews said he'd be there alone this morning, having feigned illness while his parents went off to work.

The door swung open, and a boy about Lanny's age stood there. A bright red birthmark on his left forearm vaguely resembled a dolphin and explained his nickname of Fishy. "Hey, Mr. Miller. 'Sup?"

Mason smiled and shook the boy's hand. "You're Fishy, I assume?"

"Yeah. I'm real sorry about all this. I was just goofin' off. Didn't mean to cause no problems."

He could at least put his ballcap on straight and put on a belt. "Hey, I was young once too, and I made more than my share of mistakes. Like I said on the phone, though, it's what you do to make things right that shows what kind of person you are."

"And this is just between us? You won't say nothing to my folks, right? I got enough problems with them already."

I bet you do. Mason lowered his voice. "My lips are sealed. A deal's a deal, right? Did you tell anyone I was coming by this morning?"

"Naw, man. It's all good."

"Great. Now, if you'll give me the, um, decoration, I'll be on my way like this all never happened."

Fishy rolled his eyes. "Dude, seriously? I already tossed it. Got too hot, you know? Once word got around school, didn't want to leave it here. Like, my mom goes through my stuff all the time. Thinks I'm on weed or something."

Mason inhaled and clenched his fists as a wave of heat rushed through his head. "Okay. Where is she?"

"She?"

"The skull. Where's the skull?"

Fishy pointed toward the woods about a half-mile down the road. "Took it down there. Shouldn't take you too long to find it."

Mason looked around. A few vehicles had passed while he stood on the porch. No way to know if anyone noticed him there. "You're going with me."

"Dude, I've got stuff to do."

"Listen, *dude*. Either go with me or we wait for your folks. I bet your dad would be thrilled to know you tried to sell drugs to my boys."

"Man, I don't sell that stuff."

"Really? Well, it'd be your word against mine, but I guess you know your folks better than I do."

Fishy nodded toward the truck. "Come on, but you need to make it quick."

As they arrived at the stand of trees, the boy motioned for him to pull over. "Back there's where I left it."

The two walked a few steps into the woods, shuffling through a layer of maple, oak, and tulip poplar leaves. Mason didn't like thinking about Sarah lying among the dirt and insects. No big deal, though. When he got home, he'd clean her up good. A soft towel for the outside and an old toothbrush to tidy up the teeth and inside. No harm done.

"Be careful not to step on the skull," Mason said. "They're not that expensive, but it takes a while to get a replacement."

Fishy squatted and brushed away the fallen debris. "It's over here, man. It looks pretty creepy laying out here. Awesome."

Mason's grin vanished as a chill shot down his spine. "The jawbone. Where's the jawbone?"

Fishy shrugged. "Got to be close. It was there when I threw it back here."

"Threw it? You threw her back here?"

"What's the big deal? Buy another one."

Nausea flashed through Mason. "Buy another one? She's broken, Fishy. *Broken.*"

"Sorry, man. Don't know what to tell ya."

Mason lifted the skull and cradled it in the crook of his arm. Maybe the pins holding the jaw to the cranium broke when she hit the ground. The mandible's here somewhere. Got to be. And if it's broken ... He knelt and moved his hand through the decomposing foliage in ever-growing circles. "Did you tell anyone else where you put the skull?"

The boy shook his head. "Naw. Probably a coyote or something took it."

"Think. Be absolutely sure."

"Didn't tell nobody."

Was that possible? Could an animal smell bones even after they were coated with polyurethane and sealed in plastic? Maybe. And these bones hadn't been cooked. Any marrow inside could still be pungent and edible, and there were certainly plenty of stray dogs and other creatures around. If the mandible was gone, how would he find it? The answer was simple.

He wouldn't. Sarah would forever be missing her jaw. His eyes watered, and he swallowed hard. No way to fix this. And the reason for his grief stood before him.

"Sorry, man. Not my fault, though."

What? Mason squinted at Fishy. "*Not your fault?* Then whose fault is it? Idiot." He grabbed the boy's arm, squeezing hard before pulling him toward the road.

Fishy licked his lips, and wrinkles covered his forehead. "Chill, dude. Give me a couple of days and I can come up with some money. It cost five or ten bucks, right? No sweat."

A horn honked as a vehicle neared. Mason stopped, a smile frozen on his face, as one of his neighbors drove past and waved.

Mason yanked open the pickup's passenger door. "It's your lucky day, Fishy."

CHAPTER FIFTY-FOUR

Jeremy flicked through the channels on the TV in his hotel room. Sunday afternoon in early October. A couple of NFL games to choose from, which would be great if he cared for football. Hockey season started later this week, but even if it was already going, none of the games would be broadcast in Memphis. Not exactly a rabid NHL fan base.

He'd scheduled a call with Director Bailey for ten o'clock the next day. Time to finalize everything and move on. Take a few weeks to figure out what he wanted to do next. Maybe become a security consultant for businesses. Or get his private investigator's license. Or go for something completely different. Buy a food truck and drive around town selling homemade chicken salad sandwiches. And tacos. Everybody loves tacos.

He didn't know what he'd do, but he did know where he'd do it. Somewhere close to Maggie and Rebecca. Past time to pick up the pace of their relationship, and Maggie had made it clear she felt the same way. Absence may make the heart grow fonder, but you can't hold hands via Skype.

He glanced at the digital clock beside the unmade bed. Less than an hour since he'd talked to her for the third, no, fourth time that day. He sighed and made the complete cycle of TV stations again, muted the volume, and dialed her number.

. . . .

The ringing buzz of his cell phone awakened Jeremy from a deep sleep. Something's happened to Maggie or Rebecca. He took two measured breaths to gain focus and slow his heart, then checked the time. Eleven o'clock. He snatched the phone off the nightstand and peered at the illuminated screen. Troy Obion? He cleared his throat, determined to sound awake.

"Hey, Troy. What's up?"

"Sorry to wake you, Jeremy."

"Huh? I was up. Just cleaning out some emails before tomorrow morning."

"Sure you were. Don't know why you can't admit you were sleeping. People do that, you know. Sleep. Nothing wrong with it."

"I'm gonna have to take the Fifth Amendment on that one. What are you doing up this late?"

"Late? It's barely eleven. Anyway, I've been spending some vacation days helping with the search for the Palmer boy, and I thought you'd want to hear we had a break. The TBI got a call a few hours ago from a farmer up in the Friendship area. Said a pack of dogs was stalking around his chickens so he grabbed his shotgun and fired off a couple of rounds."

"At the dogs?"

"In the air. Didn't want to hit his chickens. Anyway, the pack tucked tail and ran. The farmer went to count his chickens and see if he lost any. He didn't. But he found something the dogs dropped. Part of a human jawbone."

Jeremy bolted upright. "Did it belong to the boy?"

"Well, that's the thing. At first, they weren't even sure it was real. Pretty chewed up by the dogs, and the bone had been coated in plastic or something. The TBI's still testing it, but they're almost positive it's genuine."

Jeremy flopped back onto his pillow. "DNA or dental records?"

"The part of the bone they have isn't the jaw. I mean, it is, but not the part with the teeth. They told me what it was called. Ramus or something like that. But not enough of anything for dental records to help. Be later tomorrow before the preliminary DNA results are in. Could even be Tuesday morning. That's kind of the reason I'm calling."

"You want access to the FBI's testing? Honestly, it's not much faster."

"Maybe not the standardized tests."

"You talking about the Rapid-DNA machines? Troy, those aren't approved yet. Certainly not admissible as evidence. I'm not even sure Memphis has one. The Bureau hasn't bought any as far as I know. There were some floating around for demos, but it'd be a pretty big coincidence if we've got one locally."

"Can you find out? It could save us a lot of time."

Jeremy sighed. "Troy, even if there is a machine here, those things can't detect mingled DNA. I'd have to get a pure sample. No dog slobber or anything else that would contaminate the specimen. Most likely be a waste of time."

"Maybe, but I'm asking. Can you at least find out if there's one of those machines anywhere close to Memphis? If there's not, then we don't have to worry about it. But if there is ..."

"I'll make the call, Troy, but don't hold your breath. Even if I find one, can you talk the TBI into handing over a sample?"

"You forget who you're talking to here?"

"Give me half an hour."

"You're not going to fall back asleep, are you?"

"Told you. I wasn't asleep. Talk to you in a few."

CHAPTER FIFTY-FIVE

After several phone calls, Jeremy learned that yes, the Memphis FBI office had tested a Rapid-DNA machine, but no, they didn't still have the unit. Lester Truett, the Special Agent in Charge, raved about its possibilities, but only in limited situations. His concerns were more procedural than technical in nature. He feared it could become easy for investigators to rely too heavily on DNA evidence without doing the legwork to back it up. Got half a dozen suspects? Swab them and in ninety minutes—voila!—suspect confirmed or eliminated. Of course, a court order would be needed if the suspect wouldn't provide a voluntary sample, but if you knew the right judge, it'd happen.

Truett had sent the machine to the Little Rock office, about a hundred forty miles away. After a three-way phone conversation with the head of the Arkansas FBI office, it'd been agreed that if a sample from the jawbone could be obtained, it would be sent there for testing to save time. Bringing the machine back to Memphis would require an additional two hours for breakdown and setup, and no one was eager to process the paperwork that went along with transferring the device.

At two a.m., Troy called back to confirm he'd be able to secure a sample within the hour. The TBI lab would extract marrow and provide it with no guarantee as to its viability. All parties understood any information obtained as a result of this test would never be admissible in court.

Troy would pick up Jeremy at his hotel at three-thirty for the bumpy ride on I-40 to Little Rock. Barring traffic or construction, they'd be there and have the test underway no later than six a.m., with results due by nine o'clock.

Ten minutes early, Troy's red Jeep Wrangler pulled in front of the hotel. Its oversize tires and high chassis promised a rough trip, but at least he'd put the hardtop on. Jeremy grabbed two cups of coffee from the urn in the lobby and braced himself against the wind as he moved from indoors to out. Gonna be another cold, dry day.

"Mornin', old man," Troy said. "Hate to say it, but you definitely didn't get your beauty sleep last night. Appreciate the coffee, though."

"Oh. I suppose I could have brought you a cup, too. Sorry."

"Ha ha. I take it back. You look wonderful."

Jeremy handed him the java. "You got the DNA sample?"

"Yep. What time's your guy going to open up in Little Rock?"

"I told him I'd call when we were about thirty minutes out. He said he'd meet us at the office and have everything ready. Here's the thing though—apparently the device is made to run off cheek swabs. We're kind of crossing our fingers this will work."

"Only one way to find out, and the TBI said their results won't be back until late tonight. Worst-case scenario, we make the hour and a half drive for nothing."

"It's about two hours to Little Rock."

Troy adjusted his rearview mirror, took a sip of coffee, and slipped the Jeep into gear. "Buckle up."

CHAPTER FIFTY-SIX

"**M**aybe we should shut everything down for the season," Paula said. "Say it's out of respect for the Palmer boy."

Mason sat beside her on the porch, watching the clouds morph from gray to orange as the sun poked over the horizon. "What? Why? We've got an awful lot invested. If we closed now, we'd be worse off than when we started. Might as well stick a *For Sale* sign out front."

"I figure it's just a matter of time till the police come poking around here. They've been everywhere else. Might be best to put everything away out of sight."

Mason placed his hand over hers. "And if we shut down, what does that look like? That we're hiding something? No, we stay open. It's the best thing for us and the community. And anyway, it's not like we've seen a drop-off in attendance. People need to forget their problems. Have some fun. And there's safety in numbers, right? Folks are glad to let their kids come out here and burn off some energy. Heck, they'd probably be up in arms if we closed."

"Then we just keep going. I suppose that's for the best. I've run through this a hundred times, and I can't see as how there's anything to connect us to Lanny. And you're sure about Fishy?"

Mason chuckled. "Wish you could have seen him when I drove him home. Scared to death I was gonna come back when his parents got off work and make him tell them what he'd done. I don't think we need to worry about him."

"You did the right thing, honey. Would've been trouble if you'd brought him back here."

"Since I was seen with the boy, didn't make any sense to take any chances. Got what I was after, most of it anyways. Besides, Fishy doesn't know where the rest of Sarah is. I'm sure of it."

"What about the missing jaw?"

"I'll go back once the sun gets up a bit and see if I can find it. If a critter did take the bones, they're long gone by now. Nothing to be done about it except hope they're eaten or buried. Still, Lord knows I'd feel a whole lot better to get that jaw back with Sarah where it belongs."

"Me too. Before you go out, why don't you stop in for coffee at the diner and get the latest gossip? Maybe you'll learn something new."

"Not likely. Bunch of crotchety old men sitting around complaining about everything from the government to their bunions. Always talking about the rain too. Either how much we got or how much we need."

Paula smiled. "Uh-huh. That's why you fit in so well."

He winked at her. "Of course, the waitresses there are pretty nice."

"Well, if you can find one that'll put up with the likes of you, be my guest."

"Eh, I finally got you figured out. Don't need to start all over again. I'm going to check on a few things around here and then head out. Probably skip the diner today and spend a little more time searching. I'll go tomorrow."

She shrugged. "Suit yourself. Want me to come look with you? The boys will be catching the school bus in about half an hour, and I can put off some of my chores until this afternoon."

"I wouldn't mind the company. Just got to promise to behave out there."

"Behave?"

Mason rested his hand on her leg and leaned closer. "I seem to remember this one time we were out in the woods. Course it might have been twenty years or so back, but I remember it clear as can be. If it wasn't for the poison ivy, would've been the perfect day."

Her face reddened, and she lifted his hand and placed it on his own leg. "I'm quite sure I don't know what you're talking about. I'm a lady."

He kissed her cheek. "Yes, you are. But be sure to check the first aid kit for calamine lotion before we go."

CHAPTER FIFTY-SEVEN

Troy stopped his pacing and plopped into the breakroom chair. "Is it always like this? Hoping it is the kid's DNA while praying that it's not?"

Jeremy placed his hands on his hips and arched his back. The drive to Little Rock had been mercifully quick and painfully bouncy. "Yeah, it is. Seems like for every bit of good news in this job, there's a hundred bad pieces. Way of the world, I suppose."

"That's a tad cynical, isn't it?"

"Danger of the job and one of the reasons I'm ready to get out. I don't want to be that guy. The one always looking for the negative. Or maybe I'm already him and need something different. Can't keep a rosy outlook when you deal with this kind of stuff all the time."

"You had your out, though. Moving more into white collar crime?"

Jeremy shook his head. "I did. I don't know. Could be I'm an adrenaline junkie, and I'll be bored to death when I leave. But chasing insurance scammers? Not for me."

"Heh. Try sitting by a state road for hours, hoping a speeder comes by just so you have something to do."

"Apply to the Bureau, Troy. Put me down as a recommendation."

"You serious?"

"I am. Looked over your resume and sent it in. I might have already mentioned your name to my boss, in fact."

Troy drummed his fingers on the table. "Can't say I haven't thought about it."

"No guarantees, but I'll do what I can for you. Not sure if that'll help or hurt, though."

"I'll look into it. I mean, if it gets me—"

Little Rock's Special Agent in Charge walked into the room, a sheet of paper in hand. "Results are in."

Troy licked his lips and exhaled. "And?"

"Not the boy."

Jeremy frowned and nodded. "Hundred percent certainty?"

"According to the machine, yes. Sample was clean. No contamination. When the TBI gets their official results back, they'll say the same thing."

"Well," Troy said, "I'll make the call and give them a heads-up. The Palmers will want to know."

"If it's not the boy, who is it?" Jeremy asked.

The agent traced his finger down the paper. "Ran it through the database. Missing girl out of Indiana. Sarah ... here it is. Sarah Goldman."

Troy spun around, his mouth and eyes open as far as they'd stretch.

Jeremy tried to speak, but no words came out for several heartbeats. "Sarah Goldman? French Lick, Indiana?"

"Um, yeah. How'd you know that?"

"Let's go, Troy. We need to get back to Memphis. And I'm driving."

....

Jeremy pressed the phone against his ear, dodged another eighteen-wheeler, and shot a blast of air through his nostrils. "Yes sir, I understand. But doesn't it seem a bit *too* coincidental? Sarah Goldman's body found in the same area as the Lanny Palmer disappearance?"

Director Bailey sighed. "The girl's killer is already sitting on death row, remember?"

"Assuming he's guilty."

"The jury certainly did. That's good enough."

"He wouldn't be the first innocent person convicted of a crime. And if he didn't kill Sarah Goldman, this is the first real break in the case, and it's ours now. Body transported across state lines and dumped conveniently close to the site of a missing boy. Could it be coincidence? Sure. But if it's not, sir, do you want to risk letting a killer get away?"

"Of course not, but I'm still not assigning anyone else to this. There's already a task force from the TBI and local PDs looking for the kid, right? What's the point of throwing more people in the same area? If they find something else, we'll go from there. If not, well, maybe this gives some closure to the girl's parents."

Jeremy massaged his forehead. "Sir, this isn't merely a bone. Someone went to a lot of trouble to preserve it. Sealed it in plastic. Why do that if you're just going to dump it in the woods somewhere? It doesn't make sense."

Bailey exhaled. "I'll hold off on your retirement paperwork for another few days. Get me more to work with, then we'll talk. End of discussion. Got it?"

Jeremy clenched his teeth. "Understood. Oh, and sir, did you get that resume I sent? Troy Obion?"

The sound of papers shuffling filtered through the phone. "Yeah, I got it. No promises and no favors, but I'll look it over. He meet the qualifiers?"

Jeremy glanced at Troy. "Yes. College graduate, no problem passing the physical requirements, and nothing in his background as far as I know."

Troy shook his head and pointed to a slow-moving U-Haul in the left lane.

"Okay," Bailey said. "I think the online application period's open for the next three or four weeks. If he's serious, tell him to start there. We'll see what happens after that, but again, no promises. I'm not pulling any strings here. Either he gets in on his own merits or he doesn't."

Jeremy swerved around the rental truck. "Wouldn't have it any other way, sir."

CHAPTER FIFTY-EIGHT

Troy stretched, yawned loudly, and took a sip from his Dr Pepper. Jeremy leaned back in his office chair and resisted the urge to finish off his fifth cup of coffee. "You doing okay there?"

"Not enough sleep, and the adrenaline rush from your Nascar slalom back from Little Rock is wearing off. I'll live, though. At least as long as I get to drive from now on. You do know I-40's a major interstate, don't you? The shoulder's not a passing lane."

"Yeah, but in that monster Jeep of yours, I'm not sure it makes much difference. And I'd say you drive like an old woman if that wasn't such an insult to old women everywhere. Cut almost twenty minutes off your time, I believe. Of course, young as you are, I figure you're still using your learner's permit, right?"

Troy rolled his eyes and grinned. "Mandatory driver retesting every six months once you reach your age. That's what I think."

"Well, I guess when you get old enough to vote you can have a say in it."

"Har har. So what's our plan?"

Jeremy tapped his finger on the desk. "Our plan? Nothing's changed. You're needed most on the Palmer case. Help them locate the boy, and when you do, if there's a connection to Sarah Goldman, we'll find it. In the meantime, I'll head out to where they found the jawbone. See if anything there stirs up new ideas."

"You do think the cases are related though, right?"

"No doubt in my mind. And if they are, then something happened to spook this guy. The Palmer boy's disappearance doesn't match his MO. Presumably taken off a public road while waiting for the school bus. That's risky. Not like grabbing someone hiking alone in a thousand-acre state park. He wouldn't bring this attention on himself unless he had no choice."

"He panicked."

Jeremy leaned forward. "Maybe. But why the Palmer kid? Did he see something? Know something? He's the key. Figure that out, and you'll find whoever took him."

"They're trying. The TBI won't say whether they think there's a connection between the jawbone and Lanny, but they have to at least suspect there is. For now, though, they're keeping the discovery secret. Need-to-know basis only."

"Makes sense. Nothing to be gained by making the info public. I assume they'll search the area where the bone was found?"

"That's the plan. Cadets from law enforcement around the state are coming in today. They've had so many locals helping they're afraid somebody's going to trample some evidence. Good luck getting them to stay away, though."

"You going out with them?"

Troy frowned. "Don't think so. Planning to talk to a few people who knew Lanny. A couple of kids from his school seemed a little iffy. Maybe speak with his basketball coach and his boss at the Dairy Queen. Honestly, though, nothing that promises to be very helpful. They've all been interviewed before."

"The TBI ask you to do that?"

"Course not. They don't even want the local PD too involved in their interviews, much less one from out of state. Muddies the water too much, they said. Still, a man's got to eat, right? And if I happen to be around the DQ when I'm hungry, or the high school when classes let out ..."

Jeremy chuckled and shook his head. "Follow your instinct. You never know. Oh, and get your application in to the Bureau as soon as you can. If you're still interested, that is."

Troy couldn't hide his grin. "Definitely interested. Got to do my part before they start issuing walkers to you guys. Do they at least let you pick the color of tennis balls on those things?"

"Sure, as long as you requisition them six months in advance. Otherwise, you take what you can get. Pink balls or whatever."

Troy nearly spit his soda across the room. "Oh, man. I can't believe you said that."

Jeremy laughed and threw a stack of post-it notes at him. "Idiot. Get out of here before this old man teaches you a thing or two about respecting your elders."

The policeman stood at attention and saluted. "Yes, sir."

"Hey, Troy. Good luck today. Be nice to get a little good news for a change."

"Yeah, it would. We're due, right?"

Due? He used to think that way. In the end, it all evens out. Might be true for some, but not in this job. There's always another killer. Always. And no matter how many people were slaughtered, no matter how many grieving family and friends were affected, there was only the killer. No balancing of the scales.

Jeremy forced a smile. "Yeah, Troy. We're due."

CHAPTER FIFTY-NINE

Mason huddled over the upstairs workbench in the old barn and inspected the timeworn pliers. Most of the rust was gone, but they'd need another night in the vinegar bath. After that, a dab of oil would keep them shiny and protected. Grandpa would be proud. His made-in-America Craftsman tools were still going strong. Good old USA steel forged into a—

The thunk of a closing car door echoed through the building. He edged to the barn entrance and cracked it open. A stranger stood beside a bright red Jeep Wrangler, its hard top removed. Oversize tires, winch on the front bumper, chassis sitting high off the ground. The boys could have some fun in that thing.

The visitor scanned his surroundings and headed for the house, pausing to look over the pumpkin patch before climbing the steps to the porch and knocking on the screen door. After a moment, Paula answered and the two shook hands. The stranger pulled something from his pocket and showed it to Paula. She smiled, nodded, and motioned him inside. The law.

Mason scooted back to the workbench and reviewed his options. He chose a large crescent wrench, feeling its heft before sliding it into his back pocket, then smeared a bit of grease on his hands, picked up a dirty rag, and headed for the house.

The two were in the kitchen when Mason arrived, the stranger seated at the table while Paula poured some coffee. Both looked up and smiled when he walked into the room.

"Honey," Paula said, "this is Officer Obion. He's down from, I'm sorry, was it Kentucky?"

Troy stood and extended a hand to Mason. "No, ma'am. Indiana."

Mason wiped his hands with the rag before clasping Troy's hand. "Out working on the equipment. Always something to fix around here, and the day's not done unless I get my hands dirty."

"I understand completely. I've got an uncle in Iowa who used to farm. I remember spending a few summers there when I was a kid. Hard work."

Mason nodded. "Used to farm?"

"Yes, sir. Ended up selling the place off several years back. Made him an offer he couldn't refuse, as they say."

"Uh-huh. I suppose to some people money might be more import—"

"Mason, dear, would you like some coffee?" Paula held up the pot, her plastered smile belying the look in her eyes.

"Sweet tea, please. Now then, Officer, what brings you out this way? You helping hunt for that missing boy?"

"Cream or sugar?" Paula asked as she placed the coffee on the table.

"Black is fine," Troy said as he sat back down. "Yes, Mr. Miller. I'm here as a volunteer, assisting the TBI in the investigation."

Mason took a seat across from the officer. "Lots of folks helping out. Wouldn't expect nothing less around these parts. Wish I had the time to join them, but between the farm and the corn maze, I've got my hands full."

Troy nodded. "Your Halloween events are why I'm here. I stopped by the Dairy Queen to speak with Lanny's boss, and he told me the boy worked here also."

"Of course. We already told another officer the whole story. Lanny worked out in the corn maze. Had to let him go, though. Got a little rude with some of our customers. Can't have that. We run a family business and expect folks to show respect to each other."

"Sure. Got all that info in the notes from the earlier visit. Never hurts to get a second set of eyes on stuff, though."

Paula leaned against the stove. "Maybe Lanny up and ran away. Seems to me that's the most likely situation. All this talk about kidnapping, well, things like that just don't happen around here."

Mason grunted. "Don't be ridiculous, Paula. That stuff happens everywhere. We've been lucky, that's all. But how do you know he *didn't* run away?"

Troy shrugged. "We don't. Could've, but doesn't seem likely. Most of the time when kids his age run away, there are signs. Broke up with his girlfriend, problems with parents, drug abuse. None of the indications are there. At least with what we know so far."

Mason sipped his tea. "How can we help?"

Troy pulled a notepad from his shirt pocket and clicked a pen. "I was hoping you could give me more information on what happened that caused Lanny to get fired."

"If you gentlemen don't mind," Paula said, "I've got some laundry to do."

"Certainly," Troy said. "Thank you for the coffee, ma'am."

"My pleasure." She nodded toward her husband. "Just don't get him started on any of his farming stories. How his grandpa did this and his father did that. You'll be here till Christmas."

Troy smiled at her and turned his focus back to Mason. "Now then, sir. If you could walk me through the night you fired Lanny?"

"Sure. He was working out in the maze. Got a dozen or so kids who dress up as zombies and wander through to, you know, spook things up. Make it a little scarier. Course, we don't do that when the little kids are out there. Not until after dark when it's mostly teenagers."

Troy scribbled a note. "How long had Lanny worked here?"

"It was actually the first night we were open. He was here last year too, helping out down with the pumpkins. This was his first year to be in the maze."

"Uh-huh. Any problems with the other kids working out there?"

"None that I know of. It's a small town, and they all go to the same school. I imagine if there were any serious problems, somebody would've heard about it."

"Gotcha. Now, exactly what did Lanny do that caused you to fire him?"

"We tell our workers not to touch anyone. Scaring them's fine, but don't get too close. Even showed them some YouTube videos of workers at haunted houses getting punched by customers. Folks get scared, you don't know how they'll react. It's best for everybody to keep their distance."

"And I take it Lanny broke that rule?"

"He did. Group of four or five girls around his age came through his area. Near as I could figure, he jumped out behind them and scared them pretty good. They screamed and he started chasing them. One of the girls fell and he grabbed her arm. She kicked him hard and he backed off. When the girls came out of the maze, they told me what happened. Course, they were laughing about it by then, but rules are rules."

"And what did Lanny say about all of this?"

"Said he was just trying to help her up. Didn't matter, though. Look, my single largest expense for this whole deal is the insurance I pay to protect us and the folks that come through here. I don't need that cost to go up, so when someone does something risky, I cut them loose. Not much choice."

"Makes sense. And how did Lanny take it when you let him go?"

"Not good. He apologized. Said it wouldn't happen again. I tried to explain why I couldn't keep him on, but a boy his age just doesn't get it sometimes. Kept talking about it not being fair, that other workers did the same thing. I told him I could only deal with the incidents I knew about. He was pretty mad."

"Angry enough to run away?"

Mason shrugged. "You got any kids?"

"No, sir."

"Well, when you do, you'll understand. Who knows what goes on in their heads? I imagine by the time he got home, he'd forgot about it. Could be wrong about that, but I don't think so. Besides, it was almost a week later when he disappeared. Don't think he'd stew on it that long and then decide to up and leave, you know?"

"Uh-huh. Did you see him again after that night?"

Mason scrunched his forehead. "Not that I recall. I mean, it's possible, but I don't think so. We get an awful lot of folks out here, especially on weekends. And it's not like he was banned or anything. He's a good kid. Made a mistake, that's all. I reckon as how we'll hire him back on next year if he wants. That is, well ..."

"Sure. Would it be okay if I took a look at the maze? Get an idea of where he worked?"

"If you think it'll help, of course. Can't imagine you'll see anything except corn and decorations, but you're the expert, not me."

Troy downed the last of his coffee. "Just want to make sure we cover all our bases. I'll need to get the names of those girls before I leave so I can follow up with them too."

Mason walked to the sink, dumped the remainder of his tea down the drain, and called for his wife. "Paula, we're going out to the maze for a bit. Officer Obion wants to get a feel for it. See where Lanny worked."

"Of course. Can I fix you a Thermos of coffee to carry with you, Officer? It's quite chilly out there this morning."

Troy stood and shoved his chair back under the table. "That's very kind, ma'am, but I'll be fine."

She smiled and flicked the switch on the coffee pot. "It was very nice to meet you. If there's anything we can do to help, you let us know. We're all tore up about the boy."

Mason nodded and motioned toward the back door. "Hope you wore your walking shoes today."

Troy patted his stomach. "I could use the exercise. Already had a Blizzard for breakfast."

"Honey," Paula said, "put on a heavier coat. Wear some gloves too. Don't need you catching a cold."

"I'll be fine. Keep your phone close in case we need anything." He followed Troy out the door and down the steps into the yard that opened onto their land. The sun had warmed the ground enough to send up tendrils of steamy heat waves, and the slow breeze struggled to blow ripples through the corn. In the distance, the cattle were hollering to each other, most likely wondering when their hay was coming. The bucolic quiet of late morning on the farm.

Mason casually reached back and squeezed the cold steel of the wrench. Craftsman tools came with a lifetime warranty. Far as he knew, they never really specified whose lifetime.

CHAPTER SIXTY

M ason led the way through the maze. "Not quite so scary during the day, huh?"

"Looks like a lot of work," Troy said. "Was it hard to set up?"

"Not too much. We've done this for a few years now, and it gets easier and bigger every fall. We make enough money off it to help out with repairs and stuff around the farm, but truth be told, we'd probably do it even if we didn't clear a cent. The community's really taken a liking to everything. Gives them something to do without having to drive too far. Lots of families will come out several times during the season. Good way to keep in touch with neighbors. Hold on to that small-town feeling, you know?"

Troy ran his hand along the stalks as they walked. "How do you get the corn so dense in here?"

"Double planted. One way and then again at ninety degrees off that."

"Anybody ever get lost back here?"

Mason laughed. "All the time. That's why all the workers have to know the closest way out. I try to keep enough people in here so they can keep an eye on the customers. Make sure everybody stays in the paths. Course, every now and then somebody'll take off trampling through the stalks. We tend to frown on that. It's a lot of work to repair the damage."

The men walked past some stacked hay bales with a ghost peeking from behind.

"Kids ever mess with your decorations?" Troy asked.

"Not really. A few busted pumpkins now and then, but that's about the extent of it. Like I said, we try to keep enough workers back here to keep an eye on things."

Mason licked his lips and flexed his fingers. The first skelcrow waited around the next corner. Demond Houston. Wearing a dirty blue button-down shirt with brown tweed jacket, khakis, cap, and a pipe wired to his mouth. Looking rather dapper and plasticky. Officer Troy Obion's future depended on his reaction to Demond.

The men turned left, and Mason lagged behind the policeman.

Troy slowed and glanced at the display. "Cool. You light it up at night?"

Mason traced a finger along the wrench. "Sort of. Battery powered LED lights inside the skull. Also got a few spotlights spread around, but they run off solar. Don't last too long. Plus, we give out flashlights."

"If I get time, I'd love to come back after dark and go through. Seems like it'd be fun."

"You're welcome any time. On the house, of course."

"Appreciate it. Much farther to Lanny's work area?"

"Another ten minutes or so if we get a move on."

Troy moved to get a closer look at the skelcrow. "Great. I'm trying to get out of here before lunch. Maybe swing back by the DQ before heading to the search area."

"Shouldn't be a problem. Lanny worked right up this way. Coming?" Mason moved off and glanced over his shoulder to ensure the policeman followed. He didn't.

Troy stood with his arms crossed, reviewing the scene before him. "Never seen a scarecrow like that before?"

Mason cleared his throat. "We call them skelcrows. My youngest son came up with the name. Got the idea from the Dollar General in town. Helps make a five-dollar skeleton look more real. Anything to increase the spooky factor, you know? Kids these days. Almost impossible to scare them, what with all the gory stuff they see at the movies."

Troy scratched his bottom lip. "Uh-huh. Interesting. Looks good."

Mason scooted closer to the officer. "I hate to hurry you, but—"

Troy whipped around and faced the farmer. "Sorry. I get distracted sometimes. Don't mean to take up too much of your time. I know you've got a lot to do. Lead the way."

Mason studied the policeman's face. If he had any suspicions, he hid them well. "Okay then. Like I said, just a bit farther."

"Great. I'll be out of your hair in no time."

They passed one more skelcrow on the way. Gloria Mathias, tastefully attired in a purple blouse and black pants, accessorized perfectly with a huge golden brooch, black handbag, and floppy red hat. Troy slowed and smiled at her but kept walking.

"This is the spot," Mason said. "Lanny worked around here. Right over there's where the incident happened. Not much to see, I'm afraid."

Troy paced the area, scanning the ground and scribbling notes in his pad. A couple of times, he pushed the corn aside and peered into the depths of the field.

"Whatcha think?" Mason asked.

Troy slid the pen into the spiral rings of the notepad and slipped it into his back pocket. "I think that's a lot of corn."

Mason laughed. "Give it another month and this field will be bare. The cows will be well-fed, though."

"I appreciate your time, sir. Wish I could say it's been helpful, but there's nothing here. Didn't figure there would be, but leave no stone unturned, isn't that what they say?"

"I suppose it is. Just wish I could do more."

Troy nodded. "We all do. Tell you what. If you don't mind, I'd like to spend a little more time out here. Walking in the quiet's really felt good. Cleared my mind."

"Farming will do that for you. There's a tie to the land. Not an easy life, but it's a good one. You take all the time you want."

"Thanks. I'll wander back the way we came in and poke my head in to let you know I'm going."

"You sure you can find the way?"

"Honestly? No, but I'd like to try."

"Well, if I haven't seen you in an hour, I'll come looking. Deal?"

Troy shook hands with Mason. "Deal."

Mason moved quickly, wanting to put some distance between the two of them. He passed Gloria, her outfit fluttering in the slow breeze, rounded the next corner, and stopped. No sound except the dry rustling of corn stalks. A few turkey vultures circled lazily overhead, the only dots in a pastel blue sky.

A perfect day. The kind of day only someone in touch with being outdoors could understand and appreciate. Hunters or farmers or fishermen or—

There. The unmistakable click of a cell phone's camera. A cough, then another click. And another.

Mason sighed. A perfect day ruined or improved, depending on your perspective. He needed to get back to Paula. Make sure she was ready.

Her lucky day.

CHAPTER SIXTY-ONE

Mason paced the kitchen. "Pictures. He's out there taking pictures. Not good, Paula. I wish I could—"

"Enough," Paula said. "We knew this might happen. Now we'll deal with it. Try to settle down. Don't want to make him any more suspicious than he already is."

"How long's he been in there? He could be calling the police. Waiting for backup to arrive. It's all closing in around us. Too fast. Way too fast. We need to get everything ready. Go ahead with—"

"Honey, you're making me nervous. Sit. He's been out there alone for almost thirty minutes. I'm sure if he was calling for reinforcements, they'd be here by now."

Mason peered out the window over the sink. "If he's not out of there soon, I'm going to find him."

"And?"

"And ... doesn't matter. There he is. You ready?"

She took a deep breath and nodded. "For our family."

"Always." He glanced at his wife and walked down the back steps, waving toward the officer. Troy returned the wave and accelerated his pace.

"You made it out alive, I see," Mason said.

"Touch and go there for a while. But I appreciate it. Seriously. Felt good to be outside and let my mind wander. Forget about all the mess that's going on."

"I know just what you mean. A man needs to clear his head once in a while or it's liable to explode. I sometimes look back at my daddy and granddaddy and wonder if it was easier for them. Simpler life, you know? Less to worry about. Eh, what am I saying? Farmers always worry. It's who we are."

"Tough way to make a living, I'm sure. Don't think I could do it. Too much stuff out of my control."

Mason shrugged. "You learn to deal with it any way you can. Be thankful for what you've got. Beyond that ..."

"I suppose so. Listen, thanks again. I may take you up soon on your offer to go through the maze one night."

"You're welcome any time. Bring some friends if you'd like."

Troy headed for his Jeep. "Might just do that. We could all use a distraction, even if it's only for a couple of hours."

"I imagine this stuff, the missing boy and all, eats away at you."

"I'm finding that out."

They rounded the house and approached the driveway. "Well, we're hoping and praying for the best. We know y'all are doing everything you can."

Troy opened his vehicle's door. "Give my best to your wife."

Mason nodded and leaned against the tailgate of his old pickup. Still no other visitors to the pumpkin patch this morning. A blessing to have such a peaceful morning after the last few hectic days. "Know what else eats away at you? Beetles. Can't blame them, though. They're only doing what the good Lord created them to do."

Troy's eyebrows squished together. "I'm not sure I understand."

Mason leaned back and casually scratched the back of his head. "You will."

The deer rifle's report tore through the late morning calm, startling the few birds loitering on bare tree branches. Within seconds, all was quiet again.

CHAPTER SIXTY-TWO

Jeremy stared at his phone's screen. Four calls to Troy since yesterday afternoon, all going straight to voice mail. Either he'd turned off his cell or he was in a dead zone. Neither scenario seemed very likely. Not for this length of time. The fact that his friend hadn't returned to his hotel last night wasn't helping. Checks of local hospitals had turned up nothing.

He laid the phone on his desk and ran through the possibilities again. After so many years, seeing too much, he gravitated toward the darker options. Something had happened. Something not good. Any other conceivable situation and Troy would've called. Maybe he found—

His phone vibrated and he snatched it, his heart sinking when he saw the caller ID.

"Good morning," Maggie said.

"Hey."

"Well that's certainly a cheery way to start the day."

"What? Oh. Sorry. I'm a little preoccupied."

"Can I help?"

"It's Troy. I can't get in touch with him, and I'm starting to get worried."

"Maybe his battery's dead?"

"Yeah, maybe. I stopped by his hotel this morning and had them check his room. Bed was still made."

"Huh. Well, he's a young single guy. Could be he found somewhere else to spend the night."

"Maybe, but I doubt it. That's not Troy. And he didn't check in at the command post this morning."

"He probably decided to take the day off. It is his vacation, right? You know what they say. All work and no play makes a man healthy, wealthy, and wise."

Jeremy snorted and pressed a hand against his lips. "Yep. That's what they say. But it doesn't feel right, Maggie. Troy wouldn't just drop off the grid like this. I'm afraid something's happened."

"Then I say go with your gut. Put out a BOLO on his vehicle. See if anything turns up."

"Thought about that. Don't know how much good it'll do, but I guess that couldn't hurt. At least get his plates in the system."

"It's a start. Think this has anything to do with your case?"

"The missing Palmer boy. Sarah Goldman's jawbone. And now Troy gone missing? So much happening in such a short time. Too much to be coincidence."

"Need me to come down? I can take a couple of days off. Let Rebecca spend some time at her dad's."

"Appreciate the offer, but no thanks. I don't need any distractions right now. Better if I stay focused on wrapping all this up."

"A distraction, huh? That's what I am to you?"

Jeremy grinned. "Uh-huh. The best kind of distraction."

"Good answer. Call me as soon as you find anything on Troy. Oh, and I checked on Cronfeld's Marine unit. Looks like he was telling the truth. The men did sign a confidentiality agreement when they left Afghanistan. Pretty close to the same one Cronfeld gave to you."

"Not surprised. Stick a piece of paper in front of a bunch of tired Marines and tell them if they sign, they can go home. Who wouldn't agree to that? Thanks, Maggie. Don't know what I'd do without you."

"Me neither. Now hurry up and solve this thing. A couple of girls in Virginia wouldn't mind seeing a bit more of you. And don't worry about Troy. I'm sure you're being your old paranoid self. He'll turn up."

"Wish I could be that confident. Give Rebecca a kiss for me. I need to get to work. Going to try to retrace Troy's steps yesterday."

"Jeremy? Be careful."

"Yeah. Sometimes we paranoids get it right."

CHAPTER SIXTY-THREE

Three hours since the BOLO was issued and nothing. Jeremy considered trying to get a warrant to track Troy's phone, but knew it was pointless. No evidence of a crime. Besides, if the phone had been turned off, it wouldn't do much good. Cell towers in the rural areas where he suspected the policeman had gone were few and far between. Triangulating wouldn't be very helpful in narrowing down a search area.

Troy's boss hadn't heard from him. Neither had his soon-to-be-girlfriend Peggy or any other friends. It'd now been over twenty-four hours since anyone had contact with him. Something was dead wrong.

Local law enforcement had their hands full with the Lanny Palmer investigation. The Bureau wouldn't get involved without evidence of a crime falling under their jurisdiction. Jeremy had no choice. He'd search alone.

First stop, the Dairy Queen. The manager confirmed meeting Troy yesterday and shared as much of their conversation as he could remember. Lanny was a good employee. Worked a couple of hours in the evenings cleaning tables and emptying trash. Missed a shift now and then, but what boy his age didn't? No problems with any customers. Hung out with a group of boys from school. Seemed like a good kid. And worked some nights at the Miller farm over near Friendship.

Jeremy reviewed the grainy security footage from the day before and confirmed Troy left alone. Nothing out of the ordinary. The manager offered Jeremy a complimentary meal. He thanked him and declined. Next stop was the Millers' place.

The farm was a little ways off the beaten path, though handmade signs pointed the way from the main road. He turned into the drive and drove past a minivan in a grass parking area. Pumpkins, decorations, and other wares were strewn about the area. A young mother wrestled with her two kids in an attempt to pose them for a photo beside hay bales and mums. He slowed and continued up the gravel drive to the house.

An old pickup truck sat by the home, its muddy tires, sporadic rust, and numerous dents proclaiming this vehicle was proud of its hard work. Off to the left, an ancient barn braced itself against the years and strutted under its shiny metal roof. In the distance, the sound of machinery. Jeremy hoped he wouldn't have to walk all the way to the noise before he found someone.

"Can I help you?" A woman stood on the porch, shading her eyes against the noon sun's brightness.

Jeremy waved and walked to her. "Yes, ma'am. I'm Special Agent Jeremy Winter with the FBI. Wondered if I could ask you a few questions."

"The FBI? This about the Palmer boy? You're the third one who's come up here. Don't mind telling you what we told the others, but it won't be much use I'm afraid."

Jeremy flashed his badge. "Did you say I'm the third person who's been here about the case?"

"Oh, where are my manners? Would you like to come in and sit down? Mason, he's my husband, will be in for lunch soon. You're welcome to join us."

"Thank you, but that won't be necessary. I'm in a bit of a hurry. I was hoping you could tell me if anyone from the police came by here yesterday."

"They did. A young man with a Jeep, as I recall. Nice young man. Had some coffee with us while we talked."

"Do you remember his name?"

"Last name O'Brien or something like that. Took his coffee black."

"Can you tell me what you discussed?"

Paula shifted her stance. "We talked about Lanny and what his job was here and why we had to fire him."

"Fire him?"

"Nothing big. Broke one of our rules. That was the last time we saw him."

"Officer Obion ask about anything else?"

"No, sir. Not that I can recall. He couldn't have been here more than ten or fifteen minutes tops."

"Did he give any indication where he was headed next?"

"Uh-uh. What's going on here? Has something happened to him?"

He pulled a business card out and handed it to her. "Not really sure. If you or your husband think of anything else, would you call me?"

"Of course we will. What's the world coming to?"

"Ma'am?"

"Just not safe anywhere, is it? I remember when folks didn't even lock their doors at night. Suppose those days are long gone, huh?"

Jeremy nodded. "I've been locking my doors for a long time, ma'am. A very long time."

CHAPTER SIXTY-FOUR

"He's ruined," Mason said. "What am I supposed to do with this mess?" The cutting work was finished, and Troy Obion's remains lay scattered on a table in the root cellar. His legs were already back in the freezer and the rest needed to go soon before it started to thaw.

Paula scrubbed both hands across her face, then wrapped her arms tightly around herself and swayed back and forth. "I'm sorry my first *murder* didn't meet your high standards, but don't put this on me."

"I'm just trying to explain that—"

She covered her mouth and dry-heaved several times. "He moved at the last second, okay? Do you even understand what just happened here? The danger we're in?"

He narrowed his eyes. "There's nothing left of one side of his face. You act like a little duct tape and glue will fix this right up. You aimed too high. Center mass, I said. And if that didn't finish him, I was right there. He wouldn't have suffered. And shooting people is just like shooting deer. If I had a trophy buck in my sights, I wouldn't aim for his head, would I?"

She took a step back and pulled her lips into a thin line. "Maybe it's the same for you, but you're not ..."

"What? I'm not what, Paula? Normal? Is that what you were going to say? You think I'm some kind of psychopath?"

She sighed and let her shoulders drop. Her hands twitched, and she shoved them into her jeans pockets. "Do we have to do this? We both know the situation. You're my husband and I love you, but normal people don't go around killing folks. I've never asked you to stop, only to make sure you put our family first."

He closed his eyes and inhaled deeply. "Killing people *is* putting my family first."

"I know that. All I'm asking is that you don't get angry at me for not being as good at it as you are. Being around dead bodies isn't the same as shooting someone."

He sighed and twisted his head, stretching his neck as far as possible. "You're right. You got the job done. Suppose you did good for your first. Now let's hope nobody else comes here looking, but if they do, remember. Fifteen minutes or so. That's all he was here. Asked a few questions and moved on."

"Maybe we should've waited and seen if he came back before we killed him."

"No, he was too suspicious. If he left here, he'd of come back with his friends. Maybe even a search warrant. I couldn't let that happen."

"I know. It's just that things seem to be occurring so fast. Too fast. That's how mistakes get made. We've got a family, Mason. You, me, two boys. Maybe it's time to stop, or at least take a long break before one of us gets hurt. The risk is too much. Let's figure out what to do with him and hope they don't find that Jeep."

"The grinder. That's all we can do. Nothing but blind luck that we weren't caught hiding his car. Moving the body now, what with the FBI around and all, is too dangerous. Gonna take a while, though. He's got to get in line. Lanny won't be finished up for another few days."

"Can't you just toss some of him in there with the boy?"

"Doesn't work that way. Each beetle eats what it eats. Tossing more in there doesn't make them go faster."

"More beetles then?"

He exhaled a torrent of air and shrugged. "Yeah, we could do that I reckon. Need to pick up a couple more tubs down at Walmart. I can probably have it all up and running in three or four days, maybe sooner, depending on how quick the bugs get here."

"You tell me what you need, and I'll take care of it."

"I'll get a list together. Shouldn't be too much."

"Anything around the farm need doing? I can help with that too, you know. Don't want you to feel overwhelmed."

"Naw. Not much happening other than the corn maze. Another three weeks, and we'll be closing it down too. Be a good time for a break. Maybe plan a trip to the mountains. Take the boys up to Gatlinburg when they get out for Christmas."

Paula swallowed hard. "Sure. A trip sounds nice. Let's talk about it later though, okay? We need to think through some things. Make sure we've got everything covered, you know?"

"Whatever you want, babe." He gestured toward the torso lying atop a tarp at his feet. The cop had been a big man, and with time against them, they'd opted to forego the normal procedures and get him in the freezer as quickly as possible. "Looks like most of the blood's drained out. You want to hold or wrap?"

She shuddered violently and grabbed the oversize roll of plastic wrap. "I hope you've got more of this somewhere."

"I've got a whole case upstairs. You never know how much you're going to need."

CHAPTER SIXTY-FIVE

Jeremy forced himself to breathe through his nose and checked the GPS again. ETA twelve minutes at posted speeds. He'd be there in half that time. The narrow, twisty roads wound through farmland along the edge of the Forked Deer River. Open brown fields of harvested corn and cotton, bordered by dense clusters of trees, flew past. If a deer decided to make its appearance on the road now, they'd both be done for.

He swung wide around a sharp right turn, ignoring the slip of his rear tires. Near Buck Creek, just west of Eaton Brazil Road. That's where the deputy sheriff said he'd be. Another glance at the GPS. Two minutes. Maybe three.

His phone rang and he risked a glance. Maggie. Too dangerous to talk at these speeds. Let it go to voice mail. On the horizon, a row of trees ran left to right. That's got to be the stream.

Jeremy braked hard and craned his neck, searching the dirt path that bisected the street. West. Left. He bounced off the pavement into the ruts paralleling the creek. A hundred yards in, the stream meandered off to the left and allowed a strip of arable land to arise. Broken corn stalks dotted the tiny field. Two turns, maybe three at the most, of a combine would handle the whole patch. How did they get such big equipment into places like this? No land went to waste.

A couple of hundred yards later, the trees moved back in, hemming the road in on both sides. Jeremy's vehicle bounced along for another half minute before a clearing opened up. A white car, "Crockett County Sheriff" emblazoned in green along the side, sat parked beside a silver pickup truck with a blue/red light bar atop its cab.

Jeremy pulled close and hopped out. His leg didn't bother him often since the blood clot, but today it was angry. He moved quickly toward the two men waiting for him.

The man in the uniform raised a hand in greeting. "You the FBI guy?"

Jeremy showed his ID. "Yes, sir."

"I'm Deputy Claymore. This here's Deputy Branson. He was off-duty when I got the call."

The men exchanged handshakes and head nods.

"Where's the vehicle?" Jeremy asked.

Claymore gestured to a thicket of trees behind him. "Back about fifteen feet or so. The pine trees get pretty thick so we're lucky the copter spotted it."

"Any idea how long the vehicle's been there?"

"None. This area's been searched from the air two or three times already. You know, just hoping to spot something that might help us find the boy. It's a little far from where the TBI's focused, but we're looking everywhere. And like I said, thick as them trees are, the boys in the sky could've missed it before."

"Got it. You tape it off yet?"

Both deputies shook their heads. "Ain't touched it. Took a look inside and figured that's all we needed to see. Nobody in the Jeep or surrounding area near as we can tell."

"Who else is coming?"

"The sheriff, of course. The TBI is supposed to be sending somebody too. Want to make sure there's no link between this and the boy. Don't see how there couldn't be, though."

"And why is that, Deputy?"

"Lots of stuff happening around here at once. Too much to not be connected. Look, we're not exactly Mayberry. Got our share of problems. Meth, domestic violence, the occasional shooting or stabbing. But a kidnapped boy and a missing cop in the same week? And rumor is the TBI found some bones that don't belong to either one of them. I might look young, but I wasn't born yesterday."

"Uh-huh. Don't solve the crime without getting the evidence first. Kind of hard to get a conviction that way."

The deputy rested his hand on his service weapon. "Yep, it is. Conviction or not, I'd be happy just to get the two of them back alive for now. Worry about the rest of it later."

Tensions in the community were high and if—when—they caught the kidnapper, he'd need some serious protection. Wouldn't be the first time law enforcement looked the other way. "Got it. Show me to the vehicle?"

"Right this way, sir."

Decades of pine needles covered the ground, and Jeremy paused before going deeper into the trees. He squatted and peered intently ahead. Two slight parallel indentations led to where he assumed the Jeep was parked. Any potential evidence should be fairly easy to spot as long as it wasn't any shade of brown.

"Stay to the left," Jeremy said. He motioned along the vehicle's path. "It came through here and I don't want to disturb anything that may be on the ground."

"You're the boss," Deputy Branson said. "If you stand over here, you can just make out the back of the Jeep. Looks like they drove it up there as far as they could, then took a sharp right to get it as far out of view as possible."

"All right. Gentlemen, if you don't mind, could you wait here for the TBI? I'd like to get a look at the scene by myself."

The deputies exchanged a glance. "Whatever you want."

Jeremy nodded and moved toward the vehicle, checking the ground before gently stepping straight down, careful not to shuffle his feet. After four steps, hope was sucked from his chest. Bright red. Sitting high atop huge tires. And an Indiana license plate. Troy.

Doesn't mean anything. This is good. A clue. Troy found something. Someone.

Now I have to find him. That's all. Done it before. Do it again.

He paused to review the scene. Woodsy pine scent mingled with river odors. Isolated location, so most likely the vehicle had been driven back here intentionally. Had to be someone familiar with the area. He tilted his head back and stared at the sky. Not much opening between the trees. A miracle anyone had spotted the Jeep.

Jeremy slipped latex gloves on and approached the vehicle from the driver's side. The door was closed. The window down. No sign of trouble thus far. Another step and he could get a look inside the—

The window wasn't down. It was gone. Pieces of glass littered the driver's seat and the space behind. The black leather interior had a speckling of red, some dots the size of quarters, some the size of pinheads. The bigger ones had a trail where gravity had drawn them down.

Jeremy spun from the vehicle and staggered as far as he could before falling to his knees and throwing up. When finished, he moved farther away and sat with his back against the scratchy bark of an old pine.

When the deputies arrived with the TBI almost twenty minutes later, he was still sitting, carefully inspecting each hollow point as he snapped them back into his Glock's magazine. This same weapon had almost killed a man in Afghanistan. There'd be no *almost* in Tennessee.

CHAPTER SIXTY-SIX

"Give me an update. What do we know?" Director Bailey said. Jeremy edged closer to the speakerphone. "The Jeep was located almost seven hours ago. We're waiting on DNA analysis to confirm, but I'm confident it's Troy's blood. The TBI is bringing his vehicle in for more testing."

"Okay. Get the Rapid-DNA back from Little Rock. Priority One on my authority. I want confirmation as soon as possible. Is the location of the vehicle the crime scene?"

Jeremy cleared his throat. "Not likely. We found a few shards of window glass outside, probably tracked out by whoever drove the Jeep there. No blood or drag marks to indicate Troy was removed from the vehicle at the site. Most likely happened elsewhere and the perpetrator dumped the car there. Figured no one would find it for a long time. Maybe even planned to move it again when things calmed down."

"Theories?"

"Gunshot through the window. Based on the glass dispersion inside and bloodstains on the doorjamb, Troy was standing there with the door open. Either getting in or getting out. No way to know. Any glass that remained intact was knocked inside the vehicle. My guess is so they wouldn't attract any attention when moving the Jeep."

"Physical evidence besides blood splatter?"

Jeremy sniffled and grabbed the desk's edge to stop the sudden dizziness. "Um ..."

"Agent Winter, listen. You don't have to do this. There may be no connection between Officer Obion's disappearance and the Palmer boy. And certainly nothing that indicates either case is tied to your serial killer theory. You can back off. Let the locals handle it."

"Not going to happen. The TBI is going to formally request our assistance if they haven't already. Law enforcement is swamped, and the Palmer case is going to be officially designated a child abduction. They need help, sir. And they need it fast."

"When I get the request, I'll give them what I can spare. Until then, we'll assist only when asked. Too many agencies involved and things get lost in the shuffle. Nobody wants that. And I know what I say isn't going to have any impact on whatever you're going to do. Now, besides the blood splatter in the Jeep, is there anything indicating Officer Obion might not have survived the shooting?"

Jeremy brushed a hand under his eyes. "Possible bone fragments and brain matter."

Bailey grunted. "The bullet recovered?"

"No, sir."

"Who's got jurisdiction?"

"The local sheriff's handling it for now. The TBI is hanging back and will assist as needed. Troy's vehicle's being taken to Jackson so their crime scene techs can go over it. Memphis is on standby if they're needed. Any prints they find will be uploaded as soon as possible."

"What're you thinking?"

"Troy found something. Whether my case or the Palmer case or both, I don't know. It's the only thing that makes sense."

"Your plan?"

"I've retraced what I know of his day. No one stood out. Nice, quiet folks."

"Always the way it is, isn't it?"

Jeremy cleared his throat again and straightened in his chair. "Mostly. The neighbor on the news saying they had no idea the guy next door stored body parts in his basement. Such a nice boy. Kept his lawn mowed. No wild parties. Waved when he got his mail. Such a pity."

"Keep at it. If there's a connection, find it before someone else gets killed. I'll see if I can get you some help in the meantime."

"I appreciate that, sir, but it's not necessary. I work better alone."

"I'm not so sure about that."

"Um, sir, unless you're ordering me to—"

A gentle tap on his office door and a redheaded, green-eyed vision appeared.

Jeremy swallowed hard. "Maggie?"

Her wrinkled brow and slight frown pulled all his emotion to the surface. The pain and anger. The grief and frustration. Energy bolted from his body and he slumped back in the chair.

She moved behind him and placed her face next to his. "We'll find him."

He pulled his lips into his mouth, sniffled, and shook his head. "He's gone, Maggie."

CHAPTER SIXTY-SEVEN

"You're sure that's all?" Mason asked. "He didn't say anything else?"

Paula refilled his sweet tea and topped the drink off with a fresh lemon wedge. "Honey, we've been through this several times already. I told you everything. He was FBI. Asked a few questions about that cop and left. That's it."

He bit into his BLT, heavy on the B and mayo, then brushed a napkin across his lips. "Jeremy Winter, huh?"

"Yeah. Seemed to be in a hurry. He knows something's up, just doesn't know what, I think."

"You still got the cop's phone?"

"In the bedroom gun safe."

"Grab it for me, would you?"

Mason's sandwich was gone by the time she returned and handed him Troy's cell.

"Can't believe a police officer didn't have a password on his phone. Guess he figured nobody'd mess with him," he said.

"Lucky for us though."

"Maybe. But at least when they go looking for him, the last place his phone was won't be here."

"And you're positive you popped the battery out at the high school before you came home?"

He turned the cell over in his hand and nodded. "Yep. Best get rid of the thing, I suppose. If they come back here looking, don't need them to find that."

Paula chuckled. "Honey, if they come back here with a search warrant, there are a whole lot worse things they could find."

Mason stared out the kitchen window. Acres and acres of farmland. The story of a family. "I don't want to lose it, Paula. Can't."

She moved behind him, wrapped her arms around his chest, and bent to his ear. "Never. This is the Miller farm. Always has been. Always will be. We have a plan, remember? I just wish there was a way to test it beforehand."

He dabbed at the bacon crumbs on his plate, then sipped the last of his tea. "Might could on a smaller scale, but it'd be hard to do without someone noticing. It'll work. I've triple-checked everything."

She straightened and patted his back. "Then we've done all we can do. Now then, you plan to sit here all day or you gonna get your chores done? I swear, I never thought I'd marry such a lazy man."

Mason rubbed his stomach. "Lazy? Feed a man a meal like that, what do you expect? All I can do to keep my eyes open."

"Uh-huh. Best get on out of here then before I start giving you some jobs around the house. Got a list of stuff needs doing."

He raised his hands in surrender. "I'm going, I'm going. Got a lot of work to do in the barn. Those new beetles came in and I reckon they're hungry for their lunch too."

"Everything ready for the pumpkin patch tonight?"

"Near enough. I'll have the boys go through the maze again when they get home from school. Changed the batteries in the flashlights yesterday, so they'll be good for another day or so. Thursdays are always slow anyway. Tomorrow and Saturday will be the big days. Last weekend before Halloween. All sorts of ghosts and goblins be about, I reckon."

Paula planted her hands on her hips. "Uh-huh. And when it's over, I expect we'll be planning that vacation?"

Mason pulled his ball cap down low. "Yes, ma'am. Oh, and I'm thinking about heading over to the search area. Maybe volunteer later this afternoon."

"You sure that's a good idea?"

"Haven't been there yet. Don't want anyone to think I don't care. Might even pick up some information. You never know."

"If you go, hang back with the others. Don't act too nosy. They say on those TV shows that the police watch the crowd. The suspect always returns to the scene of the crime. Can't stay away."

"Well, good luck to them then. Been a good hundred and fifty folks there on most days. Oftentimes a lot more. That's what I love about living here. People pretty much stay to themselves unless somebody needs help. Then we all pitch in. That's what neighbors do."

She wiped the table with a dishtowel. "Just be careful. Don't ask any questions. That's how they get you."

He winked. "It is? Good to know you've got it handled."

She shook the rag at him. "Go on now before I have you mopping this floor. I swear, you'd think pigs ate lunch here today."

CHAPTER SIXTY-EIGHT

"Still no request for assistance from the local PD?" Maggie asked. Jeremy scanned his list of emails. "Nope, but would it matter? We're not backing off it. They're investigating, and we'll share anything we learn. If they ask the Bureau to come in, well, we're ahead of the game, right? Oh, and have I said how glad I am you're here?"

Maggie rolled her eyes and glanced at her watch. "Not for about ten minutes. But don't stop."

"Never. Now you know everything I do about missing persons, Lanny Palmer, and Troy Obion. Thoughts?"

She tapped her finger against her bottom lip. "I don't know, Jeremy. When you lay it all out like that, it's not hard to imagine there's some connection. But I could easily see the opposite as well. There's no physical evidence connecting any of these cases."

He held out his hands, both palms up. "So ..."

"So we go with your instinct. But how does that help us? Where do we focus?"

Jeremy licked his lips and planted his elbows on the desk. "We focus on Troy. Best physical evidence we've got so far. We find the crime scene and go from there."

"And we do that how? You've already retraced what we know of his day. Cell phone's turned off or dead so can't track that. If you've got any—"

Of course. "His cell phone."

"Yeah?"

"When I first met Troy at Catherine Mae Blackston's house, he told me something. Said he always took photos with his phone any time he did an investigation. Didn't matter what it was. Said the pictures helped keep everything fresh in his mind."

"Don't see how that's very helpful without having the cell."

Jeremy traced his finger across the desk. "Auto backup. All of his photos were automatically saved online. He could look at them from any computer. And if he could look at them—"

"We can too. Do you know the website?"

He shook his head. "Can't imagine it'd be that hard to find, though. Maybe he had an app or something that did it for him. We figure that out, and we're halfway there."

Maggie pulled her phone from her jacket pocket, tapped a few buttons, and passed it to Jeremy. "Pictures of Rebecca," she said. "Lots of them."

Jeremy's heart fluttered. "I could look at her all day, Maggie."

"Let me have the phone." She scrolled through a couple of apps and looked up. "Check your email on your laptop."

He found the message, opened it, and clicked a link. Photos of Rebecca filled his screen.

She studied her phone for a moment. "I think it's built into the operating system. Pictures back up to a Google site. The whole setup's password protected, and I honestly never even think about it. Here's the thing though—mine only backs them up when I'm connected to Wi-Fi. Saves on data usage."

"Then maybe Troy's backed up to Google too. We just need his password."

Maggie nodded. "And hope he didn't set his options so it only worked when he was connected to Wi-Fi."

"I've got to believe he didn't, Maggie."

"What makes you so sure?"

He folded his hands together. "I've got no choice."

. . . .

The crowd at the search area milled about waiting for the afternoon update and instructions. Several TV station vans sat clustered to the side, their cameras and reporters ready. A field full of pickup trucks, four-wheelers, and towed fishing boats grew by the hour. Most people wore the same attire as yesterday and the day before. Camo or jeans. Decent weather to be outside. Full sun and gusty winds. Weeks since the last rain or even a heavy dew. The briefing would include another warning from the TBI. Be careful with discarded cigarettes. We don't want grass fires making the search that much harder.

"How long until we hear back on the warrant?" Jeremy forced himself to keep his eyes scanning the crowd. Hard to do with Maggie standing beside him.

She'd changed out of her business suit to jeans, hiking boots, and a sweatshirt. Her identification and Glock were attached to her belt, and a black ball cap with gold "FBI" was pulled low. He'd noticed several men cast glances her way and he sidled closer. No sense letting anyone get any ideas.

"It takes however long it takes," she said. "Troy's phone uploaded his files to a folder on Google's servers. The warrant's issued, but Google said it could be up to two days, not that it necessarily would."

He pulled up the sleeves on his bright orange sweatshirt. "Sun's getting hot."

She glanced at him and grinned. "Planning on doing some hunting? The space station can probably spot you with that thing on."

"What? University of Tennessee. Go big orange. Or something like that."

"Uh, yeah. Looks great on you. Really."

The squeaky whine of a microphone's feedback echoed across the crowd as a TBI agent climbed into the back of a pickup truck and gestured for quiet.

"Good afternoon," he said. "We appreciate you coming out again. I can't emphasize enough how important your help is, not only to us, but to the Palmer family too. We're going to move the search area a bit farther west today. Team captains already have the grids. I assume most of you have been here before and are familiar with the process. If today's your first day, please check in at that white tent over there. The ground's still dry, so no problem with the four-wheelers going out, but watch the cigarettes. And remember, this isn't a race. Speed still kills. Take your time. Look everywhere. That single piece of evidence you find could be what gets Lanny back to us. Now, before we go out, let's ask for some help."

He handed the microphone to an older looking guy in faded jeans and a striped sweater. After clearing his throat, the man began to pray. Jeremy took a moment to glance around. Hats off, heads bowed. A few looked around but kept respectfully silent. Something brushed his hand, and he looked down as Maggie slipped her fingers between his and squeezed.

When the prayer ended, another man stepped forward, his arm around a woman's waist. Both appeared exhausted. Their clothes looked like they'd been slept in, and dark bags drooped under their eyes. Had to be the boy's parents.

The man took the microphone and stared at the crowd for a moment before speaking. "Lanny never hurt nobody. I know he wouldn't just run off. Fourteen years old. Just a boy. If someone took him, if they hurt him ..." He tried to say more but choked up, then dropped his hands to his side. The woman slipped her arm through his and took the mic from him.

"Y'all can't understand," she said, "what it means to see you out here helping look for Lanny." Her shoulders slumped, and she dabbed her eyes. "We appreciate it more than you'll ever know. We just want our boy back home. If anyone knows anything, if you're watching this, Lanny, please just come home."

She buried her head in her husband's chest, and her sobs echoed through the speakers. The preacher stepped close and wrapped his arms around the couple.

Jeremy closed his eyes. All around him, people were sniffling or outright crying. The family must be in agony. He understood what it was like to have people taken from you. Wife, daughter, friend. None deserved their fate. All deserved justice. Vengeance is mine, saith the Lord. He'd heard it many times. Might even be in the Bible somewhere. But sometimes vengeance is too slow. And when it is—

"Ow!" Maggie yanked her hand away.

Jeremy looked over the crowd. Could be that Troy's killer was here. If so, he'd better be praying for a miracle. Praying hard.

He'd need one.

CHAPTER SIXTY-NINE

Mason stood with a group of men from his church. They'd been assigned an area down along Epperson Creek, far from the abduction and murder site. Not that any of them knew that, of course. It'd be a boring afternoon, but you do what you have to do.

The pastor from the Friendship Community Church was praying now. Something something protect us. Something something Jesus.

Few people looking around. Not very reverent. At least they had the sense to keep quiet till the prayer was over.

Huh. Cute redhead in the black FBI cap. Haven't seen her around. Would've remembered. How sweet. Holding hands with her boyfriend. Seen him somewhere. Could be the agent that came by the farm. Right size and build.

Grant us peace and favor and something something Lanny safely. Amen.

Mason replaced his ball cap and moved toward the portable toilets. "Be right back. Gotta take care of some business before we head out."

The crowd moved off in dozens of directions, creating a traffic jam of bodies weaving through the field. Heads nodded as folks recognized each other. A low murmur flowed through as if everyone was afraid to speak too loudly. The mood was serious. Mason knew what they were feeling.

Most every man there, and the majority of women too, were hunters. Brought up on it from the time they could walk. This afternoon was a new opening day to the season. Confidence and hope that they'd bag their quarry. Locate something—anything that could bring this chaos to a close and let the community return to normal.

Rumors were out about a missing policeman. Anger and frustration was building. Fear had seeped into their little corner of the world, and no one was happy about it. Mason guessed that three-quarters of the people were armed and wouldn't have been surprised if the number was higher. Carry permit or not didn't matter. One way or another, these folks were going to put an end to it.

A flicker of red in the sea of camo caught his eye, and he spotted Miss FBI again. The redhead's boots looked almost new. Hope she doesn't get any blisters. I'm sure her boyfriend there will help her out.

The man glanced up and caught Mason looking his way. Had to be the same guy who talked to Paula. Sunglasses hid his eyes, but his face left no doubt. Wrinkled brow, lips pressed together and turned down at the corners. The man was working, scanning the crowd. And he was angry. So be it.

Mason offered a polite nod and half-smile before stepping into the rankness of the portable toilet. Take care of business here then maybe introduce myself. Apologize for not being there when he came by the farm. Give him a chance to ask a few questions on neutral ground.

Mason stepped outside and looked around. No sign of red hair and none of the half dozen orange sweatshirts marked Mister FBI. Oh well. Maybe next time.

He picked up the pace and hustled to rejoin his church group. Such a pleasant day for a snipe hunt.

CHAPTER SEVENTY

"Told ya," Maggie said. "Just got to have a little faith." She scooted her chair closer to Jeremy to get a better view of his laptop's screen.

He angled the computer on his desk and leaned toward her until their shoulders touched. "Exactly what I've got. A little faith, although I'll admit that three hours has to be some sort of record for a company to provide access to online data."

Jeremy typed the Google-given password and watched as photo after photo loaded. The pictures seemed to be in reverse chronological order. A large, older brick building. The county high school. No people in the photo but plenty of cars. A cornfield. Some Halloween decorations. Paula Miller and a man who was probably her husband. An oversize Blizzard in the cup holder of the Jeep, likely a combination of Reese's and M&Ms knowing Troy. The Dairy Queen manager and his store. Dozens of other pics of trees, streams, and people, all presumably in the search area.

"Troy likes to take pictures, I guess," Maggie said.

"Know anybody his age who doesn't use their smartphone constantly? At least he's not snapping selfies and photos of his dinner every night."

"Other than the ice cream, you mean."

Jeremy smiled. "He does—did love his Blizzards. Based on these, looks like the high school was his last stop. That's within the range of the last cell tower that picked him up. The time stamp says he was there at 11:03. Maybe he talked to someone."

Maggie rubbed her hands together. "You keep assuming he's already dead."

"You don't? I saw the Jeep. The DNA's a match."

"Yeah, on a blood drop. Nothing else yet. People can survive bullet wounds. Happens all the time."

Jeremy shook his head. "Can't do it, Maggie. Can't get my hopes up. Possible bone and brain matter there too. I've seen enough to know you don't live through something like that. If I allowed myself to think, even for a second, that Troy's still alive, I'm not sure I could take it when we find out the truth."

"Then I'll hope for the both of us."

How does she stay optimistic in spite of the statistics? Not naïveté. More like innocence that won't fade. Had he ever been like that? No. Of course not. At least not since Holly and Miranda. "Do that, Maggie. I say we start at the high school and work our way backwards."

"You're the boss."

"Sure. You say that now."

"Well, of course. There's no one else around to hear me. It's all about plausible deniability."

....

Jeremy switched his view between the photos and reality. "This looks about right. Troy took the picture somewhere in this area. Recognize any of the vehicles?"

The high school's parking lot was full of cars, and in another ten minutes, classes would be letting out for the day. No sign of security cameras on the side of the building. Not likely this was the crime scene. Too public. But it was possible someone had spotted the Jeep. If nothing else, it was more than they had.

Maggie scanned the printed photo and pointed out a few cars that matched the picture. "Assuming Troy came straight to the school after leaving the farm, he'd have been here around lunch time. A bunch of the seniors probably leave then to go get something to eat. Maybe Troy talked to one of them."

Jeremy scrunched his mouth to the side. "Law enforcement's been keeping a pretty tight watch over this place since Palmer disappeared. His friends all swear they don't know anything. Troy told me he saw the police reports. Separate interviews all telling the same story. Nobody knows what happened."

"It's funny. You watch this stuff on TV, and it's the same thing. The police always say somebody knows something. We just need them to come forward. Tell us what they know." She sighed and frowned. "Too bad that's not always true."

"If Troy's death—"

"Disappearance."

"If Troy's disappearance is related to the same guy who's grabbing people from parks, fact is that probably no one knows except the murderer himself. And unless he gets drunk enough or high enough or boastful enough to tell someone, nobody will know until we catch him. Truth is, the hard part of the investigation is already over, at least in my mind."

"And that is?"

"Figuring out the killer exists. Random murders and disappearances in multiple states. If Randy Clarke hadn't called me about his missing ex, I'd have no idea this guy was out there."

"I don't get it. No real evidence your serial killer exists, yet you're convinced he does. No real evidence Troy's dead, but you're certain he is. What's the difference? I mean, if the lab confirms brain matter with his DNA, then okay. But until then ..."

He tilted his face upward. "I don't know. Experience? Fear? A hunch? You tell me. All I know is we've got to keep moving forward. Find this guy before anyone else dies. We're close, and he knows it."

"And when we get him?"

"We do whatever it takes to make sure he stops."

"And after that?"

"I'm out. Done. No longer a public servant. Moving back east where my girls are. And where I'll be free to, um, do something I should've been done a long time ago. Put it to rest."

She moved so she faced him and stared, her eyes narrow. "You're going after him, aren't you? Whoever killed your wife. That's why you're okay with leaving the Bureau. This whole thing with Cronfeld is just a convenient excuse."

Jeremy brushed an eyelash from her cheek. "And daughter. He killed my wife and daughter. And I swear, Maggie. This was never my plan. Never. But I keep thinking about them. How I've spent my whole career chasing these murderers. And since Troy disappeared, it's gotten worse. We'll find whoever killed him. He deserves that. But it's not right. My wife and kid stuck in a cold case file somewhere. If I don't look ..."

She moved closer and clasped her hands in front of her chest. "Honey,

I understand that. I do. I'd feel the same way. I won't try to tell you what to do. I just want to make sure it doesn't, um, it doesn't ..."

He pulled her into a tight hug and scratched his hand along her back. "It doesn't, and it won't. We're together. You, me, Rebecca. It's what I want more than anything."

Maggie nuzzled under his chin. "And when you catch him?"

"We all have a price to pay. An eye for an eye and all that stuff."

"Be careful, Jeremy. Don't let the anger win."

Why not? Anger wasn't always a bad thing, right? Not when good things came of it. He stared at the clouds meandering across a crystal blue sky. The problem was figuring out if the good outweighed the bad. Or maybe more accurately, deciding if killing the past was worth jeopardizing the future. His friend dead. His wife and unborn daughter brutally taken. No justice, at least not yet. Both killers free to live their lives, never having paid the price for their sins. That had to change. Had to.

He told himself he should hate the thoughts that came. That justice comes from the legal system, not him. That the desperate rapture he'd felt when deciding he could kill the Afghani wasn't real. That the guilt and remorse would be far worse than anything he felt now.

He should hate the thoughts that came.

He couldn't.

....

A few students trickled out of the school a minute or two early and then the floodgates opened. A mass of people dispersed in the parking lot accompanied by yelling, waving, and honking horns. Maggie stood near two of the target vehicles with Jeremy a couple of rows over. As the kids neared their cars, each FBI agent held up a photo of Troy and his Jeep and asked questions. Curious students gathered around, shook their heads, and moved off to their cars.

Within six minutes, the parking lot was empty except for a few vehicles still in the teachers' area. Jeremy motioned for Maggie, and they strolled over.

"Any luck?" she asked.

"None. You?"

"No. Most of the boys said that if they'd seen it, they'd remember. Big Jeep, nice tires, winches on front and back. Perfect for, um, I believe 'muddin' was the word they used."

"I got the same response. One kid said to tell the dude to get in touch with him if he wanted to sell the Jeep."

Maggie shivered as a hard gust swept over the parking lot. "I don't know, Jeremy. Doesn't seem like we're making any headway here. Somebody should've seen him or his vehicle if he spent any time here."

"Yeah, so maybe he didn't. Quick drive through the parking lot and then on to wherever. Don't think so, though. Why come here just to snap a photo? Doesn't make any sense."

"Let's check in the office. If this is like every other school I know of, visitors should sign in. If Troy did go inside, we should see his name on the log."

Less than five minutes later, the two sat in Jeremy's car pondering their next move.

"One photo," Maggie said. "Never went inside the school, and no one saw him or the Jeep."

"And no broken glass in the area where the picture was taken. Can't imagine this is the crime scene. Send his photos to the Bureau and have them take a look. See if there's anything we missed."

She tapped her phone and forwarded the encrypted information to the Memphis FBI crime lab. "Got it. Where did he go from here?"

Jeremy shook his head and started the car. "No idea, but I do know where he came from."

"Back to the farm?"

"Yeah. Back to the farm."

CHAPTER SEVENTY-ONE

A lackluster sun and gray cloudless sky welcomed Jeremy and Maggie to the parking area in front of the Masons' home. Several vehicles clustered around three school busses. A few families milled about, picking over the few melons that remained. Staked crookedly in the ground, a handwritten sign announced all pumpkins were now only a dollar.

The revving of ATV engines attracted the agents, and they moved behind the house. Off to the left a bit, near what he assumed was the exit to the corn maze, Jeremy spotted Paula near a wooden concession stand. A couple of four-wheelers headed into the maze, probably the family's kids getting everything ready.

A cluster of nearly a dozen teenagers gathered around a table near the house, each of them busily applying zombie makeup. With the wind gusting and spooky sounds filtering through speakers in the yard, it'd be a perfect night for a haunted field. Already, the agents could hear shrieks and screams from kids wandering through the maze.

Maggie nodded toward Paula. "That her?"

"Yeah. She wasn't much help. We need to talk to her husband. Find out what he knows. Maybe their stories will be different."

"Wishful thinking, I imagine. Even if one of them does know something, they've had plenty of time to get their stories straight."

The sound of crunching gravel came from behind, and the agents turned to see a pickup truck pulling into the driveway and stopping beside the house. A man stepped out, waved toward the families in the pumpkin patch, and walked inside.

"Got to be the husband," Maggie said. "How do you want to handle this? Both of us with him, or me chatting up Paula?"

"You talk to her. Even if you don't learn anything new, at least she'll be distracted. I'd rather talk to her husband alone."

"You got it. Take your time. If that stand's got any hot apple cider, I'll be fine."

He glanced around before bending down and kissing her. "Be there quick as I can. Save some cider for me."

She brushed her hand casually against his. "No promises."

His chest and stomach filled with the same momentary weightlessness he got when speeding over a hill on a high-speed chase. "Uh-huh. I've got the car keys, remember? No cider, no ride back to the hotel."

She laughed and moved toward the concession stand, flicking her hand in a backward wave.

Jeremy climbed the steps to the deck, knocked on the screen door, and stepped back to wait for an answer. Training had taught him that standing too close to a door that opened his direction could be a very bad decision. One quick shove from inside the house and he'd be flat on his back. A shadow moved behind the curtains, and Jeremy tapped the butt of his holstered Glock with his palm. The interior door opened, and a man dressed in jeans and a white T-shirt greeted him.

"Can I help you?"

Jeremy showed his identification. "Yes, sir. Jeremy Winter with the FBI. You Mister Miller?"

The man chuckled and gestured toward the concession stand. "Well, if I wasn't, I reckon that woman over there'd sure enough run me off right quick."

"Yes, sir. Mind if I ask you a few questions?"

Mason swung the screen door open. "Want to come inside? I was just about to jump in the shower, but I can hold off for a few minutes. Been out looking for Lanny all afternoon."

"I understand. This won't take long. Any news on the Palmer boy?"

Mason arched his eyebrows. "Well, I figured you'd know before I would."

"I'm actually not working on that case."

Mason gestured into the house. "In or out. Can't stand here with the door open. It may be October, but we haven't had a hard freeze yet, and dry as it's been, still plenty of flies and the like around."

Jeremy entered the home and stood in the kitchen. Blue-checkered curtains framed a window over the sink that looked into the backyard. On the gas stove, a cast iron skillet sat ready for its next use. The refrigerator had a few photos and a calendar from the local pharmacy. Off to the left, a table and four chairs nestled beside a bay window.

"Something to drink?" Mason asked.

"I'm fine, thanks."

"Suit yourself then. Now, if you're not looking for Lanny, what *are* you doing?"

Jeremy moved away from the door and stood with his back to the refrigerator. "Actually, I'm looking for a friend of mine. Troy Obion."

Mason's eyes widened. "That police officer? He didn't turn up yet? Paula told me y'all came looking for him."

"No, sir. He hasn't checked in anywhere. Not answering his phone either."

"Hope he's okay. Pretty big guy, though. I imagine he can take care of himself."

"Uh-huh. So you spoke to him when he was here, correct?"

"I did. He was asking about the Palmer kid, of course. Lanny worked here when the maze first opened this year. Like I told that officer, I had to let the boy go. Got too close to some of the kids. We've got a strict hands-off policy for everyone's protection."

"Anything else?"

Mason slowly shook his head. "Not that I recall. I mean, all he wanted to know about was Lanny. I told him the same thing I told you. He hung around for a few minutes then headed off."

"Any idea where he went?"

Mason scratched his forehead. "None. Last I saw of him, he got in that big red Jeep of his and took off."

"You said he hung around for a few minutes. Doing what?"

Mason glanced out the screen door. "He, uh, wanted to see where Lanny worked. In the corn maze."

"And you showed him?"

"Yeah. It's not far in there. Took him in and left. Had to get back to work. Busy time of year as you can imagine."

"I can. How long would you say he was in there?"

Mason shrugged. "Maybe fifteen, twenty minutes? Something like that. I kind of kept an eye out for him. Easy to get lost in there, but that's the whole point, isn't it?"

"Mind if I take a look in the maze?"

"Suit yourself. Got to warn you though—there's a passel of kids from the elementary school out there. Reckon you probably heard them. Might be a little chaotic, and it's going to get a whole lot more crowded here before long. But I can have one of the boys take you if you'd like. Honestly though, you'd have the place to yourself in the morning if you'd rather. Be able to see better too. Either way."

"You get that many people out here on a Thursday night?"

"This close to Halloween we do. Take a look around the county. See much going on? Folks get a chance to do something different, 'specially kids, doesn't really matter what night of the week it is. And with all this mess with Lanny, well, people need something to take their minds off the situation. Even if it's only for a little while."

Jeremy extended his hand. "Thank you for your time, Mister Miller. If you don't mind, I think I'll take you up on your offer and stop by in the morning."

Mason shook hands and locked eyes. "Looking forward to it. Before you leave, be sure and stop by Paula's stand out there. Get you something warm to drink. On the house."

"I'll do that. Until tomorrow then."

Jeremy left the house and strolled toward Maggie and Paula. Mason Miller had seemed genuine. A good neighbor who wanted to help. A family man. An asset to the community.

All of which meant exactly nothing. A shudder shot across Jeremy's shoulders. He resisted the urge to look back at the house. No need. He knew what he'd see.

Mason Miller, standing at the screen door, staring.

CHAPTER SEVENTY-TWO

Maggie smiled at Jeremy as she filled her glass with apple juice. The hotel's breakfast buffet wasn't going to win any gastronomical awards. "Sleep well?"

He gestured toward his coffee cup. "On my third dose. Not helping."

She sat across from him and poked at her plate of fruit. "Think this is fresh?"

"Sure it is. Saw them open the can myself."

"Good enough for me. Talked to Rebecca this morning. She said to tell you hi and she wants you to come over soon."

For the briefest of heartbeats, Jeremy's frustration faded, and he grinned in spite of himself. "Can't wait."

"What's the plan?"

Good question. "Already made a few calls. Nothing shook loose last night on Palmer or Troy. I'm going back to the Miller place. Get a closer look at the maze."

"Want me to go with you?"

"Might be better if we split up. Cover more territory that way. You check out his Jeep. See if the lab's found anything helpful. Make sure you keep in touch, and don't wander off alone anywhere. I'll talk to Miller and have him retrace Troy's path through the maze."

"Got a hunch?"

Jeremy sighed and stared into his cold coffee. "Got nothing. No time. No clue. And not much hope. Yesterday I was so sure we'd find something at the school or farm."

Maggie scooted her chair closer. "You've got me. Don't forget that."

He placed his hand on hers. "Never."

"You sure Miller wasn't hiding anything? Putting you off until today?"

He pushed his coffee away and worked at spreading frozen butter on an untoasted bagel. "Am I sure? No. But if he's hiding something, he's good at it. Didn't seem evasive. I'm pretty sure he stared a hole in my back as I was leaving, but that seems to be the norm around these small towns. Don't get me wrong. They're friendly enough, but you're either born here or you're not. And if you're not, well, Godspeed and don't let the door hit you on the way out."

"Hang in there. We give it our best and move on. Either that or sink into the pit. Start wondering that if maybe we'd done something different ..."

"I've been there and don't want to go back. Be nice if just this once we got the happy ending. The one where I find Troy still alive. The one where Lanny Palmer walks back in his front door and hugs his parents. Not gonna happen."

She sighed and brushed the back of her hand across his cheek. "Maybe not, but that doesn't mean we can't push forward. What you do is important. The problem is, you only get to see the victims, not the people you saved. The ones who are still alive because you stopped a killer."

"Where does this end? Do the best I can and be happy? Not sure I can do that this time. Too personal, you know?"

"Yeah, I do. I can't imagine the pain you've gone through. Afghanistan, your family, Troy. But don't let it take away who you are. Who we love."

He stretched, letting his left arm drag down her back. "Enough of the gloom and doom. I say we—"

"Mind if I join you?"

Jeremy's knife clattered to the table. "Colonel Cronfeld."

The man dragged a chair over, the scent of cigarettes enveloping him. "And a hearty good morning to both of you as well. Miss Keeley, I don't believe I've had the pleasure."

Maggie kept her expression neutral. "What can we do for you, Colonel?"

"You can talk some sense into your boyfriend here."

"He's more than capable of making his own decisions, and not that it matters, but I fully support him in this."

Cronfeld shook his head. "You two just don't get it, do you? I'm offering you a chance to punch your own ticket. All I want in return is assurance that you'll keep doing what you've done all along."

Maggie pushed her plate away. "A deal with the Devil, huh?"

The colonel tilted his head and raised an eyebrow. "Look, I know you don't care for me. I won't insult you by pretending I have only your interests in mind. This is obviously important to me, and if I can help you two out in the process, why not?"

Jeremy stood and extended his hand to Maggie. "Let's get to work. And Colonel, please give my best to your wife."

Cronfeld slid Maggie's fruit in front of him and used her fork to take a bite. "Agent Winter, I'm afraid that, once again, you've misread the situation rather badly. There are no secrets between my wife and myself. I know all about your clumsy attempt to turn her against me. Really now. Threatening to go public unless I back off? You've watched too many movies."

Jeremy leaned close to Cronfeld. "Interesting. Is that what she told you our meeting was about? Now, I'm going out to find the person who killed my friend. Somewhere in all the research you did on me, I'm sure someone mentioned I might have a problem with anger management. Let me assure you, Colonel, that I don't consider it a problem. In fact, anger's one of my better qualities. We're done. Understood?"

Cronfeld removed his glasses and cleaned them with a napkin. "Perhaps now's not the best time, but we will resolve this issue to my satisfaction. If not today, then next week or next month or next year. But rest assured, we will settle this."

"It's already settled. You just don't know it yet."

The colonel took another bite of fruit from Maggie's plate. "And I could say the same. Tell you what. You wrap up your investigation here, then we'll talk again."

"We have nothing else to discuss."

Cronfeld smiled at Maggie. "Please, dear, give that sweet daughter of yours a hug from me when you see her. Rebecca, is it? I can see where she got her good looks."

Jeremy slammed his fist on the table, sending pieces of fruit flying into Cronfeld's lap. "They're not part of this."

The colonel stood and brushed a peach tidbit from his slacks. "Really, Agent Winter. You should see someone about that temper of yours. Now, we all have a busy schedule so I'll be on my way. We'll talk later, though. Give it a week or two. Let the emotion of your friend's disappearance fade. I'll be in touch."

"Don't bother."

Cronfeld used another napkin to wipe fruit juice off his shoe. "Oh, it's no bother. Miss Keeley. A pleasure. I do hope we can meet again under more pleasant circumstances."

Maggie's lips formed a thin line. "The Bureau doesn't know about *my* anger issues, Colonel. But my ex-husband does. Look him up. Ask to see the x-rays. And stay away from my family."

The man winked at Jeremy. "Quite the feisty one, isn't she? I guess what they say about redheads is true. Mother *and* daughter."

Jeremy moved toward the colonel, stopping inches away. "I lost everything once. I won't let it happen again."

Maggie grabbed his arm and eased him backward. "Let's get to work, Jeremy. We'll deal with this vermin later."

Cronfeld laughed. "Really, there's no need for name-calling, is there? I truly hope you find the person who killed your friend. And when you do, we'll talk. Good day to you both."

The couple watched until the colonel was out of their sight.

"Now then," Jeremy said. "I'm not sure I know the story about your ex. Something about your anger and his x-rays?"

She wrapped her arm around his. "Self-defense."

"I'm going to guess it only happened once."

"My ex is many things, but stupid isn't one of them. He's a fast learner. Slow healer, though. Had to sign the divorce papers with his left hand."

He kissed the top of her head. "Remind me to stay on your good side."

She squeezed his arm. "Not too worried about that. Still, I'm pretty sure I could take you if I needed to."

He chuckled and poked her side. "Yeah, I am too."

CHAPTER SEVENTY-THREE

Jeremy drove past the parking area and pulled next to the Miller house. The sun shone low in the sky and bounced off the light frost covering the brown lawn. Smoky whispers of steam drifted from the ground and faded to oblivion. He opened his laptop and pulled up the satellite image of the farm to orient himself, then stepped outside.

He slammed his car door, hoping to get the attention of anyone around. These days, being a stranger on private property could get you killed. A greeting echoed from somewhere behind the house, and Jeremy zipped up his black windbreaker before heading that way.

Mason Miller stood near a woodpile, tossing a few pieces into a wheelbarrow. "Mornin'. Just got to get the fireplace going and then I'll be ready. Looks like it's gonna be a warm day, but got to get the chill out of the house. Keep the wife happy. Get you some coffee?"

"No thanks. Already hit my limit for the day. Can I give you a hand with that?"

"Thanks, but I've got it. The boys were supposed to take care of this before school today, but that didn't happen. I imagine we'll be having a discussion about their chores when they get home."

"Got to raise them right."

Mason paused and stared at the FBI agent. "That's true. You do. The preacher says to train them up in the way they should go, and when they get old, they won't depart from it."

Maybe, but he'd seen plenty of kids deviate from their upbringing, much to the chagrin of their parents. He waited as Miller toted the firewood inside and quickly returned.

"Ready?" Mason asked.

"Yes, sir. If you could just show me what you showed Officer Obion,

I'll be out of your way as soon as I can. I know you've got a busy day ahead."

Mason chuckled. "I'm three hours into the day. Slept in this morning, but don't tell nobody. Last Friday before Halloween, they'll be swarming all over this place today, especially once the sun sets. Be lucky to survive the night."

"Pays the bills though, right?"

"Eh, it helps. By the time you back out all our costs, we're sure not getting rich. But folks like coming out here, and we enjoy putting it together for everyone. That's good enough."

They continued in silence until arriving at the maze. Jeremy used his phone to snap a few pictures of the area before motioning for Mason to lead the way.

"Your buddy asked how we set this all up," the farmer said. "Double-planted, crisscrossed. Get the plans off the Internet. Not too hard after the first time, and we keep making it bigger. Decided to do a clown's face this year. Next Halloween, who knows?"

Jeremy walked on without responding. Occasionally, he'd stop to take a picture of the paths, cornstalks, or decorations. Nothing.

Mason removed his ball cap and ran the back of his arm across his forehead. "Warming up."

"Uh-huh."

They turned a corner in the path, and Jeremy slowed to study the decoration. A skeleton, definitely one from Troy's photos based on the attire. Jacket, khakis, pipe. Why the interest in it?

"Lanny's work area is just up here a little ways," Mason said.

Jeremy moved closer to the skeleton. "Give me a minute."

"Get 'em online mostly. Tried using some of the cheaper ones from Walmart, but they're not heavy enough to hold up in the weather."

The skull was clearly heavy-duty plastic. Generic and no match for the found jawbone. No surprise. Serial killers didn't leave their trophies out in the open. "Bet this looks good at night, all lit up in the dark."

"That's what the folks want to see. Always surprises me that people pay me to scare them, 'specially the kids. Listen, I don't mean to rush you, but I've got a big day ahead of me, and like I said, got kind of a late start. So maybe we could—"

Jeremy snapped a few photos of the area and pointed to the skeleton.

"Oh, sorry. Just one more. Quick selfie with this guy if you don't mind. Something to send to a little girl I know. She'll love it."

"Of course. Daughter?"

Jeremy stood by the decorations and stretched his arm, turning the camera until he got the image he wanted. A couple of quick snaps, and he placed his phone back in his pocket. "No, at least not yet. Not married."

They walked farther into the maze. "Got plans though, huh? That redheaded FBI agent? Lucky man."

Jeremy glanced at the farmer.

"Oh, sorry. Paula told me about her. Saw you two kiss last night and assumed ..."

"Yeah."

They came to another skeleton, this one dressed as an old woman.

"Want to stop here?" Mason asked.

"No, thanks. Just show me where Lanny worked, and I'll get out of your way."

"Okay then. Right up around this next corner."

A few dozen steps later, Jeremy stood in a small opening cut back into the corn. A few hay bales stacked on each other. Couple of pumpkins. Wooden box behind the hay with spare flashlights. A bunch of nothing.

"This is it," Mason said. "He'd hang out here or move up and down the paths a little. Jump out and scare folks, then slip back into position and wait for the next group."

"Did Officer Obion have any questions about the maze? Anything unusual?"

"Nope. Nothing out of the ordinary. Fact is, there's not a lot to it. A few decorations stuck in some trails surrounded by corn. Throw a bunch of dead ends in the mix, and you've got all you need."

"And no idea where the officer went when he left here?"

Mason shook his head. "Sorry."

"Okay. Lead me out of here, and I'll get out of your way. I really appreciate all your help."

"Glad to do it. Just hope you find your friend soon. Lanny too. This is usually a quiet community, and we'd sure like to get back to that."

The men exited the maze and strolled toward the house.

"Best of luck to you," Mason said.

"Thanks. Hope you guys have a big turnout tonight."

"We will. Good weather, no moon, and date night for the high school boys. Gives their girlfriends an excuse to hold onto them."

Jeremy moved down the gravel driveway to his car. What am I missing? Did Troy suspect something here? Maybe ask Miller if it's okay to look around on my own. See how he reacts. Better yet, wait an hour or so, come back, and ask his wife. More likely she'd give permission.

He ran his hand along the side of Mason's old pickup truck as he walked past. Dented, rusted, and dirty. The sun was up, bouncing its glory off his windshield. He squinted and shielded his eyes before tossing his jacket into the passenger seat of his car and sliding behind the wheel.

What now? The high school would be a waste of time. The DQ, no better. Maybe go back to where they found the Jeep. Couldn't hurt. He reached to close his car door and froze. Amid the dull grayness of the gravel, a few specks shone brightly.

Glass.

He leaned down and picked up a few pieces, rolling the shards in his palm. Studying them. Hard to be sure but could be from a car window. Could be.

He pulled the door closed and peered toward the house. Mason Miller stood there. Watching.

Jeremy smiled and gave an unreturned half-wave. He backed his car in an arc, glanced at the special agriculture license plates on Miller's pickup, and drove toward the road.

A quick look in his rearview mirror told him all he needed to know.

The man still stood there. Arms crossed. Wide stance.

A spasm shot through Jeremy's left leg. He winced and gripped the steering wheel tighter. Momentary pain. A bare hint of the agony he would inflict on Mason Miller if—when—the evidence of his crimes was found.

The car bounced through a rut, and he reached over to keep his laptop from sliding onto the floor. The touchscreen flicked on, and he glanced at the image. A magnificent creature with a fluffy orange body accented with thin black stripes. Two long fat legs and two short skinny ones.

Rebecca's tiger.

CHAPTER SEVENTY-FOUR

"You can't be sure," Paula said.

Mason brushed back the living room curtains and stared out the front windows. "I'm as sure as I can be. I know what I saw. That FBI agent may not be positive, but he's suspicious enough."

"Based on what? Some broken glass in the driveway? Good Lord, honey. That's a stretch, don't you think?"

"His whole demeanor changed. I don't know. Maybe we missed something last night."

She shook her head. "No, we didn't. We followed the plan. Replaced every skull with the plastic backup. There's nothing out there that's incriminating."

"Except in the barn. He'll be back, and maybe not alone."

"Fine. If he comes back, we'll deal with the situation then. Take the next step in the plan if we have to. But worrying about it never solved anything."

He sank into the worn leather recliner and raised the footrest. "Not worried, Paula. We both figured it'd come to this eventually. I'm ready as I can be."

Her jaw jutted forward. "We could leave. Take the boys from school and just go."

He yawned and scratched his stomach. "Could you do that, baby?"

She sighed. "No more than you could. I'm not leaving the farm. It's who we are."

"Ashes to ashes. Dust to dust. No matter what happens, this is where I want to be. Understand?"

"I do."

"Fair enough then. If he comes back, you know your job?"

"I'll do what I've always done, Mason. Protect the farm and the family."

He stretched and leaned his recliner all the way back. "Got a big afternoon ahead. Moving the old tools to the new barn's gonna take a couple of hours. I believe I'm going to take a nap, long as you don't tell nobody. Don't want word getting around that I'm lazy."

Paula walked across the room and kissed his forehead. "Get some rest. I'll wake you if I need to."

Mason snuggled into the chair and closed his eyes. "Honey?"

"Yes, dear?"

"I'd like a BLT for lunch. Maybe even two of them."

"Extra bacon?"

He smiled, laid his hands on his belly, and drifted into a hard sleep.

CHAPTER SEVENTY-FIVE

Photographs covered the conference room table. Troy's Jeep. The corn maze. Skeletons. The high school. And Mason Miller.

Jeremy bent close to two of the pictures. "No question. They're different. The skulls in Troy's photos are not the ones I saw."

"That doesn't make sense," Maggie said. "Nobody would be stupid enough to put murder victims' skulls on display. Why would you risk it?"

"I'm not quite ready to make that jump yet, but I'm getting there. He probably doesn't see it as a risk. Said he's been doing the maze for years, and if no one's questioned anything before, why worry about it now?"

"But trophies are personal, right? Why share them?"

"Don't know. Remember though—the killer also took Sarah Goldman's hands. And Barry Thornquist's arm bones had cut marks. Could be he kept the hands as trophies. The skulls are just a bonus. His way of bragging to the world."

"It's thin. Maybe we should talk to the local cops. See if they've got any info on Miller that might enhance the theory."

Jeremy scratched his cheek and tapped a finger on one of Troy's photos. "Miller's got no criminal record, and I don't want word to get back to him that we're considering him a suspect. We need more. Something that'll get us a warrant. We just have to find it."

"If he's got the Palmer kid—"

"Then the boy's already dead."

She bit her bottom lip. "Kind of harsh, don't you think?"

He rubbed her arm. "Sorry. But we both know the statistics. And if Miller is a serial killer, another murder wouldn't mean much to him."

"I know. The way you said it, though, hit me kind of hard."

"I'm sorry, babe. Listen. We'll head back in a couple of hours. Two off-duty FBI agents out looking to relax on a Friday night. Check out the maze first. See if anything suspicious turns up. Then you chat with the wife. Maybe see if you can tie Miller to some of the locations of the victims. I'll dig around the rest of the public areas, and we'll end the evening with a hayride."

She picked up one of the photos. "Look at him. The way he's staring at you. I don't like it."

"Can't arrest a guy for looking at me. I told him I was taking a selfie to send to Rebecca. He's got no idea I took his picture."

She smiled. "I'm sorry. I never thought I'd hear you say you took a selfie. It's so ... not you."

"I feel like an idiot even saying it. Look at how Miller's standing."

"Left hand at his side, right hand in his jacket pocket, right foot slightly back. He's ready to go into a shooting stance. Think he's carrying?"

"You think he's not?"

"Doesn't prove anything either way. Permit or not, he's on his own property. And he didn't seem at all nervous?"

"Not a bit. Wasn't very talkative, but so what? Said he had a lot to do but didn't really seem to be in any huge hurry. And he didn't try to hide anything from me as near as I could tell."

"To recap, you've got a few photos that really don't prove anything, broken glass that the lab confirms probably came from a car window, and a license plate that's the same as a couple of hundred other vehicles in Miller's county alone. It's risky going there tonight, Jeremy. Friday before Halloween? They'll be packed."

"That's what I'm counting on. Miller will be distracted. Give me time to wander around on my own. If we find anything, we back off and surveil. Call in the info and get some support before we grab him. Maybe even hold off until tomorrow morning when everyone's gone."

"Can't do that. If Miller's the guy, he'll know about Troy and the Palmer kid. If there's a chance either of them are still alive, we can't wait."

Jeremy scooped the photos into a pile and slid them into a folder. "We'll make that call when the time comes. Let's grab some dinner before we go. Barbecue sound good? My treat."

She crinkled her nose. "Sounds kind of heavy, doesn't it?"

"Tell them you want slaw on top. Trust me on this. Oh, and bring your laptop."

"For what?"

"Thought we might Skype with a little girl I know. Help me get my head on straight before we go out to the Miller place. I mean, if it's okay with her mom."

She stood and scooped up her computer. "Slaw, huh? Sounds disgusting."

CHAPTER SEVENTY-SIX

"Guess your FBI friends aren't coming," Paula said.

Mason watched another group of teenagers enter the maze. "Not today at least. Getting dark and too many people around. Too risky."

"Maybe they're not coming at all."

They'll be here. He wrapped his arm around her waist. "Maybe."

"Just checked on Lucas out front. The parking area's full, and he's directing people into the field beside the house. Looks like it's going to be a record night."

"Where's Andy?"

"Got him helping out at the concession stand. Popcorn and candy bars only. He spills too many of the drinks."

"Uh-huh. It might be a record night, but I imagine that boy will eat up our profits in Snickers and Baby Ruths."

They stood in silence watching the crowd. Listening to the laughter punctuated by the occasional scream from within the corn maze. Feeling the gusty breeze as it rolled over their land.

Mason sighed. "Wouldn't have it any other way, Paula."

She sniffled and wiped her eyes. "Me neither, honey. You're a good man. Good father and husband."

He pulled her closer and nuzzled his face in her hair. "Enough of that foolishness. Folks will be thinking we've gone soft or something."

"Don't much care what they think."

He swatted her rear. "I know, baby. Now let's get to work. I'm going to check on the maze. You best get Andy away from the concession stand or we'll be hauling him to the hospital to get his stomach pumped."

She rolled her eyes, took a step, then froze.

Mason followed her gaze.

"They're here."

CHAPTER SEVENTY-SEVEN

"How much?" Jeremy asked the teenage girl sitting behind a table at the maze's entrance.

"Ten dollars each," she said.

"Seems kind of steep."

Maggie swatted his arm. "You're not going to find a cheaper date than me. Pay her."

Jeremy handed over a twenty, and the girl pushed two flashlights toward him.

She placed the cash in a metal box and spouted her spiel. "We'll blow an air horn when we're getting ready to close. If you're still stuck in there, someone will guide you out. That's a few hours away, though. There's spare flashlights and batteries in there, so if yours dies, just let one of the workers know. There'll be a box at the exit for you to leave your flashlights. Oh, and please don't touch any of the decorations."

"That happen a lot?" Jeremy asked.

The girl squished her nose and peered at them through her red-framed glasses. "Does what happen a lot?"

"People mess with stuff in the maze."

"Not really. We're just supposed to say it. I mean, sometimes a pumpkin gets busted, but that's about it."

Jeremy flicked on the flashlights and checked the brightness of the beams. "Wish us luck."

"Oh, and somebody stole one of the skeletons once. Least that's what they said at school."

He glanced at Maggie, then back at the girl. "That so?"

"Yeah. That's what Lucas told me."

"Lucas?"

"The Millers' oldest boy. Y'all have a good time now." She smiled and held out her hand to the teenage boy in line behind them. "Hey, Billy. You by yourself tonight?"

The agents moved a few steps into the maze and stood to the path's side.

"What're you thinking?" Maggie asked.

"The jawbone they found. That's the connection. If one of Miller's skulls did get stolen, maybe that's where the jawbone came from."

"Could be. But even if it did, you're not going to find others in here. These skulls aren't the same. Miller will say he swaps them out every now and then for whatever reason."

"Yeah, but think about it. What if Lanny saw something? Figured it out? Or asked the wrong question?"

Maggie frowned. "That might explain a lot. Like why Miller would strike so close to home. It's a panic move. But without some evidence, still not enough for a warrant."

Jeremy stared off into the corn, listening as the piped-in Halloween music overpowered the rustling of the dry stalks. Groups of people, mostly kids, ran past, eager to dive into the dark maze. One couple strolled by, holding hands and whispering to each other. He watched until they rounded a corner, then spun toward Maggie.

"The hands. Where is he keeping the victims' hands? Miller wouldn't let them get too far away. Maybe they're tucked in the scarecrows. Hidden so only he knows."

"Why would he?"

"Same reason as the skulls. The thrill. Knowing that all these people see his work but don't understand who he is. It's his way of getting the publicity virtually all serial killers crave."

Maggie took a step into the maze. "Simple enough to check out and won't need a warrant."

He grabbed her arm. "No. I don't want us both to be in here if something does turn up. You go back. Tell that girl you forgot your phone in the car. Make a call and see if you can get a few more people out here in case we need them."

"Jeremy, look around you. It'd be too obvious if we brought out more cops. Besides, there's no way we could control the scene even if we had a hundred officers out here. Too many people around, and half of them are probably armed. That's the way it is around here. I say we check out the maze and see if we find anything. If we do, we come back in the morning when there's no crowd."

"No. Gives him time to dispose of evidence. If he thinks we're onto him, the longer we wait, the worse our chances. These kids are going to be out here for another few hours at least. If the evidence is in the open, Miller's not going to be able to do anything until they're gone. Go to the car and make the calls, but tell everyone to keep it low-key. Personal vehicles only. The last thing we need is a bunch of lights and sirens pulling up in here. If it is Miller, and we spook him, no telling what he might do."

"Why can't I stay with you? I can make the calls here just as easily and watch your back too."

"We need eyes outside the maze in case Miller makes a run for it. Chances are he knows we're here."

"I don't like it. Sounds like you're protecting me."

He kissed her forehead. "Heck of a date, huh? And I'm covering all the bases, not protecting you. I'll call you in a few minutes."

Jeremy waited until she was out of the maze before heading to the first scarecrow. The crowd thinned out the farther he walked, but running kids bumped into him often. He kept the palm of his right hand pressed against his pistol. Just in case.

Flashlight beams bounced across openings in the paths. Stars popped in and out of view as thin clouds floated across the sky. A teenage zombie leapt at Jeremy, then retreated after getting no reaction.

There were far scarier things on his mind tonight.

The first skeleton was just as he'd last seen it. A young couple handed him their phone and asked him to take their picture with the decoration. He smiled, obliged, and told them to have fun.

The setting seemed different at night. Much more realistic. A spotlight cast shadows that fought against the LED lights inside the skull. The skeleton's teeth scowled or grinned, depending on your mood.

He massaged the scarecrow's arms, squeezing and twisting the shirt until he was sure. Nothing but hay. He ignored the noise from passing teenagers and ran his hand inside the shirt and pants. Still nothing.

Three scarecrows later, the story was the same. Hay-stuffed shirts and pants. Plastic skulls. Good luck getting a judge to issue a warrant with what they had now. Time to find his way out of the maze and talk to

Maggie. Have her casually chat with Paula Miller while he scoped out the rest of the operation.

He stood on tiptoe and strained to see above the corn. Useless. He'd find one of the teenage zombies and get them to show him out.

Might all be for the best anyway. So many people here that it'd be impossible to ensure everyone's safety. If the two of them didn't come up with anything tonight, there was always—

He froze. The laughter and yelling and music and screams faded into the background. Strong gusts shoved thicker clouds across the sky and obscured the moon. The same wind carried a message to Jeremy that things had just become much more complicated. An unmistakable odor.

Deadly.

Smoke.

CHAPTER SEVENTY-EIGHT

Jeremy grabbed his cell phone and hit the speed dial. "Maggie, I smell smoke. Can you see anything?"

"Yeah, I smell it too, but I don't see anything. I'm out front where the pumpkins are. Could be someone down the road burning trash. Maybe a bonfire. I made the call to the TBI, and they're rounding up some … There—looks like smoke coming from the old barn. Wonder if Miller's in there burning evidence? Heading over there now."

"Maggie, stop. Call 911 and wait for me. If that thing's on fire, we've got to get these people out of the maze before we do anything else. This thing will go up like a tinderbox if sparks hit the corn. I'm going to head to the entrance. You get them to sound the air horn to evacuate."

"On it. Call me back."

He ran to the closest scarecrow, stacked a few hay bales, and climbed on top. The entrance was off to his left. Two minutes away, maybe less if he took a straight path through the corn. No way to keep his orientation, though. He'd have to—

An orange flicker caught his eye. Flames licked through openings between the old barn's boards and fought to climb higher. The wind was in his face, and already, tiny specks of ash drifted through his flashlight's beam. Another group of kids passed him, laughing and oblivious to the danger. No more time. These people needed to get out of the maze now.

A screech shot across the field. The air horn. Maggie. The teenagers paused and looked confused before ignoring the signal and continuing into the maze. The music stopped, and another squawk echoed through the maze. This time, a few kids yelled that it was too early to close. Others stood around, confused by what was happening.

The cindery odor grew stronger by the second. Within a minute, two at the most, there'd be no mistaking it. The kids would figure out something was burning, and it'd only take one or two people to panic before the situation turned from dangerous to deadly. He had to get them out. Now.

He pointed at one of the older boys. "You!"

"What's going on?"

Jeremy pointed toward the entrance, the shortest path out of the maze. "Take them that way. Straight through the corn. Trample down as much as you can on your way out, but hurry."

"Mr. Miller will get mad if we—"

"Go! Ten steps, then turn around and look for me. I'll direct you. Ten more steps, then turn back around. Got it?"

One of the girls in the group tilted her nose into the air. "Smoke? Do you smell smoke?"

The others' eyes widened, and they began scanning the area with their flashlights, searching for the source of the potential threat.

Jeremy pointed at the boy again. "Hey! That way. I'm counting on you to get them out. Others will be behind you so leave a trail. Move fast, but stay focused on me."

The air horn sounded again, this time one long continuous blast. Yelling erupted from other sections of the maze. Hopefully, the zombie guides were doing their job and clearing the cornfield. The distant wailing of a siren echoed. Fire or police. At this point, it didn't matter. He'd take any help he could get.

He motioned slightly left to the boy leading the group out. Another minute and they'd be safe. So many others, though. There was time. As long as no one panicked, they'd make it out safely.

A loud series of screams came from his left, then another from behind him. He spun around and paused a nanosecond before cursing.

Tiny flickers of orange grew everywhere. The sparks had found the maze.

CHAPTER SEVENTY-NINE

Mason Miller perched in the combine harvester watching the FBI agent move farther into the maze. From this vantage point in the machine's cab, a good nine feet plus off the ground, he could still make out shapes as flashlight beams danced through the cornfield. Such a shame it had to end this way, though it was worth it. His family and his farm would be protected. They'd go on without him. They were strong. He'd made sure of that.

The boys knew their duties. How to farm and hunt. Take care of the land and the animals. Love their family. Watch over their mom.

And Paula. His sweetheart since high school. Love without limits. Willing to accept him as he was. He'd given his permission that if she found another man, she was free to remarry. She'd rolled her eyes and laughed, told him she already had a couple of guys lined up, then kissed him deeply and wept.

But the farm goes to the boys.

A twinge of regret that there could be others hurt. His neighbors. Good folks. Mostly. Lanny had been a mistake, but an unavoidable one. In a minute, the boy would be nothing more than bits and pieces of bone scattered across acres of farmland.

Paula had started the fire right on time. Anything they feared might not be completely destroyed otherwise—clothes, shipping boxes, Troy Obion—had been soaked in gasoline and ignited. The barn would be an inferno before long. There'd be no evidence Paula had ever been in there. All that money wasted on the metal roof, though. Couldn't be helped.

A high-pitched squeal sounded, and Mason squinted toward the maze entrance. Someone had signaled a warning. No matter. He sighed and picked up his cell phone.

Funny what you could learn on the Internet. All you had to do was search for stories on the Oklahoma City bombing back in 1995, and you'd learn most of what you needed to know. All you needed was a detonator, some fertilizer, a diesel fuel mixture, and nitromethane, all fairly easily obtained by a farmer.

Another blast of the air horn.

His eyes watered, and he pulled his lips into his mouth. His granddaddy's barn. Built by hand and made to last. Could survive anything short of a tornado.

Or bomb blast.

One continuous shriek of the air horn.

Mason cleared his throat and sat up straight. He cranked the combine and switched on the overhead lights, illuminating a section of the maze. Some kids still wandered about, either ignoring the warnings or confused about the way out. A couple of them turned toward him and began moving toward the combine. By now, Paula would have their kids safely away from the danger.

He shook his head and dialed the phone number for the detonator, pausing before he hit the send button. The barn, built by hand by his grandfather, was about to disappear with a simple press of his finger. The materials he'd labored to get into the root cellar would destroy everything down there. Tubs and beetles and tools and the freezer and any evidence of his activity. There'd be no trace of Paula anywhere in the barn. Plausible deniability for her.

He'd have to close his eyes so he wouldn't see that piece of his heritage destroyed. The barn would remain in his memory for the next few minutes until his own death. The FBI agents made it easy. He'd attack them, maybe even kill the man or his girlfriend. There'd be no joy in it. No pleasure. Simply a necessary act in order to ensure the outcome he wanted. Death by cop sounded so much better than suicide. Made him appear crazy, like he was imbalanced or something. That'd give the boys something to hold on to until they were ready.

The crowd in the maze seemed to be moving quicker now. Some running toward the barn, others away from it. Time to go.

He closed his eyes and pushed the send button.

CHAPTER EIGHTY

Not where he'd been a second ago. That's all Jeremy knew. Flat on his back. No noise save a dull ringing in his ears. Smell of fire. Gunpowder. Another grenade. The dark Afghanistan sky overhead. Pain in his ... everywhere.

He forced his head to turn to the side. Nothing except a few dark strands of something. He blinked several times.

Had to get his weapon. Get ready in case more came.

His right hand dragged across scratchy vegetation. Not right. Something's not right.

He grabbed a handful and lifted it to his face.

Blink.

Concentrate.

Corn stalks.

Not Afghanistan. But ...

The maze. Flattened as far as he could see.

What ...?

Kids.

Maggie.

Got to go. Get moving. Find help.

He pushed himself into a sitting position, gasped, and fell backward. His brain performed triage. Metallic taste of blood. Chest and stomach felt like he'd swallowed razors. Legs were there, but ignoring him. Arms cooperating.

He felt for his phone. Gone.

Flipped his head the other way. A light.

Bright.

High.
Coming directly toward him.

CHAPTER EIGHTY-ONE

Mason dabbed at the blood on his forehead. He'd hit the steering wheel hard, though hadn't lost consciousness. His fault. He'd badly misjudged the size of the blast. Overcompensated for the depth of the root cellar. Somehow, the combine's windshield remained intact, though covered in dirt, debris, and who knows what else. A piece of clothing—T-shirt?—hung limply on the outside left mirror.

The old barn was gone, obscured by a cloud of dust. Wouldn't be anything except a crater to see anyway. The explosion would've ripped everything apart, sending wood shrapnel in every direction. The cast iron stove might've survived, but he didn't see how anything else could have. Bits of that cop and Lanny and Sarah and Blue Shirt and Catherine Mae Blackston and everyone else now scattered over rich farmland.

Ashes to ashes. Dust to dust.

People to fertilizer.

Car alarms echoed across the field. Lights from inside the house cast a dim circle around the home, revealing broken windows. Soon, the farm would be covered up with emergency personnel. Two things. That's all he wanted.

First, Paula and the kids surrounded by friends. Comforted. Consoled. Told they couldn't have known. It wasn't their fault. It'll take time, but they'll get over it.

Second, that any cops or FBI agents who showed up were good shots. Don't let the prey suffer.

He put the combine in gear, switched on the cab's interior light, and moved toward what remained of the maze. People were stirring now. Staggering around. Helping others. That's what neighbors did.

A few waved at him. Motioned for help. He ignored them and kept moving.

Searching.

The male FBI agent had to be somewhere in this area. The blast would've blown him toward Mason, though how far was anyone's guess.

No bodies on the ground. Good. No serious injuries, at least at this distance.

Only one person had to die today. Two, if the Fed or his girlfriend didn't kill him in time.

But he was ready. A farmer working his land. Harvesting his crop.

No better way to die.

CHAPTER EIGHTY-TWO

Jeremy struggled onto all fours and closed his eyes. Deep breaths. There'd be injured. And Miller still out there somewhere. Had to make sure help was coming.

A wave of nausea pounced, and he spewed his lunch on the ground. Too dark to be sure, but likely there'd be blood mixed in.

He straightened and ran the back of his hand across his mouth. Hearing was returning in his right ear, and he could make out the wah-wahing of car alarms nearby. Shadowy figures moved about, a few running, some staggering, one falling.

He pushed himself off the ground, stood for a heartbeat, then dropped to one knee.

A hand on his back. A young voice. "You okay?"

He nodded. "Help the others."

The voice hurried off, and Jeremy stood again, extending his arms to maintain his balance. Electricity shot a warning signal down his left leg. It wasn't going to hold him up for long. Too much damage, both new and old.

He searched for a landmark to regain his bearings. Figure out where to go.

A flashing blue light bounced off the house. The police were here. More would come.

Many more.

An enormous cloud of dust now filled the sky. Whatever had exploded had been big. Fuel drums stored in the barn probably.

More voices filtered in now. Somewhere behind, screaming. Pain or grief, he couldn't tell.

There. A broken board, part of a plastic skull still attached. He shuffled to it, knelt, pushed himself up again, and wedged the wood under his left armpit. A makeshift crutch.

The white lights. Brighter now.

He shaded his eyes and squinted. Farm equipment. Lighting up part of the area. Smart move.

Needs to stop though. Going to run over someone if he gets much closer.

CHAPTER EIGHTY-THREE

That's him. The FBI agent wobbled but remained standing. Mason turned slightly right, placing the man dead center in his windshield. He switched on the sixteen-foot-wide front reel and set its speed at maximum. Broken corn stalks sailed through the air as the contraption shoved everything in its path toward the cutter bar, up a conveyor, and to the augers and threshing drum. Effective for grain. Probably make quite a mess with flesh and bone.

But as you sow, so shall you reap.

Large pieces of debris still fluttered to earth around the combine. Paper plates. Candy wrappers. Styrofoam cups. The concession stand must've been hit hard.

Mister FBI hadn't moved. Had no idea what was coming. And once he figured it out, well, Mason played fair. The cab's light remained on, illuminating the driver. If the man was fast enough, he could get off several shots. If not, the redhead would have to finish the job. Of course, by then her boyfriend would've made it through the combine's threshing drum. Not as thorough as the grinder, but quite effective nonetheless.

Off to the left, several people shouted and waved their arms over their heads, motioning for his attention. Yell all you want. Not stopping for anyone. Not now. Not ever.

One of the group broke off and ran toward him. A kid. Pointing back at something. Mason leaned forward over the steering wheel. Not something. Someone.

A figure on the ground. Kind of small and not moving. Had to be a kid. Mason ran a hand across his mouth and squinted toward the scene. This distance from the explosion, they'd be okay. Injured maybe, but not too bad.

He angled the combine to the left, keeping the FBI agent in his line of vision. The harvester's overhead lights flooded the area around the injured child. A teenager, his zombie makeup smeared, hunched over the youngster. Three others stood in a semi-circle around him.

On the ground beside them ...

Mason swallowed the bile rising in his throat and wished he was already dead.

A camouflage ball cap. Faded orange *T*. No. Lots of kids wore those, didn't they? Paula would've protected the boys. Andy was safe somewhere. Had to be.

But he knew.

A spasm shook the boy, and the others moved a step back. One of the teenagers turned and threw up. The combine's noise hid the screams, but his son's face told him. Andy—his boy—was in terrible pain.

The children should've been far enough away, safe from any danger. But the explosion had been bigger than expected. What about Lucas? And Paula? Were they injured? Or worse?

He'd been forced to act too quickly. If the FBI agents had stayed away, this wouldn't have happened. Why come here when they had to know something like this could happen? If they wanted to arrest him, they could've done it when he was alone. Not here when his family might be in danger.

His body shook as if a cold chill gripped him and wouldn't turn loose. They'd pay for hurting his boy. For making one so young suffer.

He looked away from Andy, unable to bear the agony. In his back pocket, the Buck knife waited. Handed down to him from his dad, its whittling days long past. The blade still sharp and eager.

One more job to do.

He stopped the combine, brushed a hand under each eye, and climbed down.

CHAPTER EIGHTY-FOUR

Finally. The combine stopped, and Jeremy shaded his eyes to get a better look at the driver.

Mason Miller.

Jeremy's fingers closed around his Glock's grip, and he exhaled deeply. Thank God it hadn't been thrown clear. His throat burned, whether from dust, blood, or both, he couldn't tell, and his midsection begged him to fall into a fetal position or risk ripping his insides apart.

Two police cars pulled behind the house. Distant sirens echoed that additional help was closing in. Within minutes, the confusion of the blast was going to give way to the chaos of emergency personnel.

Sporadic yelling surrounded him. Some calling names, others crying for help. Smoldering pockets of cornstalks and barnwood dotted the field. People began to fan out, looking to help.

Miller climbed down from the machine and hurried toward a group of three or four people. Teenagers from the size of them. If he got hostages ...

Even without the pain looping through his body, no way Jeremy could hit him from here. Not at this range in these conditions. Had to buy time. Get closer.

Jeremy fired a shot into the air.

Miller turned toward him and slowed. The newly arrived cops squatted and pulled their weapons, sweeping the field for the source of the gunshot.

"Jeremy!"

Maggie. Good. He raised his hand.

"Don't shoot," she yelled. "He's FBI."

Miller held both hands in the air and jerked his head toward the body on the ground. "That's my boy. I need to see him."

Jeremy shuffled closer, the board's splinters digging into his palm.

"Get on your knees. Now."

Mason shook his head. "Can't do that. Got to take care of my boy."

"Maggie?"

"With you," she answered.

Jeremy cut his eyes toward the police cars. Maggie was moving toward the suspect, flanked by the two local cops. "Miller," he said, "enough people have been hurt today. Get on the ground so we can get some help in here for your son."

The group around the fallen figure began to back away toward Maggie, their bodies in her line of sight.

Near the house, a scream pierced the air, and a woman dashed toward Mason. One of the cops grabbed her and held her back. The screaming faded to sobs.

"That you, Paula?" Mason hollered. "Just stay back now. I'm sorry about all this. Real sorry."

Jeremy edged closer. "Your family's hurt. We can help them. You just need to back away so we can secure the area. We'll take care of them. Promise."

"Need to see how bad the boy's hurt first. Got to know."

"Uh-huh. Just stop. No closer. People are on the way. Paramedics. We'll fly him to Memphis. Make sure he gets whatever care he needs."

Mason edged toward his son. "I won't let him suffer. Can't do that."

"I understand. But I can't let you get any closer to him. Stop now. Get on the ground and let us help your son."

Another spasm rocked the boy's body for several heartbeats. A low moan, a gasp. Nothing.

Mason hesitated, shoulders slumped, then resumed the slow walk toward his son. "I love my family. Make sure they know that."

Not good. Miller had already decided how this was going to end. Jeremy kept moving. Another ten yards at least before he'd have any chance of hitting Miller. He fired another shot in the air. "It doesn't have to be like this. We can all go on. Live another day."

Mason stopped, held his hands out, and squatted. Slowly, he scooped up some dirt and watched it drift through his fingers. "Don't think so. Locked in a cell's no way to live."

"Let my partner check the boy. Just lie on the ground there and—"

Mason leapt and came at him in a full sprint, his right hand reaching for his back pocket. Five seconds max before he'd close the distance between them.

"Gun! Jeremy, get down!"

Maggie.

The harvester's lights outlined Miller, casting a long shadow bouncing directly toward Jeremy. He let the crutch fall and swung his left hand up to support his weapon before squeezing off two shots. Center mass.

Miller careened into him, sending both men to the ground. Jeremy gasped in pain as the farmer's knife sliced into his shoulder. He rolled to his right and screamed as a coughing fit brought new levels of agony to his body. Got to get up. Find Maggie. Warn ... his vision blurred, then went black as the pain became secondary to letting go of life.

A voice yelled through a tunnel.

"Stay down!" Maggie. He forced one eyelid open.

Miller, now on his knees, swung his right arm toward Maggie.

A two-shot burst from her, then the man's torso slumped backward on top of his legs.

More screaming. Paula Miller.

Sirens. Lots of them.

Hands on him. A face. Maggie, surrounded by disappearing stars.

Her mouth moving. Gibberish.

He coughed again. A thousand tiny steel knives sliced through his organs.

Smile at her.

Beautiful Maggie.

EPILOGUE

Jeremy stared at the IV as it dripped its contents into the tube snaking from his arm. Third bag this morning, the doctor had said. No wonder he had to pee so badly.

"Babe, I hate to ask but ..."

Maggie rolled her eyes. "I'm telling the nurse to put the catheter back in. I'm pretty sure she'd be happy to get a little payback."

"Hey, I can't be responsible for how I treat people when I'm in this condition."

"Uh-huh. Word on the floor is they're planning a party on your discharge date."

"Which is when?"

She shook her head and handed him a stack of envelopes. "When you're healed, and not a minute before. Between the concussion, collapsed lung, stab wound in your shoulder, and the spike of wood they pulled out of your leg, it'll be a while."

"Got nowhere to go anyway." He winked at her. "Food's not very good, but my nurse is kind of cute."

She rolled her eyes and shook her head. "Seriously, if I was looking for another job—and I'm not—I'd go to nursing school. Seems like I spend more time in hospitals with you than I do anywhere else."

"Anytime you want to practice playing nurse, I'll be happy to assist."

She blushed briefly. "Easy there. Don't want to get that heart rate up."

He yawned and stretched his arms. "Whatever you say, nurse. Anything new on Miller's wife?"

"Nope. She's sticking to her story that she had no idea what he was doing."

"You buy that?"

"I'd like to, but I don't. Maybe it's because I'm a mother too. Watching her bury her son was tough. But the crime scene techs will be at their farm for at least another month. If there's evidence of her involvement, maybe they'll find it. Doubt it though. Not much left. The press is saying it's a miracle only three people were killed."

"Not counting Miller's victims, however many that may be."

"Probably never know for sure. Of course, you could stick around at the Bureau and help them investigate the scene. The press would have a field day if someone hinted to them you were being forced out."

He shook his head. "Time to move on. Best for all of us." He sorted the morning's mail delivery. Most were from people at the Bureau he didn't know. "Huh. This one's from Randy Clarke thanking me. Says he wants to get together when I feel up to it."

"Randy Clarke?"

Jeremy handed her the card. "Catherine Mae Blackston's ex-husband. Put it up there next to the one from Rebecca. You know what to do with the rest."

Maggie dropped the cards in the trash. "What's in the big envelope?"

"No return address." He tore it open and pulled out the contents. Three pages, official forms with redacted information. He scanned them quickly and pulled a post-it note from the last page.

The heart rate monitor alarm sounded, and Jeremy ground his teeth together.

Maggie's forehead creased, and she scooted closer. "What is it?"

"We've got a problem." He handed her the post-it note.

She read it, frowned, and tossed the crumpled paper into the garbage can.

"Get well soon. Colonel Ramsey Cronfeld."

AUTHOR'S NOTE

Thank you for reading *Coming of Winter*. I hope you've enjoyed the start of this new series.

I'd greatly appreciate it if you'd take the time to leave a review of the book online when you get the chance. Other than buying their work, the best thing you can do for an author is write a short review.

There's more to come from Jeremy Winter. If you want to be among the first to know the latest news (and maybe win a free book), you can subscribe on my website, www.tomthreadgill.com. You'll receive a short email occasionally with things like publishing dates and special offers. I promise not to spam you or give your email address to anyone else.

Thanks again, and watch for more books in the series coming soon.

Made in the USA
Monee, IL
10 January 2022